ICY
BETRAYAL

DAVID G. KEITH

Good Egg Press

ICY BETRAYAL

Library of Congress Catalog Number: 2015930983
ISBN: 0986370606
ISBN-13: 978-0-9863706-0-1

Icy Betrayal is a work of fiction. Names, characters, places, and incidents are the products of the author's imagination or are used fictitiously. Any resemblance to actual events, locales, or persons, living or dead, is entirely coincidental.

Cover Design by OMG Media
Interior Design by Lorie DeWorken, MIND*the*MARGINS, LLC

Published in the United States by Good Egg Press
www.goodeggpress.com

PROLOGUE

The human body is no match for a three-thousand-pound vehicle; even at twenty or thirty miles an hour, a car can be lethal. The sound of the bumper connecting with bone cut her to the core just as the sickening thud of his head hitting the windshield pierced the still of the Colorado night. Then, there was silence, less the idling of the vehicle at rest. Lisa Sullivan knew the man was dead.

I firmly resolve, with the help of Your grace,
to confess my sins, to do penance and to amend my life.

—Excerpt from the Act of Contrition

ONE

The red LED readout on the electronic sign outside the Bank of Colorado branch in Greenleaf hypnotically flashed between the time and temperature.

5:29 a.m.

11°F, -12°C.

It was late November and unusually cold, even by Colorado standards.

Rocklin County Sheriff's Deputy Victor Brooks drove past the bank and into the parking lot of the GreenMart on North Main, hoping to score some hot coffee to help get him through the tail end of a ten-hour graveyard shift. He was working "beat two," an area that covered the rural, western part of the county at the base of the Front Range Mountains.

Working "two," as deputies called it, meant a lot of driving and no shortage of boredom. It was the largest beat geographically among the four under the 350-square-mile territory of the Rocklin County Sheriff.

He watched as the drip of fresh coffee made its way into the pot the all-night clerk had started at his request. Another forty-five seconds and he'd be good to pour. If it took any longer, the scent of the fresh Danish in the display case an arm's length away would lure him into 450 calories he could do without.

"C'mon, baby," he muttered.

"SD-21," screeched the handheld radio clipped to his belt. "TC, possible fatality, car versus pedestrian. Highway 46, mile marker 28."

Brooks had fifteen years on the force, but the location of the call surprised him. Victor Brooks knew every inch of road in his beat, and his brain was faster than Google Maps, but this particular location was one he couldn't quite frame in his mind.

"Roger that, this is SD-21, my ETA is 15 minutes," he responded back to dispatch. If the drip would stop, he might be able to pour a quick cup.

"Dispatch, Sam-9, en route to Highway 46 TC, ETA 35," the radio squawked.

TC was police code for a "traffic collision" and "Sam-9" was the call sign for Sergeant Jason Valenzuela, the shift supervisor for beat two. The radio transmission meant Valenzuela was leaving department headquarters in Castle Springs and heading to the scene as well. Brooks knew he would have to get through the rest of his shift without coffee.

"Shit."

Highway 46 was a seldom-used, two-lane road in the far northwest corner of Rocklin County. There were cabins scattered here and there, but there were a lot more deer in the area than people. Accidents involving pedestrians happened in town, not on Highway 46, thought Brooks.

Deputy Brooks was responding "code 3," meaning lights and siren, but he never topped forty miles an hour due to the winding road, the darkness of the hour, and the icy road conditions. After passing the 28-mile marker, Brooks slowed his cruiser. Good thing, too. As he negotiated a slick, tight turn, the blinking hazard lights of a yellow Ford Fiesta were suddenly right in front of him. Three-day-old snow crunched beneath his tires as he braked and maneuvered his squad car to the side of the road. He positioned the vehicle so he could aim his floodlights on the car.

As he came to a stop, the driver stepped from the Fiesta and looked back in his direction. Brooks could see the driver was a woman, appearing somewhat disheveled, with mascara stained tears streaming down her pale cheeks. The red knit cap and light coat she was wearing were no protection from the harshness of the cold morning. She looked to be in her early thirties with long, blonde hair. Brooks let out a slow whistle as she approached. She was knock-out gorgeous, he thought to himself, like something you'd see on a magazine cover. She was shaking and appeared to be close to hyperventilating.

"You okay, ma'am?" he asked, climbing from his patrol car.

"I'm okay. I didn't see…"

"Where?" he began to ask.

"Back there," she said, pointing to the roadside some forty feet behind them.

The woman turned to him sobbing and asked, "Am I under arrest? I swear I didn't see him!"

"It's okay, let's calm down. I'm Deputy Brooks, what's your name, ma'am?"

"Lisa Sullivan," she said, wiping her cheek and smearing more of her mascara across her face as she looked up at him.

"Okay, let's get you out of the cold," he said, leading the woman to his car. He opened the passenger door of the cruiser and helped the woman inside. He reached across her, turned the heater on full blast, and told her he'd be right back.

Brooks closed the door and walked back to where the woman had pointed. A few seconds later, he was standing next to a figure laying face down in the snow on the shoulder of the road. He knelt down and checked for a pulse, but there was nothing. The deceased was a male, likely in his mid to late fifties, wearing an orange hunter's vest. Brooks was surprised at how cold the man's body felt.

"Dispatch, SD-21, I've got a 10-55, Highway 46, mile marker 28," he reported into his handheld just as Sergeant Valenzuela pulled up to the scene and rolled down his passenger window. Brooks heard his last few words echoing from the supervisor's radio inside the car. 10-55 is the RCSO radio code used to request that the County Medical Examiner respond to the scene.

"The driver?" the sergeant asked.

"She's back in my unit. Gotta get a statement."

"You got enough flares?"

"Fresh case."

"Put 'em out. That's a nasty turn. I'll get the tarp. Looks like we're stuck with more OT."

The RCSO was under a mandatory overtime order—they were severely short staffed, but those who controlled the purse strings in the county wouldn't authorize any new deputy positions. The consensus was that it was less expensive to use overtime. The deputies liked the extra cash, but it had been going on for months and burnout was becoming a very real issue.

"I'd rather go home," Brooks said, leaning on Valenzuela's patrol car. "I got thirty hours of OT already this pay period. It's getting to be too much."

"Save up and spend it on a trip to Hawaii. Bet it'll hit eighty there today," said the sergeant.

"You and the captain wanna give me some time off for that trip?" Brooks responded.

"I'll get right on that, Brooksie. Right after that trip to Cabo I've been promising my old lady," Valenzuela said, and then added, "I'll call Serrano."

It's during REM sleep or "rapid eye movement" when most dreams take place. Mia Serrano's pupils darted back and forth beneath her eyelids. They followed the bright, lively colors as they exploded to blood red then broke apart and disappeared, like fireworks fading on a flat sky. But the sharp "crack" that preceded each explosion wasn't the sound of an Independence Day celebration. Each was distinctive and ominous and caused her body to jerk beneath the covers. In her mind, she screamed at the colors. In bed, she whispered…

"Get down. Get down."

The TEC-DC9 semi-automatic rang out. The red spray dissolved away as the marimba sound coming from her nightstand jolted her awake and upright.

"Get down," she repeated out loud, trying to focus her eyes.

The ring tone was all the way up, and the mobile phone vibrated as it rang. In between the sounds, Mia emerged from her Ambien haze.

"Serrano," she said into the phone, glancing at the clock. 6:18 a.m. She was starting to focus. "Where?" Mia closed her eyes, trying to pinpoint the location in her mind.

"Okay. Got it. Be there in ninety minutes."

Mia ended the call, rolled onto her side, and reached for Sasha, her Beagle/Jack Russell mix.

"Sorry, Sasha, I gotta go."

Sasha slowly opened her eyes as her master kissed her head, climbed out of bed, and headed for the shower.

Mia Serrano had never given much thought to being a cop. Growing up in suburban Colorado, her mother was a high school teacher, and her father worked for WellRock Technology. He was a real life "rocket scientist" and successful enough to keep the family firmly ensconced in the middle class community of Centennial. Chuck Serrano had hoped his daughter would follow his path and work in the aerospace industry, but it wasn't to be. While Mia excelled in all academic subjects, it was clear she gravitated toward the liberal arts, particularly English.

After graduating with honors and earning her teaching credential from Colorado State University in Fort Collins, she found a job teaching English literature to high school students not far from her hometown. But over time she became frustrated with the mindless bureaucracy of the public school system. Mia loved her students, but she longed to do something else, something that would allow her to leave a mark on the world.

She had noticed a billboard on the outskirts of town—a recruiting tool for the Rocklin County Sheriff's Office, which piqued her interest. Mia looked at that billboard every day as she drove home from the school campus, pondering a possible career change from teaching high school into law enforcement.

The decision to make that career move became clear on one fateful day in April 1999 when the world would come to know Columbine High School as a killing field. It was the last day she ever set foot on that campus.

It was also the day the nightmares began.

As a woman, Mia Serrano had been welcomed into the RCSO with open arms. In the days of affirmative action, she was quite a find for the RCSO, and her Latina heritage was a bonus. She immersed herself in her career, never finding the right man, though there was no shortage of interested men. Mia Serrano was a beautiful woman. She had dark hair, cut a couple of inches below shoulder length, with natural curls and auburn highlights. Men certainly noticed her quiet elegance when she walked into a room. She never talked about it, but she was voted homecoming queen in high school some twenty years earlier and hoped no one at RCSO would ever learn that about her.

Her transition from high school teacher to cop was surprisingly easy. Keeping peace among teenagers in a high school classroom was not that different from keeping peace on the streets of Rocklin County.

She still chuckled to herself on those occasions when upon arresting someone and placing them in handcuffs they would suddenly look at her and say, "Hey, wait a minute—weren't you my English teacher?"

The morning sun began to faintly illuminate the sky as the four members of the RCSO traffic investigations review team, led by Mia Serrano, arrived on scene.

"Good morning, Mia," offered Sergeant Valenzuela, his breath hanging in the very cold morning air. "Want the dime tour?"

"Sure, that'll work."

As Valenzuela walked Mia through the accident scene, her team went right to work, dividing the tasks between the four members of the squad. They measured the distance between the Fiesta and the deceased and noted the skid marks left behind. They checked visibility and road design, and they ultimately would check the mechanical condition of the car. The braking system, lights, steering mechanism, and other key components of the vehicle would all be thoroughly checked out at the RCSO CSI lab.

Accident investigations were highly technical and often took hours to process at the scene. Then, additional days or sometimes even weeks were needed to complete the investigation, depending on when toxicology results on the victim and the driver were completed. Once all the pieces of the puzzle came together, investigators would be able to draw an official conclusion of what happened.

Mia's lead assistant, Deputy Larry Voss, was handling the video and still camera duties. He followed behind Mia and the sergeant, snapping away as they walked toward the victim.

"Did you or your deputy move anything, Sergeant?"

"Pulled his ID and covered him up, that's it," Valenzuela said, handing her a worn brown leather wallet. "There's the ID and..." he said, pulling back the tarp carefully so as to preserve the scene, "here's your vic."

Mia opened the wallet and eyed the Colorado driver's license in the faded yellow plastic window of the wallet. A hunting license was tucked behind it.

"George Myron Lombard," she said to no one in particular, "of Castle Springs."

"You're a long way from home, Mr. Lombard," she added in a quiet, contemplative voice.

The wallet also contained several credit cards and $70 in cash.

"Larry, be sure and get video of the roadway and the curve of the road where this happened," said Mia. "And get me Mr. Lombard 'in situ.'"

"Will do," Voss said respectfully. He was nearly fifteen years her senior but sincerely liked his boss. The work they did wasn't pleasant but Mia was, and it was better than pulling overtime on the beat.

Voss had recorded hundreds of victims "in situ," a Latin term meaning that the object has not been "newly" moved. In essence, Mia wanted video showing the victim exactly as Deputy Brooks found him when arriving on scene. The position of the body was something Investigator Serrano would include in the final report.

After five years of investigating traffic fatalities, Mia could often tell as much by looking at the area around the body as at the body itself. While this one seemed to be pretty straight forward, she was careful and thorough just the same.

Mia noted that the victim was dressed in relatively light clothing given the frigid temperatures that morning. While he was wearing an orange hunters vest, his coat, pants, and shoes were inadequate for temperatures well below freezing. Mia found that a bit odd.

She noted that the victim's left leg was jetting grotesquely away from his body at an odd angle—evidence that the collision with the Fiesta likely broke the man's hip. Even a relatively slow speed collision could inflict these types of injuries.

But it was the head contusion that really got her attention. She studied it closely and then stood up looking back at the Fiesta.

"Interesting. So our driver hasn't given you much, Sergeant?"

"Nope. Deputy Brooks said she was cold and pretty shaken up. He thought it best to let you talk with her about what happened," said Valenzuela.

"That'll work. Once Voss is finished getting the video, cover the body back up, okay?"

TWO

⚍

"The Lord be with you."

"And with your spirit," they recited loudly, almost in unison.

Most days at the 7:30 morning Mass at St. Joseph's Catholic Church in Castle Springs, the "regulars," as Rocklin County Sheriff's Investigator Jack Keller called them, numbered no more than a dozen. Keller, the relative newcomer in the group, had been warmly welcomed by these regulars when he had begun attending morning Mass many years earlier. Over time he had grown rather attached to the group, even though most of the regulars were in their seventies and eighties.

"Behold the lamb of God, who takes away the sins of the world. Blessed are those called to the supper of the lamb."

Blessed and quick. That was the message Father Jon Foley had gotten loud and clear early on in his stint as the pastor of St. Joe's.

"Forty minutes max, the closer to thirty, the better," old man Callaghan had told him. Callaghan had been a parishioner for sixty years and was nearly ninety when he instructed the priest upon his arrival three years earlier. "We're burnin' daylight, me boy," he'd said in his thick Irish brogue.

"The Body of Christ."

"Amen," said Jack to the priest. They shared a quick nod.

Jack Keller was old enough to be Foley's father, but the priest was the best friend the homicide investigator had. Besides, Keller preferred morning Mass to spending evenings at AA meetings.

THREE

Brooks gave Mia Serrano a quick rundown on his version of the events before introducing her to Lisa Sullivan. The poor woman, disheveled but no longer shivering, peered at Mia through the side passenger window of the cruiser. Brooks reached over, opened the door, and made the introduction.

"Investigator Serrano will take good care of you. She's the best we've got, so you're in good hands."

Mia smiled and replied to Brooks, "There's a thermos of hot coffee in the front seat of my car. You look like you could use some."

"You're a lifesaver, Investigator."

Mia walked to the driver's side of the car, climbed in the cruiser and started in.

"I'm very sorry you had to experience this, ma'am. Can I get your full name?"

"Lisa Ann Sullivan," the woman replied, looking away.

"May I call you Lisa?"

The woman nodded as a fresh stream of tears ran down her cheeks.

"I know this is a horrible experience for you, but I do need to ask you some questions as to what happened out here this morning. I hope you understand."

"It's okay, I just feel so bad for that poor man. I just never saw him till it was too late."

"Okay, let's start from the beginning."

Sullivan told Mia she had left her home in Rosebud at about five that morning, setting out for her sister's apartment in the town of Big Pine some forty miles away. Her sister had been going through a nasty divorce and had called in the middle of the night, very upset. Sullivan decided she'd go to Big Pine to be with her sister.

"It was so dark," she sobbed. "I was coming around that corner and there he was. I wasn't speeding, honest. It was slick, and I was worried about ice."

"How fast do you think you were going?" Mia asked.

"I'm not sure. Maybe twenty-five, thirty miles an hour. I tried to stop. That's when it happened."

Sullivan described the impact with more detail than the investigator expected. She said she hit him full on, and the victim was thrown onto the hood of her car. After contact, she slammed on her brakes and the man went skidding off the hood and landed on the shoulder of the road. She stopped and quickly checked on him, trying to find a pulse but couldn't detect one. She told Mia she worked as an LVN at the hospital near Rosebud, and that from her training she knew he was dead. She then "freaked out," as she put it, and after gathering her wits about her, used her cell phone to call 911.

"I'm so sorry, Lisa. We will need to get a more detailed statement from you at headquarters in Castle Springs. Deputy Brooks will take you there, and we'll see that your car is towed. We'll need to process your vehicle as part of the investigation—this is just routine protocol in these kinds of incidents. Would you like me to call your sister?"

Lisa Sullivan shook her head. "I'll call her."

"Okay, wait here and I'll have someone come and take you to headquarters."

Sullivan agreed and Mia climbed out of the car. She shielded her eyes from the morning sun, now breaking over the horizon to the east, and walked towards Larry Voss to check in with him on the progress being made. Her crew would likely be on scene for the better part of the day completing the preliminary investigation. With traffic fatalities it was important to get everything needed from the scene the first time around, especially when weather was a factor. The forecast that day called for snow.

"Investigator, you might want to check this out," called out a deputy coming out of the trees and onto the road thirty feet beyond the body. Mia walked over for a look. There, off the edge of the shoulder, was a rifle, its barrel obscured by fallen pine branches. Mia reached into her pocket for some latex gloves, put them on and carefully removed the rifle from the branches. She examined it closely, noticing the initials GML carved in the handle of the weapon. The rifle, as well as the orange vest George Myron Lombard was wearing, led Mia to believe their victim had been out hunting when he was struck and killed by the driver of the Fiesta.

It all fit and made sense, so why was she so uneasy?

FOUR

～

The sheriff's department building was just one of several that made up the Rocklin County Justice Center complex. The two main floors of the RCSO building were above ground and served largely as office space for investigators, support staff, and administration. The underground area, known commonly as the dungeon, housed the RCSO shooting range, two squad rooms, and the intake center where arrestees were processed. Adjacent to the dungeon were the holding cells, jail lockup facility, and the "tag and bag" evidence room.

Mia nodded to the deputies as she made her way through the dungeon, carrying the .22 rifle and the ammunition she had found on the body of the deceased. Normally, the crime scene guys would bring it in, but she wanted to have someone take a quick look at it, so she had taken the initiative.

She walked through the large double doors leading into the RCSO shooting range, giving Matt Nolan a quick nod. The range was Nolan's world, and he ruled it in black SWAT fatigues, clear wraparound protective eye wear, and big black earmuffs draped around his very large neck. Though just 5'6", Nolan was still an imposing figure. He was a walking encyclopedia when it came to weapons, and while not a sworn officer, he had earned a tremendous level of respect within the department.

"Whatcha got for me, Mia?"

"I got called out this morning on a TC. It looks like our victim was hunting with this rifle. What can you tell me about it?"

"Your victim picked a hell of a day to go huntin' squirrels," he said, looking over the weapon. "Too damn cold out there if you ask me."

Mia nodded but didn't say anything.

"I'll bet you this was his first real rifle. It's just like the one my dad gave me when I was a kid," he said, lost in memories of hunting trips in the mountains with his father years earlier. "But you got a bit of a problem here, Mia."

"What's that?" she asked.

Mia qualified each month on her department issued Glock but beyond that didn't have much interest in firearms. Too many bad memories.

Nolan continued, "Was this the only rifle he had out there this morning? And is this the only ammo your boy had with him?"

"Yes and yes," she responded.

"It's deer season, so he's got the right ammo. It's .243 boat tail soft point, hundred grain. But this ammo doesn't fit in that rifle."

Mia felt a little silly at her ignorance about weapons. "And the rifle?" she asked.

"Mia, unless you sneak up on that whitetail buck and put this thing right up to his temple, it ain't killin' no deer."

Mia stood there processing what Nolan had just told her.

"Okay, thanks, Matt. Just book it into evidence for me."

Captain Mick McCallister's day wasn't off to a great start having spent the last forty-five minutes reviewing overtime logs with staff. As he stepped inside the elevator to return to his second floor office, he heard a female voice calling out to hold the elevator. He extended his arm to hold the doors open and was surprised to see his lead traffic investigator as she stepped inside.

"Hey, Mia, I thought you were out on a pedestrian TC."

"I was, but I just got back. Had to run some stuff by Matt Nolan."

"Nolan? Was there a gun involved?"

"Yeah, sort of… Stuff doesn't really add up. I'm hoping to get more from the autopsy tomorrow, and then I'll be able to fill you in."

"Can't wait," the captain said with a smile as the elevator door opened to the second floor.

"I'll keep you posted, Boss," Mia responded.

Mick McCallister was a rising star within the RCSO. Barely forty years old, he had advanced through the ranks faster than anyone else at the department. The current sheriff, Cole Connelly, was set to retire in less than a year and while McCallister hadn't announced his intentions, it was pretty clear he'd be the guy to beat—if he chose to run.

Standing 6'4" tall, McCallister was a formidable figure. His light brown hair had just a bit of gray sneaking in at the temples. He was physically fit and did his best to keep his waist at a respectable thirty-four inches. He had a true command presence, especially in uniform, and women all took notice of him when he walked into the room.

He had been a star athlete in college, excelling in both baseball and football. He ultimately chose football and was the starting safety for the University of Washington for all four of his years there. Following his graduation in 1995, he entered the NFL draft and was selected by the Jacksonville Jaguars. He was never signed to a contract but was proud of the plaque he had hanging on the wall of his office. "*Mr. Irrelevant*" it read, something instantly recognized by those who followed professional football closely. The significance of being named *Mr. Irrelevant* meant McCallister had been the very last person selected that year in the NFL draft. He kept the plaque on his wall to remind himself that he had come a long way and that good things happen to people who never give up.

FIVE

⚞⚟

The Rocklin County morgue was located in a nondescript bun-
ker-like building a half-mile from the RC Justice Center. Unlike
the morgues featured on television crime shows, the facility had low
ceilings and bright fluorescent lighting. That day just a handful of the
living were inside.

"We owe you for this one, Doc. I know you're trying to get out of
town," Larry Voss told the coroner.

Dr. David Mora was hours from departing for a pathology conference in Miami. He wasn't looking forward to the conference as much
as the sunshine and warmth.

As per RCSO policy, at least one member of the accident investigation team was required to be present for victim autopsies, and it was
usually Voss.

"I'll have a cold one for you on South Beach, Larry," Mora said as he
began carving a "Y" incision into the deceased.

"I really appreciate this, Dave. We got a call on this one yesterday
morning and there's a lot that doesn't add up."

"No sweat, Larry. Besides, with the snow we're expecting my flight
will probably get delayed."

Dr. Mora made the incision, which stretched from each shoulder
to the sternum and down to within a few inches of the waistline. He
pulled the skin back slowly with the help of a blade that sliced the

connective tissue that had, until very recently, kept George Lombard's skin attached to his body. Next, he pulled back the flesh, exposing the inside of the abdomen. He paused and peered closely at a yellow mass. "Well, that's interesting," Dr. Mora said.

It was nearly three in the afternoon as Mia sat at her desk trying to finish up some old accident reports. There was enough caffeine in her bloodstream from the double latte she had just finished to make her jump at the buzz of her cell phone. Caller ID told her the call was from Larry Voss.

"Hi, Larry."

"Hey, Mia, Dr. Mora found a few surprises with our accident victim yesterday—I think I need to give you a rundown. You gonna be around for the next half hour?"

"Is this going to wreck my weekend?" Mia asked.

"Yeah, it kinda looks that way."

It wasn't easy getting time with Captain Mick McCallister, but Mia lucked out and caught him in the break room doing battle with the soda machine. He'd put in his dollar, but the machine was refusing to deliver his Diet Coke.

"Damn it," he muttered.

"Captain, have you got a minute?"

McCallister sighed in defeat.

"Sure, come on in," he responded, nodding towards his office just around the corner. "This about your fatal TC?"

"Yep."

Mick McCallister was charged with overseeing all RCSO investigations. His office was small but had a window with a view of the parking lot and snowy grounds of the Justice Center.

"Have a seat. Whatcha got?"

"A lot of stuff that's not adding up," she said.

"Like what?"

Mia looked down at her notes and began to recite the facts of the case.

"The victim is 56-year-old George Lombard of Castle Springs. Best we can figure, he was out deer hunting off Highway 46 early yesterday morning when he was struck by a car and killed. The driver, 32-year-old Lisa Sullivan from Rosebud, says Lombard suddenly appeared out of nowhere. Speed was 25-30, she says she had no time to react and hit him head on. He was thrown onto the hood of her Ford Fiesta, his head hit the windshield, which didn't break, and he was thrown clear to the shoulder face down and dead."

"Okay, so far so good," McCallister replied.

"Well, not for him," she replied with a bit of a smile. She cursed silently to herself at the feeble attempt at being cute with her boss.

Their affair hadn't ended badly; Mia Serrano and Mick McCallister parted on good terms and remained friends, seeing each other nearly every day at the station. They both knew their relationship was against RCSO policy given Mia worked in McCallister's division. The couple had managed to keep the tryst a secret from both their co-workers and the command staff for eight months. But as Mick's career blossomed, and he became the "talked about guy" to replace the sheriff when he retired, they decided it would be best to cool it.

The relationship had started off innocently, mostly playful flirting. There were a few emails and before they knew it they were having drinks at a small neighborhood bar in Denver. Over time, the relationship became serious, but there was always concern that they'd be discovered.

A holiday weekend trip to Las Vegas turned out to be the deal breaker, thanks to a close call with a RCSO deputy renowned for his big mouth. Fortunately, they saw him before he saw them, and while they were able to quickly switch hotels, they spent the weekend looking over their shoulders. Romance is hard, they'd learned, when you're always watching your back.

Both had a lot to lose. Married and divorced in his early twenties, Mick's life was more or less the RCSO. A department romance could do a lot of damage to a career he'd poured his heart and soul into. And Mia had a lot to lose as well. If word got out there would be rumors and claims she'd slept her way to her coveted investigator position. It wasn't fair, but it was department politics and human nature. They'd both worked too hard to see it all go down the drain.

Still, neither Mick nor Mia had closed the book on the relationship completely. Maybe as they advanced, perhaps into different divisions at RCSO, they could give it another go. There were plenty of personnel at RCSO involved with each other, either in dating relationships or marriages. It was a very common thing in law enforcement. But most everywhere, relationships between bosses and subordinates were simply forbidden, and RCSO was no exception.

"Anyway," she continued, "this seemed like a pretty cut-and-dried fatality, car versus pedestrian."

"So, what's the problem?"

"The autopsy. Lots of issues, I'm afraid."

"Like what?"

"Glass splinters in the victim's scalp, for starters."

"But he didn't break the windshield," Mick said, proud that he could keep his concentration. He loved it when she wore her hair back. "What else?"

"The victim's core body temperature was much colder than it should have been given the pathology. The ME tech on scene had him at 89.3 just four hours after the accident."

"It was pretty damn cold that morning."

"We asked about that, but Dr. Mora says while the weather may have been a contributing factor, no way does it explain a nine degree drop."

"Shit."

"There's more. Mora found lividity that was consistent with a victim found on his back. My vic was found face down. He also looked at the stomach contents of our vic—looks like his last meal was a nice big steak. Problem is, unless he had that steak dinner at 3:30 in the morning, the digestive time line doesn't add up. That steak hadn't been in his stomach more than an hour or two. Oh, and there's problems with the guy's rifle and ammo. Other than that…"

Captain McCallister considered his options.

"Okay, you convinced me. It looks like this may be more than some random accident, so I want to bring in somebody to assist you."

Mia hesitated. "Okay, that's fine."

"I'm going to ask Jack Keller from homicide to partner with you on this. He's got some quirks, but he's the best guy we have, and you can learn a lot from him."

All homicide investigators with RCSO started off in small units, a few even coming from traffic. She knew this case could be a great opportunity to showcase her skills and learn at the same time.

"Okay, Captain."

"I'll email Keller and let him know."

Mia stood to leave. "Oh, one more thing. Mora said the vic had pancreatic cancer. Probably had only three or four months to live."

"Are you thinking suicide?"

Mia shrugged. "I don't know. It still wouldn't explain everything."

"Anything in the victim's car found at the scene that could point to that?"

"No note or anything. Nothing really out of the ordinary."

"You might want to check with family and friends, just the same. Anything else?"

"No, sir," she said with a smile.

Mia suddenly realized how much she had missed him.

SIX

❧

Jack Keller didn't have many friends outside the department, or inside for that matter, but the few friends he did have would do virtually anything for him. Divorced twice, he swore he'd never go down that path again. Women found Keller's distinguished features attractive, but he had rarely dated in the fifteen years since the last divorce. It had left him both bitter and broke.

He had arrived in Rocklin County almost seven years earlier after doing a thirty-year stint with the St. Louis Metropolitan Police Department in Missouri. At SLMPD, Keller spent more than half his career working homicide cases—investigating more than 250 murders and posting an unheard of conviction rate of nearly 75 percent. But burnout among detectives was commonplace in his old division at SLMPD and the late night call outs, drive-by shootings, and drug-fueled murders pushed many good, hard-working detectives to an early retirement. Jack Keller lasted longer than most but ultimately went the way of the others.

His first marriage was to his high school sweetheart; for the first few years, things went well. The marriage produced a daughter, and Jack and his young family settled in a nice middle class St. Louis neighborhood. Life was good for the Kellers and the future looked bright.

But over the next couple years, as Jack became more and more involved with his career at the PD, things changed dramatically. He landed a coveted position within the department working undercover, but the assignment took everything he had, both physically and emotionally, leaving him with very little time or energy for his young family. The time he did spend at home was spent self-medicating, with Southern Comfort being his medicine of choice. As time went by, Jack's drunken spells became more and more prevalent and the result was a very troubled marriage. Finally, on a cold January night, Jack returned home from working a double shift, only to find his wife and young daughter gone, never to return.

So, Jack Keller worked harder. The department was all he had.

"Come in," McCallister called out from his computer screen after hearing a rap on his office door.

"Sorry, Captain, quick question."

Mick looked up and saw Keller holding his cell phone, pointing to the email displayed on the screen.

"What's this shit?"

SEVEN

〜

M ia spent much of her weekend at the office reviewing everything relative to the Lombard case in anticipation of the meeting with Keller she knew would likely happen Monday. She needed to
get off to a good start with him, or he'd eat her alive—or worse, humil-
iate her in front of the other investigators.

She thought back to her meeting with Mick. He had suggested she
look at the suicide angle, essentially to eliminate it as a possibility. She
opened the Lombard file on her computer to find the next of kin. The
report showed the medical examiner had notified a nephew in Salt
Lake City. She dialed the number, got a voice mail, and left a message.
She didn't say specifically what she needed to ask, but she knew from
experience that people generally called back when police investigators
left messages.

Mia turned her attention to the accident report. A few minutes
later, her office line rang.

"Investigator Serrano."

"Uh, Ms. Serrano, this is Tim Neuhaus returning your call."

"Thanks, Mr. Neuhaus, I appreciate you getting back to me so
quickly."

"You said you had some questions for me about my uncle?"

"Yes, I'm in charge of the investigation into his death."

"Investigation? I was under the impression it was an accident."

"Well, our office looks into all traffic related fatalities. I have just a couple of quick questions, if you don't mind—just for the record."

"Okay," the nephew said tentatively.

"First off, are you the only next of kin?"

"I am. We were all each other had, family wise. My father died of a stroke when I was very young. My mother passed away my freshman year in college, so Uncle George stepped in, more as a mentor than anything. He paid for my college, hounded me about grades, and helped me with my career choices."

"So, were you close to your uncle?"

"Somewhat, but I'm in Utah and he was there in Colorado—so the visits were somewhat infrequent. But we talked quite a bit on the phone."

"When was the last time you saw your uncle?"

"He drove out and spent a week here with my family for the Fourth of July. Our kids are three and four. They called him Grandpa George..."

Tim Neuhaus started to choke up.

Mia tried to offer sympathy, but it was never easy over the phone. "I'm very sorry for your loss."

"I just don't know what we're going to tell the boys."

"Mr. Neuhaus, when you last saw your uncle, how was his health?" Mia tried to transition to her key question gently.

"His health seemed fine when we saw him in July. The kids were a handful and he got a little winded, but we had a great week. Why do you ask?"

"Were you aware your uncle had cancer?"

EIGHT

〜

On Monday afternoon, Gabe Diamond was sitting in his office in Kansas City reviewing insurance payout reports when the email arrived from claims. Diamond was in his late sixties, having retired a decade earlier from the Kansas City PD. He was a gifted investigator and was quickly hired by the Midwestern Life Insurance Company after leaving the force. Before long he rose to the level of lead investigator for the Western U.S. territory. As such, he oversaw a team of sixteen insurance investigators, each with the primary duty of sniffing out insurance fraud in an area that covered twelve states.

Diamond queried the database for the policy. It had been taken out three years earlier—one of two $2 million life insurance policies on business partners at an ice-making operation in Castle Springs, Colorado. Nothing too unusual about that; it was a fairly common practice for small businesses to take out life insurance policies on the primary stakeholders.

He pushed the intercom button on his phone.

"Giselle, I need you to find a number for the Rocklin County Sheriff's Office in Colorado. See if you can me patch me through to someone in their traffic investigations unit."

"Okay, I'll let you know when I have someone on the line."

Diamond sat back and pondered the situation. It was probably nothing, but he thought he should at least have a conversation with

26

officials investigating the accident.

"I have someone on line three."

"Good afternoon. I need to speak to the investigator handling the fatal traffic accident involving a Mr. George Lombard."

"That investigator is on another line, maybe I can help you. My name is Larry Voss—I'm assisting on the case."

"Mr. Voss, my name is Gabe Diamond, and I'm with the Midwestern Life Insurance Company. Three years ago, we wrote a life insurance policy on Mr. Lombard in the amount of two million dollars. We received a call today from the beneficiary on the policy—a Mr. Scott Lennox—who co-owned a business with Mr. Lombard there in your area."

"What can I do for you?' asked Voss, his interest piqued.

"Our claims manager says Mr. Lennox called our offices today asking when he would be receiving the proceeds from the policy. The claims rep tried to explain that it would likely be several weeks before a check would be issued, but that was not acceptable to Mr. Lennox. From what I was told, he became extremely hostile, threatening lawsuits and so on. The rep described his reaction as way over the top, so I was alerted. It's probably nothing, but I thought I should perhaps give you a call as you may want to red flag it."

"Well, I appreciate that, Mr. Diamond. Would it be possible for you to get us a copy of the policy application and paperwork?"

"Sure, I can do that," he said. "What's your fax number?"

"Hey, Mia."

"Come on in, Larry. I'm going over the discrepancies with the autopsy findings before I meet with Jack Keller. I just wish I had more to go on—I mean, there's no way this happened the way Sullivan says it did. But I can't figure out what we have here."

"Would a possible motive and potential suspect help?" Voss replied, holding out some newly faxed pages from the Midwestern Insurance Company.

"You have something?"

"I got a call from an insurance investigator an hour ago who says there is a rather sizable life insurance policy on our dead guy. Two million big ones—all to be paid to Lombard's business partner. And this partner, a guy named Scott Lennox, called the insurance company this morning raising all kinds of hell and demanding his money. The investigator was concerned enough about the guy's behavior to give us a call."

She had just enough time to go over the insurance paperwork before she met with Keller.

McCallister grabbed a chair and dragged it over to Keller's desk. Jack had spent the weekend stewing about Mick's email on Friday requesting he partner with Mia Serrano on the George Lombard death investigation. He wanted to let the Captain know just where he stood on the idea of teaming up with a lowly traffic investigator.

The captain straddled the folding chair in a backwards fashion, set his coffee down on Keller's desk and folded his arms across the chair back. Keller sat back, feet firmly planted on his desk. McCallister leaned in towards Keller and began to speak.

"I know you aren't happy about this, Jack, but we have an opportunity here, a chance for you to mentor someone who I think is a pretty good investigator. So, I need the two of you to work together on this case. She knows you're the lead, and she's excited to work with you—come on, you're a legend around here. I know I can count on your experience and professionalism, correct?"

"I don't typically partner with someone with zero homicide experience. I mean, no offense to the lady, but come on—she's working traffic for God's sake. Frankly, it's beneath me."

"Look, Jack—I know you'd rather have me just reassign this case to you so you could go solo on it, but I really need you to partner with Serrano on this. You'll remember I took a chance on you seven years ago, and it has worked out pretty well for everyone."

"Jesus, Captain, she's just going to get in my way. Let me work this thing on my own. It'll be better for everyone."

"No, Jack. You're going to partner with her and you are going to mentor her. Got it?"

Keller stared at McCallister and let a few awkward seconds go by.

"Yes, Captain."

"Good. Let's get Mia over here right now, and we can do a little debrief on where she is with this case. Will that work for you?"

"You're the boss."

Captain McCallister grabbed the phone off Keller's desk and called Mia's extension.

A few minutes later, Mia Serrano walked into the bullpen.

"Gentlemen," she offered, nodding to the men, feeling at that moment like she was back at the academy.

Mick McCallister stood and pulled up a chair for her.

"So what have we got so far, Investigator Serrano?" Keller asked. His condescending tone prompted a stern look from McCallister.

The glare was enough for Keller to take his feet down off the desk and pay attention.

Mia fired up her laptop and confidently presented the facts of the case, starting with the narrative of the accident and the interview with Lisa Sullivan. From there she talked about Sullivan's car, specifically mentioning the windshield was found intact. The car had checked out mechanically; there was no malfunction with the brakes or steering. Next she covered the autopsy, highlighting Lombard's injuries and cancer diagnosis. She noted the ME's report listing the internal temperature of Lombard's body at barely 89 degrees and lividity that appeared inconsistent with the final resting position of the victim.

As Mia gave her summary, Keller peered closely at the supporting digital images on her laptop.

"That's not a rifle someone would take deer hunting," he said enlarging the image. "That's a damn pea shooter. No way would you try to bag a deer with that thing. And that ammo—it doesn't fit the weapon. Looks to me like someone staged this to look like the deceased was out there hunting that morning. Fucking amateur."

Keller caught himself as the words came out of his mouth. Great, he thought, do I need to watch my language now that I'm working with this woman?

Mia, picking up on Keller's discomfort, quickly agreed, hoping to put him at ease.

"I was just getting to that. And there's more—I just learned our victim was an investor in a local ice company. Lennox Ice had a two million dollar life insurance policy on George Lombard. The beneficiary was his business partner, Scott Lennox.

Mick McCallister's eyebrows shot up as Keller let out a whistle. The captain stood up, slid his chair back to its original position, and said, "Sounds like a pretty good motive to me. Please update me as things progress. I'll be briefing the sheriff later today."

Left alone with his new partner, Keller continued to review the evidence. Mia watched him anxiously, as a student would awaiting an assignment from her teacher.

"Good to know about the life insurance," Keller said. "It could be a big piece of the puzzle. All these pieces are pointing to a homicide."

Keller peered up at Mia over his glasses. "Good start," he said. "I suggest we call on Mr. Lennox."

So far, so good, Mia thought.

NINE

The Lennox Ice Company was located in an isolated industrial area on the east side of Castle Springs. The plant consisted of several long, tall buildings that ran parallel to each other. Sound from refrigeration units, transport trucks, and ice cutting blades echoed throughout the area. Adjacent to these buildings was a main office with a small parking lot in front.

Keller's unmarked car had seen better days. It rattled through the potholes in the parking lot as he pulled in.

"Follow my lead and don't bring up any details unless I do first. And don't mention the insurance."

"Got it," said Mia.

They climbed the stairs to the main office and walked through a set of double doors. Inside, a man stood behind a counter, sorting through paperwork. A large doorway behind him opened to a warehouse. The doors were thick rubber with big scratched Plexiglas windows.

"Can I help you?"

Keller flashed his badge. "Yes, I'm Jack Keller, and this is my partner, Mia Serrano. We're with the Rocklin County Sheriff's Office. We're looking for Scott Lennox."

"I'm Scott Lennox. What can I do for you?"

"We're investigating the death of your business partner, George Lombard. We won't take much of your time—we just have a few questions. May we sit down?"

"Why don't we go in the back," Lennox said.

Scott Lennox was in his mid-forties, clean-cut and handsome, with dark brown hair and deep-set blue eyes. He dressed in a western-style plaid shirt, belt, jeans, and simple work boots.

He escorted them to a large room behind the reception area. There were no other employees in the administration area. The office was stark, and the sounds coming from the refrigeration units in the nearby buildings were clearly audible. The noise was offset somewhat by the country music being piped into the office.

Mia recognized the song right away. "Back to Texas" was one of her favorites from Tripp Barnes, a popular country singer/songwriter known for his good looks and deep voice.

"I'm not sure what I can tell you. I was shocked. It was a horrible accident."

Lennox offered them seats at a large wooden conference table but didn't offer water or coffee. Both investigators sensed Lennox wanted the meeting to be brief. Keller sat in silence looking intently at their potential suspect. The pause was uncomfortable, and Mia fought the urge to fill the void. Keller set the pace and the mood, and he did so effortlessly.

Lennox quickly became unnerved. He shifted in his chair awkwardly. "So, how can I help you?"

"Oh, this is all routine. Paperwork, you know. We have to interview people who knew the victim just to tie up any loose ends for the report."

"But it was an accident, right?" Lennox asked uncomfortably. "He was hit by a car."

"Yes, that's correct," Keller assured him. "But Mr. Lennox—may I call you Scott?"

"Uh, sure."

"Scott, we have all these procedures. If it was just an accident involving a car and a pedestrian, we might just call and do all this nice and neat on the phone. But because there was a gun involved, a rifle actually, it opens up a can of worms. The state requires all kinds of forms be filled out if there's any sort of gun involved. I'm sure you understand."

Lennox nodded as if he did.

"So, we know Mr. Lombard was hunting that morning. He had a hunter's vest on, and we found a rifle belonging to him near his body. But we keep asking ourselves why Mr. Lombard was out hunting so early that morning. I mean, it was bitter cold, and he was out there looking for deer? Does that seem peculiar to you?" asked Keller.

"Not at all. George lived to hunt, anytime, anywhere. He'd go out several times a week during deer season. Sometimes just to study their patterns. In fact, he kept some of his hunting gear here in his office so he could go at a moment's notice. I think it was his way of relieving stress."

"Hmm." Keller made a few scribbles in his notebook. Mia figured he was just doodling to toy with Lennox but couldn't tell.

"I don't hunt, so I don't really know. It's not my thing."

More scribbling.

"So, what exactly did Mr. Lombard do here?"

Lennox eased up a little. "He was my partner. Numbers aren't really my strength, so he brought a lot to the financial side of the business. I learned a lot from him. We've expanded quite a bit over the past three years, mostly because of George."

"I'm sure you're being a little modest, after all that's your name on the door. How did you two partner up?"

"A few years ago, a mutual friend put me and George together. I needed capital for expansion but banks don't want to give you money unless you don't need it. He believed in what we were doing here and took a percentage of the company in exchange for the investment. He also helped us on the financial side. He was great with the financial stuff, so he pretty much ran that side of the business. I couldn't have done this without him," he said softly.

"We're sorry for your loss," Jack offered. "You said he handled the finances. Did Mr. Lombard work here in the office?"

"He spent a lot of time here in the early days. But over the past year or so he started coming in less and less. George had other investments, and I think he managed them from home. These days, he's in two, maybe three days a week. Or was, I guess I should say."

Keller gave Lennox a moment and shifted gears. "So how much ice do you guys make here in a given day?"

"About eighty tons a day, sometimes more. We service grocery stores, convenience stores, fresh food producers, hospitality, and so on. Cubed, crushed, block. If you want ice, we've got it," Lennox said proudly, smiling for the first time since they arrived.

As Tripp Barnes started up in the background with a rendition of the Eagles song "Take it Easy," Keller turned to Mia, inviting her into the conversation.

"Eighty tons a day, can you believe that, Serrano?" he said, genuinely.

"That's pretty impressive," Mia replied. "I notice you're playing Tripp Barnes in here over your loudspeakers. Are you a fan?"

"Oh yeah, since before he was anybody. I got to meet him once several years ago at a little club in Boulder. A couple of us from here at the plant went out to see him perform. He was just starting out back then, but everyone knew he was going to be big. I've been to every concert he's performed here in Colorado and a few in Kansas City as well."

"I saw him at the Pepsi Center in Denver a few years ago," Mia added.

Lennox was in his element. "Crossroads tour. That was a great show. Did you see him at Red Rocks several months back?"

"Unfortunately, no," Mia said. "Work, ya know."

"A friend got me 7th row, center. It was amazing." Lennox boasted.

"Was Mr. Lombard a fan?"

"Not really. In fact, George wasn't much of a music guy."

"Do you mind if we get a look in his office?" Jack asked.

"Sure, I guess so."

Lombard's office was small and sparse. There was a modest desk, computer, and printer on one side and a clothes locker and gun safe on the other.

"Can we get a look inside these? It's just routine," Keller asked.

Lennox quickly pulled open Lombard's top right desk drawer, opened a small keepsake box, took out a key ring with two keys, and used one to open the gun safe. Inside, there were three rifles and a .45 caliber handgun, along with an assortment of ammunition. The investigators were careful not to touch anything, but Mia took notes.

"Okay if we look in here too, Scott?" asked Keller.

"Yeah, we can do that."

Using the second key on the ring, Lennox opened the locker. Inside they found an array of hunting gear, mostly camouflage, along with hats, boots and gloves. Lombard was prepared for any weather condition, even temperatures well below freezing.

Keller asked, "Does anyone else have access to this office?"

"No, just George. I mean, I have keys to everything here, but I have no reason to ever go in here."

As they headed back toward the lobby, Keller made small talk.

"How do you make so much ice, and how do you deliver it all?"

"Well the entire operation is highly automated. That's why you don't see a lot of people around. We make the ice in those buildings over there," Scott said, motioning across the small parking lot. "We do cubes and crushed from those two, there's storage in the third and we do big blocks and special orders in this building. We load the ice in freezer trucks and deliver directly to the customer."

"How cold is it inside those trucks? I mean, the ice melts if it's not kept below thirty-two degrees, right?"

"For storage and transport we try to stay between 20 and 25 degrees depending on the season. Those truck doors get opened quite a bit on a delivery route and we have to maintain quality."

"Wow, this is really some operation you got here. Well, listen Scott, you've been very helpful, and we really appreciate your time. Again, we're sorry for your loss."

"Thank you," Lennox said.

They all shook hands. "I think we have all we need. Best of luck to you," Keller said.

"You too. Have a good day," offered Lennox, seemingly relieved.

As Mia and Keller walked towards their car, the sharp "beep, beep, beep" sound of a forklift echoed between the buildings. They watched as a worker climbed down from the forklift, flipped open the latch to a delivery truck, and pushed up the heavy door. The investigators were some thirty feet away but the blast of cold air from the truck immediately took Mia's mind back to the icy cold of the other morning when she saw George Lombard for the first time.

"Well, what do you make of it?" Mia asked.

"You first," Keller replied.

Mia knew this was the first of what would be many evaluations by her new partner.

"Well, going in I figured he was the guy. Now, I'm not so sure. He's hard to read."

"Yep, he's pretty cool and collected, no pun intended," Keller said with a smirk. "Didn't seem to try to hide anything. He allowed us access to Lombard's office and lockers, and he was forthcoming about the business. He either had nothing to do with it, or he figures we don't have a clue. Maybe he thinks he's pulled off the perfect crime."

"You didn't ask him about the insurance money or mention Lombard's terminal cancer."

"In cases like this, it's better to play one card at a time. It's like poker. He gave us a bit of a tell. Did you catch it?"

Mia thought it better to be honest rather than guess. "No," she told him.

"The gun locker. Lennox knew exactly where that key was. He doesn't hunt and says they don't spend much time together, but he went directly for that key. It's possible Lombard told him where it was, but I don't think so. Why would he?"

"If Scott Lennox did kill him for the insurance money, imagine his surprise when he learns Lombard had cancer and would likely have been dead within three months anyway," added Mia.

"Yeah, bummer for him," chuckled Keller, shaking his head.

"So, what's the next step?" she asked.

"Focus on the moment at hand, be aware of the next, learn from the last. How many suspects do we have so far?"

"One. Lennox."

"So we focus on that and try and figure out if he's our guy. How could Scott Lennox make this homicide look like a run of the mill traffic accident? How did he get Lombard out on Highway 46 that morning? Did he push him in front of the car? Was he already dead when the lady hit him? Was he killed somewhere else and then dumped out there? I don't know, but this was no accident, and it ain't no suicide."

They drove quietly through Castle Springs as the heat of the sun worked to melt the recent snowfall. Keller thought about the $2 million payday that would come Scott Lennox's way if they couldn't make a case.

"I think we should go and talk with the woman who hit him," Mia said. "She was in shock that morning. Maybe by now she can give us more."

"Okay, Investigator, but what do we do before visiting the driver?" quizzed Keller.

Mia was clueless. "What?"

"What time is it?"

Mia looked at her phone. "11:45."

"Right. We get lunch."

TEN

The small town of Rosebud was a thirty-minute drive from the Lennox Ice Company in Castle Springs. It was nearly 1:30 by the time Keller and Mia pulled up in front of Lisa Sullivan's apartment building. The hour they spent at Sal's, the Jalisco-style Mexican restaurant where Jack Keller introduced Mia Serrano to some of the best Mexican food she had ever tasted, had been time well spent.

On the way out to Rosebud, Mia suggested they call Lisa Sullivan to make sure she was home. Keller disagreed. He said it was better for investigators to arrive unannounced and keep the subject off balance. It gave them less time to cook up a story—if there was one to cook up. Keller figured if Sullivan really was as shaken up as she appeared, there was a good chance she hadn't yet returned to work, so she was likely home.

The Pine Tree Apartments in Rosebud were tired, in need of paint and maintenance. Carports offered the tenants marginal protection from the harsh Colorado winters, though some appeared on the verge of collapse. The complex had a large pool, covered for the winter, two tennis courts and a BBQ area. It had been a nice family complex thirty years ago.

Keller decided Mia would be the lead on the Sullivan interview. They parked and made their way up some creaky steps to the apartment marked #238. Mia rapped on the door and waited. Thirty seconds ticked by with no response. She banged on the door again, only harder. She noticed a corner of the curtain covering the window a few feet from the door open slightly. She held out her badge in the direction of the curtain.

The deadbolt turned a few seconds later, and the door opened just a few inches. The safety chain tightened.

"Yes?"

"Ms. Sullivan, it's Mia Serrano with the RCSO. I was the investigator you talked to at the accident you were involved in last week. Can we come in and talk for a few minutes?"

"Give me a minute. I gotta put something on."

The door closed slowly and caught.

It was a long minute. The two investigators eyed each other warily. Keller's senses heightened, taking in every visual cue, sound or movement. They had no way of knowing what was on the other side of the door or around the building. Sullivan was probably touching up her makeup, but she, or someone else inside could be loading up a weapon. Far too many cops die in situations just like this, and Keller knew it.

He reached for his Glock and nodded for Mia to do the same. Both pulled their weapons, clicked off the safeties and held them low and out of sight. They stayed clear of the doorway and listened closely for anything going on inside the apartment. The seconds dragged on.

Finally, the chain shifted sharply and the door opened seemingly in a single movement. The investigators both instinctively snapped their muzzles toward the sound, but stopped short when Sullivan's hands appeared and pulled back the door. They quickly holstered their weapons. The woman hadn't even noticed.

Lisa Sullivan apologized for keeping them waiting. Mia gave her the once over. Sullivan looked better than she did the morning of the accident but not by much. She wore a large, old Denver Broncos sweatshirt with jeans and was barefoot. Her face was haggard, with black circles under her swollen eyes.

Mia introduced Lisa to Investigator Keller. They shook hands, but Sullivan paid little notice.

"Come in, if you want," she said. "But I told you everything the other day. This is such a nightmare. I wish I could forget it ever happened."

"We understand, but we are just trying to wrap up the loose ends of the investigation. It shouldn't take too long," responded Mia.

"Okay, then."

Sullivan guided them through the cramped living room to the kitchen, where she offered them a seat at a small table. Across the kitchen sat an old refrigerator, along with a stove and oven that were at least thirty years old and avocado in color. The burnt orange linoleum on the floor was cracking and peeling up in one corner.

"What do you need to know?"

"That morning, you said Mr. Lombard, the deceased, suddenly appeared in front of you. You said he looked to you like a deer in headlights. Do you remember saying that to me?"

"Not really. I just know that there was nothing I could have done to miss him. It was dark and the curve in the road—"

Mia cut her off. "No, no, I don't mean to imply there was something you could have done differently. That's not why we're here. We just need to clarify a few things for the final report."

"Well, I think I told you everything. I really just want to forget the whole thing."

"I understand. We won't take much of your time today. But that morning you said he appeared to be standing in the roadway. Could you tell us again about that?"

"Well, I'm not really sure. That may have just been the shock of hitting him. Everything seemed to be in slow motion, so in reality, I'm sure he wasn't just standing there."

"Do you remember if he was turned to either side when you struck him, or was he facing you, or did he try to turn away or move away when he realized he was going to be hit?"

"It all happened in a split second. Am I going to be in trouble now for hitting him? It was an accident, I swear. I didn't mean to do it."

"No, I don't mean to upset you. We are just trying to close out the case."

"When will the case be closed? I just want it to be over."

"It should be wrapped up pretty soon. Is there anything you've remembered since that morning?"

"No, nothing at all. I told you everything that day. I don't understand why you're here. It was an accident. Like I said, I didn't mean to kill the poor man."

"Okay, we just thought that some time had passed, and that you might recall some other details."

"No, I told you everything, I swear."

Mia eyed Keller for guidance. He offered only a blank expression. This was looking like a dead end.

"Okay, well, thanks for your time, Miss Sullivan."

Mia felt sorry for her. Lisa Sullivan clearly had trouble making ends meet and her apartment was a dump with an avocado-colored refrigerator. Like the one Mia remembered from her own home, Sullivan's was covered with magnets. They held pictures of friends, cats and an old concert ticket. Mia studied it.

"Are you a Tripp Barnes fan?" Mia asked Sullivan. "It looks like you went to a concert at Red Rocks a while back. I was there, too. Great show," Mia lied. "Wow, you had great seats," she added, glancing at Keller.

"We were so lucky to get those seats," Lisa said, upbeat for the first time. "I try to go to all his concerts. That was the first time I've ever been really close to the stage."

Keller had made the connection, but instead focused on an old photo—one with a young woman with a small girl sitting in her lap.

"Is this you in the picture?" he asked Sullivan.

"Yes, that's me in my mom's lap... I think I was about three. I really don't remember it. I was so young."

"Where did you grow up?"

"I'm from the Midwest originally, and then my mom moved us here to Rosebud. She was a single mom, and we moved to Colorado when she found work out here."

"What kind of work did she do?"

"She was an office manager for a couple of different medical supply companies. First in Denver, and then later here in Rosebud. She died two years ago."

Keller examined the photo closely. "You look like your mom," he said quietly.

Lisa smiled and nodded.

"Everybody tells me that."

"Is this your sister?" Mia asked, as she pointed to one of the girl-friend pictures that appeared to have been taken at a bar.

"Uh, yeah, that's her."

"Is she the one you were going to visit in Big Pine the morning of the accident—the one going through the divorce?"

"Um, yeah."

"How is she doing?" responded Mia.

"Oh, she's fine."

After an uncomfortable pause, the pair thanked Lisa Sullivan again for her time and left.

As soon as they were back in the car Mia started in. "Seventh row at Red Rocks? And that woman she says is her sister looks nothing like her. I don't know what she's selling, but I'm not buying it."

"We'll need more than a concert ticket for a conviction in a murder case. A hundred people could have been in the seventh row. And sisters often don't look alike. My kids don't look anything like each other," responded Keller, looking out the window at the hillsides covered in pine trees as they headed toward I-25.

"So you don't see a link with her and Lennox?"

"It's possible, I guess."

"I wish I had gotten a better look at the seat number on that ticket stub. You didn't happen to catch it, did you?"

"No, I didn't," Keller responded with a shrug.

Mia wondered why Keller was so dismissive about the concert. She decided to let it be, for now.

"Investigators were just here, and they were asking me again about what happened. I just answered the questions the same way I answered them the day of the accident. I don't understand why they keep asking me stuff," Lisa Sullivan said into her cell phone as she paced across her living room.

"It will happen, just a few more weeks and the money will be here," the man told her.

"And then we can leave?" Sullivan asked.

"Yep, we are all set. Once we get the money, we are out of here forever."

"God, I wish I could see you. I'm scared to death."

"Tell you what," Keller said as they pulled into the Justice Center complex. "I've got a buddy at Ticketline. I'll have him take a look at the transactions for the seventh row for that particular concert at Red Rocks. He works up in Denver, and he owes me a favor. It's almost end of shift, so if you don't mind, I'll just drop you off, and I'll run up there and pay him a visit. You see what you can dig up on Lennox, okay?"

"Okay, Jack."

Mia climbed out and headed back to her office. As she was passing by the admin section she decided to drop in on McCallister and give him a quick briefing. Mick was packing up a laptop and files from his desk when she arrived.

"Hey, Captain. Keller and I just interviewed Scott Lennox and the woman that hit our hunter out on 46. Do you have a few minutes for an update?"

"Actually, no—I'm off to a meeting with the sheriff. And it could run 'til six."

They eyed each other awkwardly.

"Um, what about tonight?" he asked. "I mean, maybe we could meet up somewhere, and you can brief me then."

Mia was caught off guard. "Sure, I guess we could do that."

"Okay, good."

Mia took a chance. "I could make you dinner at my place. I think I've got something in the fridge I could whip up."

"That would be great, Mia. How about seven?"

"See you then," Mia said with a smile and disappeared.

Mick stood in his office as her fleeting scent washed over him. He breathed her in as he had so many times before, then grabbed his stack of paperwork and muttered to himself on the way out.

"That was probably a bad idea."

ELEVEN

Mia quickly gathered her things and headed for her car. Once inside, she pulled out her cell phone, dialed the number, and put it on speaker.

"Hello?"

"Dad, I need you to do me a favor."

"Sure, honey, anything."

"Go to the freezer and see if we have any steaks in there. I can't remember if you and I finished up the last of them."

"Okay, hold on… Yeah, we've still got two. Want me to take them out for us tonight?"

"Well, actually—we are going to have company tonight, so I'm afraid we won't have enough steak for all three of us."

"Who's coming over?" he asked.

"Mick. We've got some work stuff to talk about," Mia replied. "In the bowl on the counter, in the corner between the sink and fridge. Do you see the reddish bag?"

"Sure do."

"There should be three or four potatoes in there. Pull out one of the potatoes, look at it closely and tell me if anything is growing out of it."

Fortunately, the potatoes were still good and over the next twenty minutes Mia was able to talk her dad through the preparations for Mick's seven o'clock arrival.

He may not have been a wizard in the kitchen, but Chuck Serrano knew a lot about igniting rocket engines anywhere NASA needed him. Aside from his work on a variety of government space programs in the 1970s and 80s, Chuck had performed some highly classified work for the military. Dr. Serrano, as he was widely known in the industry, had signed on with WellRock Technology after graduating from Cal Tech with a PhD in propulsion dynamics some forty-five years earlier.

Chuck had been working on his doctoral thesis when he met the woman of his dreams at the Rose Bowl in Pasadena, not far from the Cal Tech campus. He'd often joke to friends that the pair had met at the Rose Bowl during his very last football game, a game at which he had suffered a career ending injury. There was a grain of truth to the story. Chuck's "career" was a part-time job as an usher at UCLA football home games. He'd taken on a variety of odd jobs to make ends meet while finishing work on his PhD and ushering at the Rose Bowl was one of the better ones.

His season-ending injury occurred at an UCLA-Oregon State game in late November. The Bruins were victorious that evening and within thirty minutes most of the fans had left the stadium. On a final check of his section he noticed a young woman seated alone near the entry tunnel. She appeared worried and Chuck went to offer help. He never saw the spilled beer on the aisle and down he went, slamming his shin into a concrete step. The young woman ended up helping Chuck instead. The sight of her took his pain away; Dolores Monahan was the most beautiful woman he'd ever seen.

She was a UCLA co-ed in her senior year studying English. She never cared much for football but had come to the game at the insistence of her sorority sisters. After a last second touchdown gave UCLA the victory, there was bedlam in the stands and Dolores got separated from her friends. As the crowds cleared the stadium, she returned to her seat hoping they'd come back for her. In reality, her friends had run into a group of fraternity boys and most had already paired up and left, assuming she had done the same.

Chuck introduced himself and after twenty minutes of conversation he convinced Dolores to allow him to drive her back to the Westwood campus. He never let on about the pain he was experiencing in his leg, but he could barely manage to put his foot to the gas pedal. A hairline fracture in his tibia ended his career as an usher, but Chuck's new life with Dolores was just beginning.

WellRock Technologies was a leading player in the space program during the 1970s, keeping Chuck Serrano very busy. The 1980s brought the space shuttle program, and with satellite launches and missile development, he was in demand. In the early days of his career the job required quite a bit of travel, and Chuck and Dolores enjoyed crisscrossing the country from one project to another. With the birth of their daughter Mia a few years later, the family settled in the Denver suburb of Centennial near the company's headquarters. The crisp Colorado air suited them, and they quickly became part of the community. Dolores was very active in her church league while Chuck attended Rotary when in town. Chuck put in another fifteen years before retiring at the age of sixty-two.

Dolores's death was a crushing blow to Chuck Serrano. Cancer had taken her quickly, and Chuck struggled without his beloved wife. Mia would stop by as often as possible to make sure he was eating and getting along. Mostly she found him sitting around the house looking out the window or watching television.

By the mid-2000's, Mia had scrimped and saved enough to finally buy her own place, but when the bottom fell out of the market and the interest rate on her adjustable loan started climbing, she found herself in financial trouble. Mia went to her father and asked if he would be willing to move in with her and help with the mortgage payment. He quickly agreed and the arrangement allowed her to keep her house and gave Chuck a new purpose in life. Mia's financial troubles ultimately turned out to be a blessing for them both.

Chuck considered Mick and Mia to be a great couple. They reminded him of the early days with Dolores. He had hidden his disappointment when the pair broke it off but now was excited Mick would be returning, at least for dinner. Tonight he would simply stay out of the way.

"Wow, Mia, that was terrific," Mick said, polishing off his last bite of steak with a sip of Pinot Noir.

"Thanks, but I have to be honest. Dad helped."

"Well, both of you did a great job. Let me help you clear the dishes while you brief me on the Lombard case, okay?"

"Works for me," said Mia.

Mia gave Mick the latest on the investigation, including a rundown on the interviews she and Keller had conducted with Lennox and Sullivan. It was clear that she and her boss were on the same page with the case, with neither believing it was a random accident.

"How's it been working with Keller?" Mick asked as he dried the final dish.

"He's been fine. I'm definitely learning from him. He's an odd guy, but I think a lot of great investigators are like that."

"Not sure if you know this, but I'm the one who did his background check before he came on board with us."

"Really? I didn't know."

Mia topped off their glasses with the last wine from the bottle and suggested they move to the living room. The large picture window offered a view of the snow as it began to fall. The pair sat closely on the sofa facing the window.

"So the sheriff sent me to St. Louis so I could meet some of Keller's old co-workers, you know, off the record stuff. I learned a lot and not all of it good."

"Like…?" Mia caught herself. She didn't want to put Mick on the spot. What they were talking about was highly confidential, and she immediately regretted asking him the question. Fortunately, Mick didn't seem to mind.

"He had a pretty spotty personal life—a couple of divorces. He had a teenage son that died in a car crash, maybe a year or two before he retired. The toxicology report showed the kid had been drinking and was way over the limit. Keller took it hard, as you might expect, but there was another component to it. His buddies told me Keller blamed himself for his son's death because he himself was an alcoholic. The apple doesn't fall too far from the tree kind of thing. Everybody I talked to back there told me Keller was a serious, big-time drinker. But they said it never got in the way of his work, so the PD overlooked it for the most part. But eventually the brass got tired of his antics and he left the department."

"Did he get canned?"

"Technically, he retired, but it wasn't exactly voluntary. He started hitting the bottle again really hard after his son's death. Then Keller had his own accident. I never got any of the details, but off the record, the higher ups in St. Louis gave me the impression Keller covered it up. The brass didn't want a big scandal so they agreed to sweep the incident under the carpet, provided he retired. And so he did."

"So how did we end up with him?"

"Once he retired, he spent a year or two getting sober, down in Mexico somewhere as I recall, and he managed to put his life back together. But after being retired for that year or two he got bored and applied at RCSO. We needed someone like that in our homicide unit, so we, the sheriff really, took a chance on him and offered him the job."

"Wow, I had no idea. What a lot to go through. Gotta give him credit for getting his life back together."

They sipped wine and watched the snow starting to pile up outside. "There was something else I wanted to tell you," Mick said.

"Hmm, that sounds a bit ominous."

"No, no, it's nothing bad. As you probably know, Sheriff Connelly is planning to retire at the end of his term."

"And?"

"And I'm thinking about running for sheriff. I'm not one hundred percent sure yet, but it's something I am seriously considering, and I wanted you to hear it from me, not someone else. Word leaks out prematurely sometimes, and I just thought I'd give you a heads up."

"Wow. Sheriff McCallister. I like the sound of that," Mia replied, smiling impishly.

"Well, let's not get ahead of ourselves. It's still a ways off, but I am putting some feelers out… kind of testing the waters."

"And what kind of response are you getting?"

"Surprisingly positive, actually."

"I would expect nothing less, Mick. You'd be a phenomenal sheriff, and you have my complete support."

"Well, I really appreciate that—it means a lot to me."

"Is there anything I can do to help you?"

"Not yet, I still need to make a final decision. But once that happens I will need to put together a campaign team, and I'd really be honored if you'd be a part of it. And if your dad would be interested, I'd like to have him be a part of the effort as well."

"Of course, Mick! My God—Dad will be thrilled!"

"Please keep this to yourself for now—I don't need word leaking out prematurely."

"I won't say a word, Mick. No matter your decision, I'm so proud of you."

"Thanks, Mia. I better get going, it's already past eleven, and it looks like the weather is going to be a challenge tonight."

Mia didn't want Mick to leave, but knew it was best.

They stood and walked to the door together.

"I had a great time tonight, Mia. Thank you for dinner."

"You're welcome. I enjoyed cooking for you. It was like old times."

Mick started to speak but instead held out his arms. She instinctively moved to him. She felt safe and warm. They embraced for nearly a minute until Mick leaned in and kissed her gently on the lips.

"Goodnight, Mia."

"Goodnight, Sheriff."

Mia heard Mick's car pull away and realized how much she had missed him in her life. This, she believed, could be a new start. Decisions would have to be made and sacrifices might follow. For now though, Mia Serrano just enjoyed having Mick McCallister back in her life.

Mia wrapped herself in a warm blanket and watched the snow fall from the warmth of the sofa. Exhausted, she drifted off to sleep.

Tonight there would be no nightmares.

TWELVE

Mornings were generally quiet at the Super Discount Mart in Castle Springs, and on this particular morning the overnight snowfall had kept even the most dedicated bargain shoppers at home. Keller parked his F-150 truck and walked across the freshly plowed lot. There was no greeter inside and few staff to help him, but he quickly found the electronics section.

Pre-paid phones, also commonly known as burner phones, are marketed to lower income customers and those with bad credit. Most of the phones allow users to place calls and send texts, with some even allowing internet access. Burner phones also provided criminals with untraceable phone numbers, allowing for secret calls and texts. They were a big headache for law enforcement, as Keller knew all too well.

He grabbed two burner phones, each pre-loaded with 480 minutes of talk and text time. He paid in cash, walked outside, climbed into his truck, and headed north up I-25 toward the I-70 interchange.

Jack Keller was driving toward his past at 60 miles per hour.

THIRTEEN

Mia's phone buzzed. "Taking 2day off. Talk 2morrow." The text was from Keller.

Frustrated at first, Mia instead took advantage of the break from Keller to break down Lisa Sullivan's story. Most importantly, the sister she claimed to have in Big Pine. If there was no sister, as Mia suspected, why was Sullivan on Highway 46 that morning? Her investigation had to be low profile. If Sullivan was culpable, Serrano didn't want her to know someone might be on to her.

She started searching. If Sullivan's sister was married, she'd likely have a different surname. Standard Internet searches led nowhere, Sullivan or no Sullivan. Facebook made it easier to search maiden names, but she came up empty there, too. She searched the crime database for women 25-40 and found no decent leads for anyone near Big Pine. She even searched marriage records in all regional counties. Nothing.

Mia's eyes ached from the glare of the computer screen. It was time for plan B.

An hour later, Inspector Mia Serrano pulled into Big Pine. She drove along the main drag trying to come up with a plan. Finally, she passed by the Big Pine Post Office. Bingo. The post office was the center of every small town, she thought. She parked, went inside, and took a place in line.

"Next."

Mia looked up and saw the postal clerk looking in her direction.

"Hi, just a book of stamps, please."

"You want the new ones with the Olympic torch on it?"

"Sure, that would be fine."

As the clerk reached into the drawer to get the stamps, Mia started up a conversation.

"It's been a long time since I was in Big Pine—I see the town still looks the same."

The clerk eyed her cautiously before answering.

"You from around here?"

"No, but I had a very good friend from Big Pine, and I used to visit her a lot. Her name is Lisa Sullivan, but I'm afraid I've lost track of her."

"Sullivan, you say? How long ago was this?"

"Oh, it was a few years back. She had a sister who lived here as well, although her name escapes me right now."

"Well, I pride myself on knowing pretty much every person who lives here in Big Pine, and I know there ain't no Sullivans living here now. Now there was one Sullivan, going back maybe twenty years or so, but it was an old grouch by the name of Eddie Sullivan, and he lived alone. No way did he have any daughters. If he had any, they would have likely killed him at some point. What a piece of work that guy was."

"Well, maybe I've got my facts mixed up. So what do I owe you for the stamps?" She had come up empty on the sister, but salvaged postage for Christmas cards.

FOURTEEN

With the breakfast rush over, the parking lot of the Mountain Cafe, some forty miles west of Denver, was nearly deserted. A few minutes early, Keller sat in his truck and thought about his situation. He was starting down a dangerous path and once he started there would be no going back, but he was determined to set things right.

Keller climbed out of his truck and headed inside the café, picking a booth in the back for maximum privacy. He sat down with his back to the wall allowing for a full view of the place. He took out his cell phone and checked for any messages. There were none.

"What can I get you, hon?" the waitress asked, approaching the table and armed with a pot of coffee.

"I'm expecting someone, but I wouldn't mind a Diet Coke."

"Comin' right up," she replied as she turned and walked back towards the bar.

Keller reached into his coat pocket and took out an old tape recorder. He didn't like or trust the new digital recorders most deputies used. As an investigator, Jack made a habit of recording nearly every interview he conducted. He wasn't sure what would come of this meeting but having an audio recording of whatever was said would be something of an insurance policy for him. He only hoped he would never need it.

"Here you go, partner."

Keller sipped his drink and took a deep breath. He waited, nervously checking his watch.

The sunlight streaming through the café from a large window near the entrance made it difficult for him to see her at first. A few seconds later, a very angry Lisa Sullivan approached the booth.

"Why the hell did you drag me all the way out here?" she said angrily. "I've told you people a hundred times, it was an accident."

"Look, just calm down," Keller urged.

"You want something to drink?" asked the waitress.

"Iced tea, please."

Lisa turned her attention back to the matter at hand.

"Where's your partner?"

"It's just me today."

Lisa Sullivan tried to piece together what was happening. Her eyes narrowed.

"Wait a minute, I get it. You lure me out to the middle of nowhere. You're one of those pervert cops that take advantage—"

Keller interrupted, "No, I'm not a pervert. Look, I know this is difficult for you, but you need to understand that I am here to help you."

"Why would you help me? It seems like all you and your partner do is harass me. In fact, I'm thinking about filing a complaint against you with the department. This whole thing has been a nightmare—I keep telling you it was an accident, but you people don't get that. And then you call me and say you need to talk with me again? I'm going to ask you one more time, and then I'm going to start screaming. What do you want?"

The look on the young woman's face told Keller she meant it.

"Lisa, sit down. I need for you to listen to me very carefully. The picture on your refrigerator in your apartment... the one of you and your mother when you were three years old..."

Lisa reluctantly took a seat in the booth.

"You mean the one my dad took."

"Yes, that one... I took that picture."

A shocked and horrified look crossed her face.

"When things were still good between me and your mother."

"Oh my God."

Lisa slowly lowered her head into her hands and began to cry. Thirty years of sadness and anger poured out of her.

The waitress delivered the iced tea and glared at Keller. "Asshole," she muttered.

Keller let it go. He knew what it looked like.

"Look, I need you to understand some things," Keller said quietly.

"I'm not here as an investigator. I'm here as your father because you need my help."

"Help? How dare you!" Suddenly, Lisa picked up her glass and flung the contents at Keller, hitting him squarely in the face.

"Like the way you helped my mother when you walked out on her? Like the way you walked out on your family?"

Tea covered Keller's face and shirt. He made no attempt to dry himself off. He could see the waitress chuckling from across the restaurant.

"I know I hurt you. And you'll never begin to know how sorry I am for that. But let me be clear about something. I didn't leave you and your mother—she left me. Now, understand there were plenty of good reasons to leave me, but she's the one that pulled the plug, not me."

"You're a fucking liar. You abandoned us. You left us without a god-damn word. You are dead to me—do you understand?"

Lisa started to get up. Keller grabbed her arm and looked up at his daughter, his face still dripping iced tea.

"Okay, I don't know what your mother told you, but it didn't happen that way. We can talk more about if you'd like, but right now we need to talk about what happened the other morning."

Keller paused and looked directly into his daughter's eyes.

"I know it wasn't an accident, and you need to understand that George Lombard's death is on your hands. And if you don't listen to me, you're going to prison."

Lisa Sullivan looked at this man she barely knew. Her mouth quivered. Dazed, she slowly lowered herself back into the booth.

"I can help you. But I need to know what happened that morning."

"I need to know what happened between you and my mother. Tell me what happened that day almost thirty years ago. I need to know that before we go any further."

This was painful. In Lisa, Keller saw both a grown woman and the little girl he knew so long ago.

Lisa continued, "Mom refused to talk about it. She wouldn't even tell me your name. She said you were dead. She changed our last name for God's sake. And now, here you are sitting across from me. I'm owed some fucking answers."

"Okay, then I'll tell you. I was in my mid-twenties, a young detective with a big department in St. Louis, and I was feeling the pressure of a lot of new responsibilities. A wife, a new daughter, a mortgage on a house we really couldn't afford... I don't know. I felt like I couldn't breathe. I started working ungodly hours, which didn't sit very well with your mother and understandably so. I started drinking heavily. I was trying to find peace in a bottle—a lot of bottles, actually. I realized that years later, and I got sober. Look, I'm an alcoholic. Being a drunk is a daily battle, but I've been sober for eight years now. Anyway, I came home one night, and you and your mother were gone. No note. Nothing. She just packed up, and the two of you were in the wind."

Keller had fallen on his sword, but Lisa showed no emotion.

"Well, it sounds like you had it coming," Lisa said. "So why didn't you try to track us down? Can't you do that as a cop? If you wanted to find us, you could have. So, basically you just left us behind. What, did you start a new family that wasn't so much trouble?"

"Actually, I did, years later, but it ended in divorce. And just like your mother—she left me. We had a son. He was killed ten years ago in a DUI."

Neither knew what to say next.

"After he died, I hit the bottle even harder. I lost my job. And then one day, I just had enough and stopped. It wasn't easy like it sounds, but truth be told, his death saved my life."

"What was his name?" Lisa asked, thinking about losing a stepbrother she never knew she had.

"Brian."

"I'm sorry."

Keller nodded quietly. "I was sorry to hear your mom has passed. She really deserved better."

"She did. The cancer took her quickly. She didn't suffer much," Lisa answered, tearing up again.

"Once I got sober I thought about trying to find you, but I decided it best just to stay away. I figured I'd caused enough pain, and you were better off without me. Now, in some small way, I want to make it up to you. I want to help you."

"You want to help me now? And how are you going to do that?"

Keller slipped his hand into his coat pocket and activated the tape recorder.

"We need to talk about the accident. I need to know what happened the night George Lombard died."

"I already did this. I told you and your partner everything I know."

Keller knew this conversation would be one of the toughest of his life. He needed Lisa to trust him and given that she didn't even know he was alive ten minutes ago, it would be a tall order.

"I know I'm asking for something that I have no right to—for you to trust me. But you need to understand that I am here to help you. What we say here today will never be told to another human being. But you have to trust me. I'm sorry to put you in this position, but you really don't have much choice. I know what happened that night. And if you don't talk to me now, my partner will figure it out soon enough, and I won't be able to help you."

Keller was stretching the truth but hoped she would take the bait.

After a few minutes, the waitress reappeared. "What can I get y'all to eat?" she asked, with a sneer at Keller.

"Nothing for me," Lisa said, avoiding eye contact.

"Maybe another Diet Coke," said Keller.

"Okay. And honey, I'll get you another iced tea," the waitress said, turning away. "In case you need to reload."

Lisa took a deep breath. "You think I could go to prison?"

"Yes."

She took another deep breath and out it came.

"The whole thing was Scott's idea. He said he needed the money from some insurance policy, and once he had the money he could leave his wife and be with me. God, it sounds like such a cliché. How stupid do I look? I tried to back out, but he wouldn't let me. He kept saying we're almost there, we're almost there."

"Okay, start from the beginning. Tell me about you and Scott."

"I met him at a Tripp Barnes concert. He was there with some friends. There was no wife, no wedding ring on his finger, nothing. He was just there having fun, and my girlfriend and I were sitting in the row ahead of him and his friends. At one point, they spilled some beer on us and started to apologize. He and I locked eyes and things just sparked. He jumped the row and took the seat next to me. We just enjoyed the rest of the concert, and when it was over he asked for my number. He called the next day."

"So, the relationship began right away?"

"Yeah, it went pretty fast. We started to see each other a few days after the concert. It was just something that happened. I had no idea he was married. Not until way later. God, I must sound like such a fool."

Keller sensed the change. Her anger was an opening. Lisa was starting to understand that Lennox had used her.

"What happened with Lombard? How did that whole thing go down?"

"Scott told me there was an insurance policy for $500,000 on Lombard's life. He said they had taken the policies out when they became business partners a few years back. He kept saying with all that money we could start a whole new life together. And I believed him."

Keller wondered why Lennox had lied to her about the $2 million policy and made a mental note to consider the motives.

"Scott hit him with his car the night before the accident, on purpose. He was already dead when I called in the accident the next morning."

That explains the temperature of the body, Keller thought. It also meant Lisa hadn't killed Lombard. Still, a conviction on accessory to murder would mean serious prison time. Things could get really bad if Lennox tried to hang her out to dry for the murder.

"Tell me more about when Scott hit Lombard. You say he hit him intentionally the night before—then out on the highway the next morning it was just staged to make it look like an accident?"

"Scott knew Lombard came into the office every Tuesday and Thursday evening to check the books. He always came in after every-one had left for the day, including Scott. That night, Lombard showed up and did whatever he does in the office. Scott put me upstairs by the window in the empty second floor office overlooking the loading dock. Then, he parked his car around the corner and waited for Lombard. It was maybe an hour. Lombard closed up and as he walked to his car, Scott ran him down. I don't think he even heard it coming."

"Did Scott's windshield break when he hit him?"

"Oh yeah, he hit him pretty hard. He said he wanted to make sure he killed him."

"You saw the whole thing?"

"I could see and hear everything. It made me sick to my stomach. Scott wanted to put the body on ice—to keep it from decomposing, he said."

Mission accomplished, thought Keller. But by putting the body on ice, Lennox had given investigators a rather large clue with respect to Lombard's body temperature. That was a mistake that could haunt Lennox at trial.

"Then what?"

"Scott waved me down from upstairs. I couldn't believe how calm he was—like it was no big deal to him that he had just killed another human being. I ran to where the body was and helped Scott cover him with a blanket. He then went and got one of the refrigerated trucks and drove it over. Then we picked up the body and moved it into the truck."

"When you put him in the ice truck do you remember if you laid him on his back or his stomach?"

Lisa looked blankly at her father. She considered it an odd question. "On his back."

That explained the lividity issue.

"Okay, then what did you do?"

"Scott told me to park my car on the street. Then we went inside and waited."

Keller tried to assemble a plausible defense for his daughter. She hadn't actually killed George Lombard—that was all done by Lennox. She was, however, certainly a conspirator in the crime—that much was clear. And because of her assistance, she would also be considered an accomplice. It wasn't good, but it wouldn't be a life sentence. With a good attorney, she was probably looking at 5-10 years in prison. That's if she gets caught, thought Keller.

"Then you staged the accident?"

"We waited in the office until a couple hours before sunrise. Then Scott drove his car, and I drove Lombard's car out to Highway 46. Scott wanted Lombard's car to be found close to the accident scene."

"Did you wear gloves?"

"Yes and a hat. Scott was worried about my hair somehow being found in Lombard's car. We left it near where we planned to stage the accident and went back to the plant in Scott's car. That's when I got into mine. Scott took the ice truck and again we went back to Highway 46. Once we were there, we staged the accident. Then he left me, telling me to wait a few minutes before calling 911, and he drove the ice truck back to the plant."

"The damage to your car—how'd that get there?"

"Once we got out on Highway 46, Scott drove my car into a tree. Not very hard, just going maybe ten miles per hour. He tacked some moving blankets to the tree so the bark wouldn't come off on the car. Scott said that would leave enough damage to the front end and the police would believe that I hit Lombard on accident."

It almost worked, thought Keller. And most importantly, investigators would have no reason to look for any kind of link between the woman involved in the accident and the deceased's business partner. The plan was pretty ingenious.

"What about the hunting vest and the rifle?"

Her answers were rhythmic, recited as though in a trance. "Scott took some keys from Lombard's desk and got them from the safe and the locker. Once we got to the place on Highway 46, Scott put the vest on him and tossed the rifle into the brush. Then we took Lombard's body out of the ice truck and put him on the shoulder of the road. Scott said everybody knew Lombard liked to hunt so it wouldn't be suspicious."

"And you're sure both you and Scott wore gloves while doing all this?"

"Yes, both of us. But once the accident was staged I gave Scott my gloves, and he took them."

"And once all the pieces were together you called 911 and reported you hit someone crossing the highway?"

"Yes," she said, fighting back the tears.

"Scott kept saying it would be okay. 'I'm gonna take care of you, baby,' he told me. I guess deep down I've always wanted a man to take care of me. Ever since I was little."

Keller winced. He knew her vulnerabilities were largely his fault. He reached down into his pocket and quietly switched off the tape recorder. Then he reached out and held Lisa's hands in his.

"Listen, consider the facts. Scott lied to you about being married. And he lied to you about the insurance policy. It wasn't $500,000; it was for $2 million. He was playing you. If it came down to you or prison, what do you think Scott would do? He'd say it was all your idea, cut a deal, and hang you with a murder charge. Think about it."

"Two million dollars?" Lisa was stunned.

"Yes, two million bucks. Lisa, I know I've been a horrible father to you. I want to make it up to you as best I can. I'm gonna do what I've never done for you, I'm going to take care of you, but you have to do what I tell you to do. It's the only way to keep you out of prison."

Lisa turned toward the window. A light snow had begun to fall. She took a deep breath. "Okay, I understand."

"I promise I'll take care of you now."

"Okay."

Keller reached down for the bag he'd brought in from the truck and set it on the table. "There's one more thing. I have some phones here. They can't be traced. You and I need to stay in touch, but we have to use these phones and these phones only. Don't ever call me from your home phone or your cell phone. Don't even use a work phone to contact me. Those can easily be traced by police. Do you understand?"

Lisa agreed and took the phone.

"Here are the numbers to the phones. The first one listed is yours. The second is the one I'll be carrying. You can reach me 24 hours a day.

"Okay, thanks."

The impact of the moment reverberated through them both. A photograph, taken thirty years earlier and posted on a worn out refrigerator had led a father and daughter back to each other. Maybe it wasn't too late after all, Keller thought.

They walked from the Mountain View Café toward an uncertain future together. Jack and Lisa shared an awkward hug. Like it or not, they needed one another.

Keller watched as Lisa's car pulled onto eastbound I-70 and disappeared from sight. He reached into his pocket and pulled the audio tape from his recorder. He studied it for a moment, dropped it onto the pavement, and smashed the cartridge with the heel of his shoe.

There was no going back.

FIFTEEN

Father Jon Foley pulled into the parking lot at Rock Trail County Park just as Keller was stretching his aging hamstring.

"There's nothing like a nice run up the rock when it's 35 degrees outside," said the priest.

"Why do I have the feeling it's not going to slow you down?"

Father Jon quickly went through his warm-up routine. He was younger and in better shape than Keller. The priest routinely beat Jack up the trail and never let him forget it. Despite the friendly competition, their runs were mostly for fellowship.

As Pastor of St. Joseph's Catholic Church in Castle Springs, Father Jon first met Jack Keller when he moved to Colorado to join the RCSO. The pair had become fast friends and would often take runs together or take in a Rockies or Nuggets game in Denver. The young priest was also a great sounding board when Jack faced struggles.

It was less than a mile to the top, but the climb was steep, with an ascent of nearly four hundred feet. At the peak, the trail offered magnificent views of Castle Springs and on a clear day Pikes Peak was visible some fifty miles to the southwest. Today, the winds were so strong the men huddled behind a boulder for protection.

"So, what's going on, Jack?"

"I've got a situation, and I need to talk to somebody."

"All right, what have you got?"

"Do you remember me telling you that I got married really young and I blew it, and my wife just packed up and left one day?"

"Yes, I do. You told me you couldn't handle the pressure, and you used booze to cope."

Keller loved that Father Jon didn't beat around the bush. "Did I tell you that I had a daughter from that marriage?"

"No, I think you left that part out," said Father Jon.

"Well, emotionally abandoning my family wasn't something I was very proud of," Jack responded, his voice trailing off. "But, after nearly thirty years, I have reconnected with my daughter."

Father Jon tried to get a read. "That's good, right?"

"Yeah, I initiated it. But there are extenuating circumstances, you might say."

"Well, regardless of the circumstances, at least you made the effort to reconnect. Is that what you wanted to talk with me about? Did it not go well?"

"I reached out to her because she's in trouble. I sort of crossed paths with her working on one of my cases. It's not a good situation."

"What can I do to help, Jack? Do you want me to talk to her?"

"No, no… nothing like that. I guess I just need to figure out how to do the right thing. Father, do you ever think two wrongs make a right? Or that the end justifies the means?"

"Typically, no, I don't believe in either of those concepts. There may be rare exceptions but those are few and far between. Jack, you want to tell me what's going on?"

"My daughter conspired with someone to commit a crime. She didn't carry out the actual crime per se, but she did have a role in it—a fairly substantial role. And now I find myself in the rather unusual position of actually being able to help her, and I'm torn as to what I should do."

"I see. Would this crime she participated in be a homicide? I mean, those are the kinds of cases you work, correct?"

"Yep," Keller said as the sun set behind the Rocky Mountains.

"And you could help her because of your 'unusual position' as you describe it. Is this because you are the person who is handling the investigation of this particular homicide case?"

"Yes, sir."

"Well, I can certainly see why you are conflicted, Jack. But I think you know right from wrong. Are you looking for me to tell you that it's okay to help her, to just let this one slide, if you will?"

Jack turned to Father Jon. "From where I sit, there are two kinds of people in this world. Those who view things as black or white and others that see things in shades of gray. Personally, I'm a black and white kind of person. But now, with this case, I understand shades of gray. Look, my daughter is a good person; she just fell into a bad situation, and now I can help her. She made a mistake. She knows it. And she's suffered enough, thanks to me."

"But Jack, this goes against everything you believe. You have made a career of bringing people to justice. You aren't the judge here. You've got to trust the system. If she doesn't deserve punishment for this crime, then the system will make that determination, not you."

"Look, I haven't been the best father in the world. I screwed things up with my daughter, and I have a son who, just like his dad, was a drunk by the age of sixteen and managed to get himself killed while driving drunk. I don't exactly have a stellar record when it comes to parenting, and I think this is my chance to make up for it. Not for my son, it's too late for him, but for my daughter—because if I don't do this, it may be too late for her. The good pretty much outweighs the bad. At least, it does from my point of view."

"Sounds like you've made up your mind. Are you asking for my blessing? I'm afraid I can't give you that. And you know why."

"Thanks for nothing, Father."

"Sorry I couldn't be more accommodating, Jack. But I'll pray for you both."

The next morning, Mia ran into Keller in the hallway at RCSO. "How was your day off?" she asked.

"Good, thanks."

"If you have some time today I'd like to get with you and go over the Lombard case. I did some work on it yesterday and have some stuff I need to fill you in on," Mia said eagerly.

"What kind of stuff?" Jack asked, concerned.

"I did a little checking up on Lisa Sullivan. I went up to Big Pine and did some snooping around."

"Without checking with me?"

"Sorry, but you were off yesterday, and I didn't want to lose traction on the case. It doesn't look like she even has a sister, so her story—"

"Damn it, Mia. Next time let me know what you are doing with the case. We're supposed to be partners. I don't need you flying solo on this thing."

"Okay, Jack, okay," Mia said defensively.

Jack turned and marched down the hallway and into the bullpen. She heard him slam his briefcase on the desk.

"What the hell is his problem?"

As always, Sasha went a little crazy when Mia arrived home from work.

"Yes, baby, momma is home. Sasha, you want a cookie?" she teased, walking into the kitchen where Chuck was having a cup of coffee and reading the paper. She kissed him on the cheek.

"Good evening, Investigator, and how was your day?"

"It was fine, Dad. How were things around here?"

"All quiet. Just the way I like it."

Mia set down her briefcase and purse and began tossing treats to Sasha.

"Are you hungry, Dad? I can whip something up."

"No Mick tonight?"

"No, Dad. Look, it was nice having him over last night, but it doesn't mean we are back together."

"Okay, Mia. It was just nice to see him, that's all."

"I'm sorry, I didn't mean to snap at you. It's just that Mick has a lot going on right now, and so do I. Things are more complicated than before."

"Can I give you some unsolicited advice?"

"Sure, why not," Mia said. Her father would likely tell her anyway.

"Your mother and I had a special relationship, one that lasted more than forty years. She was my best friend, and we were made for each other; I think you know that. What we had was unusual, better than anyone we knew. All of our friends and family—no one else had the special love we had for each other."

Mia smiled. "I know, and it was pretty amazing. Mom used to tell me the same thing. You were so lucky to have found each other."

"Well, I think you and Mick have the same kind of chemistry, that same magic. The two of you remind me so much of your mother and me when we were dating. I just think you are meant to be together, that's all."

"Maybe we are, I don't know. It's complicated, and I don't really know what to do," she said as she started to prepare dinner.

"Maybe I can help, Mia. I'm a pretty good listener. I mean, if you need to run stuff by someone, I'm here, and I come at the right price."

Mia and Chuck had become very close after the death of her mother, but she still wondered if he could be objective about this topic.

"Okay, here's the deal. I'd really like to get back with Mick, but the timing couldn't be worse. Still, I've been thinking that if I made a change, we could get back on track. Problem is, I just don't know how much I'm willing to give up."

"Give up?" Chuck asked, wondering where she was going.

"Mick has done really well in the department, and there's a lot of talk about him running for sheriff when Connelly retires. Last night, Mick confided in me. He's probably going to run."

"Mick would be a terrific sheriff. But why would you have to give anything up?"

"Well, first off, he hasn't asked me to give up anything. It's my idea, really. Look, if we become involved again, and if it gets out, it could get ugly, especially in the middle of a political campaign. People could accuse him of violating department policy, which technically he is by dating someone under his command. But he's more worried about my reputation and what they might say about me. How I got my job, wink, wink. I'm sure you can imagine. He doesn't want to subject me to that, and I'd hate to be a distraction to the campaign. It wouldn't do either one of us any good if it got out. But I think we could get back together if I took a voluntary transfer out of investigations and went back to patrol. That way, I wouldn't be working for him. I'd be under the supervision of another captain in a totally different division. I love working investigations, but I can't work as an investigator and be with Mick."

Chuck nodded but didn't speak. He was so proud of his daughter and all she had accomplished. He also knew all too well that family and love were far more important than work. But he didn't like the idea of Mia going back to patrol. Any job in the department brought risk, but Chuck felt she was safer in investigations.

"That's a tough call, Mia. But if it were me..." Chuck stopped mid-sentence as Mia presented a chicken Caesar salad.

"Wow, that was fast. Looks delicious."

"Wine?" Mia poured, then dished out the salad.

"Look, I know your career is important to you, and I'm so proud of all you've accomplished. Since that day at Columbine, you set your sights on something and went after it, but..."

"Uh huh, go on..." The punchline would be next.

"Mia, like I said—love isn't something that comes around very often. Careers are important, but who you spend your life with is so much more important. I had a good career at WellRock, and I enjoyed every minute of it, but I'd trade my forty years there for one more day with your mother."

Chuck moved the salad around his plate and tried to keep his composure. "You work hard to get where you need to be, you know, financially and otherwise…then the day comes and you finally have the money and free time you've dreamed about for decades, but the person you want to spend it with gets sick and next thing you know they're gone. It's not fair, but it's life. And I'm not telling you all this so you can feel sorry for me. I'm just telling you that if you have a chance at real love…"

"I know, Dad," Mia said quietly. "And keep in mind, this is all in my head right now. I haven't discussed this at all with Mick. Who knows, maybe he'd rather not get things going again, what with the election coming up and all…"

"Well, I know what I'd do. That's all I'm going to say about it. I know you'll do what's right for you. Just know I love you and want you to be happy."

Mia hugged him tightly. "I love you too, Dad. And I know how much you miss Mom. I miss her, too."

"I know, Mia, I know," Chuck said, as tears welled up in his eyes.

SIXTEEN

Mia set out to make her peace with Keller. He was probably still pissed about her "going solo" to Big Pine, but she had every reason to check out the lead. The sooner they talked about it and resolved any bad blood, the better.

"Good morning, Jack, how you doing?"

"Hey, Mia, doing okay. What's up?"

Mia took a seat across from Keller's desk.

"I want to apologize for going up to Big Pine the other day. I should have at least told you or waited till you were back so we could make the trip together. I didn't want to lose momentum, I think we both know Sullivan's story isn't adding up."

Jack responded, "Look, Mia, we are a team, a partnership, and neither of us should be doing anything without the full knowledge of the other. If you have a theory or a possible motive in the case, then you should share it with me, and we should work together on it. If that's a problem for you, then we should talk to the captain and see if something else can be worked out."

Keller's reaction still seemed over the top, but Mia took the high road. "Okay, Jack, I will be sure to keep you posted and share anything I get."

"I'd appreciate it. Now, tell me what you learned in Big Pine."

"I started wondering about Sullivan after she seemed nervous when I asked her about her sister at her apartment the other day. So I did a bunch of Google searches, checked Facebook, the works. I couldn't find anything on a sister. Of course, you have the issue of maiden names and such, so I went up to Big Pine and asked around at the local post office. I didn't tell anyone I was investigating the case, I just said I was in town and was hoping to reconnect with my old friend."

Keller interrupted. "Did you use your real name?"

"No, of course not." Mia responded, perturbed. She was new at working homicide cases, but she wasn't an idiot.

"So, what did you learn? Does she have a sister?"

"Not that I could find. The clerk at the post office, who has worked there for thirty-five years and no doubt knows everyone in town, said there was only one person named Sullivan that she could recall and they're long gone. Besides, he didn't fit at all."

Keller shook his head dismissively. "Well, I'm not sure that means much, given the maiden name issue. There are lots of possible scenarios, and I don't think we can conclude anything about her having or not having a sister up there based on the memory of some Big Pine postal clerk."

Mia was irked. She had come up with a bona fide lead and he was dismissing it as nothing.

Jack continued, "And even if there is no sister and Sullivan is lying to us about that, remember there are lots of reasons people lie about things, but not all lies point to a homicide. Who knows, she could have been driving out there to score some dope for all we know. I'm just saying we can't jump to any conclusions at this point. I'm not saying we don't pursue it, I'm just saying let's move slowly on this. We still think Lennox is behind the murder."

"Yeah, I understand what you are saying. But my money is still on Sullivan being involved somehow. That concert ticket on her refrigerator meant something to her. Trust me, it's a clue that ties her to Lennox."

"Sure, it's possible I guess. My buddy with the ticket agency is checking on it. But Red Rocks holds what, nine or ten thousand people?

She and Lennox both went that night, that much we know. I'll tell you what—I have an old friend up in Big Pine. I worked with him in St. Louis; he retired right before I did, and he moved out here. Let me check with him to see if he can do some snooping around about a sister for Sullivan. I'm sure he'd do that for me if I asked him. Sound okay?"

"Sure, Jack."

"See, Mia, this is how partners work together. I could have saved you a trip up there yesterday. My old buddy can do the legwork on this. We'll focus on Lennox for now."

"Okay," Mia replied. She took her cue and left the bullpen.

Keller leaned back in his chair. There was no friend in Big Pine, but hopefully it would get Mia off the sister angle. He needed to think very carefully about his next steps in the George Lombard investigation. His daughter's future was in his hands, and he wasn't going to let her down this time. And he could see that Mia Serrano was going to be a big pain in his ass.

Mia considered the change in Keller. He was acting strangely; definitely different than when they first started working the Lombard case together. Maybe he'd started drinking again, she thought. That would explain the day off with no notice.

Mick's text broke her train of thought. "C me when u can re: Lombard Case."

She headed to the captain's office, and found him studying a requisition spreadsheet.

"Have a seat. I just got off the phone with the sheriff. He asked about the Lombard case... Anything new?"

"Well, sort of. When Keller took his vacation day, I took the opportunity to pursue some things."

"Like what?"

"When Jack and I dropped in on Lisa Sullivan the other day, I asked her about her sister. The morning of the accident she told me her sister was going through a tough time, and she was headed to Big Pine to visit her. That's why she was out there that morning. So when I asked her how her sister was doing she just gave me some half-ass answer. I got the distinct impression she was caught in a lie and there was likely no sister in Big Pine. Which begs the question: what was she really doing out there that morning, and why would she lie to me about it?"

"So what did you do?"

"I ventured out on my own, that's what I did."

Mia ran down her visit to Big Pine and her efforts in trying to locate a sister, adding how Keller was none too happy about her making the trip without him.

"He was genuinely pissed that I did this while he was on a day off. Said we were partners and that we need to work together and share each other's thoughts and theories about the case… It was weird. Almost like something has changed with him."

The captain understood. "Listen, Mia, keep in mind Keller is used to running the show. He's not used to having partners doing stuff on their own in an investigation that he's involved in. I'm not condoning his actions or saying he's right, but just keep that in mind."

"I know all that. Or at least I do now. He reamed me pretty good."

Mick chuckled.

"I'd like to get together with you and Jack later today to go over the case. Would that work for you?"

"Sure, I can make that work. Want me to tell Keller?"

"No, I'll call him. Better coming from me than you. Don't want him thinking you're bossing him around."

Mia laughed softly and shook her head.

"No, we can't have that."

Mick sent off a quick email requesting a three o'clock meeting to review the "murder book." Keller had taken on the task of putting the book together when he had been assigned to the case. It contained all the pertinent information—all compiled into one large oversized binder. Common in nearly all police agencies, the "murder book" allows for all information to be kept in one place relative to a specific homicide. It was an excellent investigative tool and also served a valuable purpose in preparing a case for court once an arrest had been made.

At three o'clock, Mick, Mia, and Keller arrived at the investigations division conference room and took seats around the table. Keller put the murder book on the large wooden table between them.

"Jack, can you start off by going over what we've got so far?"

"Sure, Captain."

Keller opened the book and started by explaining the initial 911 call, the response by deputies to the accident, and Mia's on-scene investigation and interview of Lisa Sullivan. From there he moved on to the autopsy, describing the findings by the medical examiner and how they were in direct conflict with what was originally believed by investigators handling the incident that morning.

Specifically, Keller highlighted the very low body temperature, lividity inconsistent with the body's position, and the glass found in his scalp. He referred to the medical examiner's findings of terminal cancer. He moved on to the rifle found at the scene, noting it wasn't a weapon that an experienced hunter like Lombard would use to hunt deer. Further, the ammo didn't match the weapon—another mistake an experienced hunter would never make. Next, he talked about the $2 million insurance policy, which listed Scott Lennox as the sole beneficiary. He concluded with highlights from the interviews with Lennox and Sullivan.

Mia detailed the discovery of the concert ticket and the possibility it could be a link between Lennox and Sullivan. "There's something going on with those two, believe me," she added.

"So, Mia, you believe that Lennox and Sullivan know each other and are both connected to this case. And I think all of us agree this was no accident and is most certainly a homicide, correct?" the captain asked.

Both Mia and Keller nodded their agreement, but Keller spoke up.

"It's no accident. Lennox no doubt is behind it, he's got a $2 million motive. Maybe Sullivan is involved too, I don't know. But the evidence on her is flimsy. Any good defense attorney could have her off the hook in a New York minute."

Mia didn't hold back. "Jack, you were with me when we interviewed her at her apartment. You saw the look on her face when I asked her about her sister. You saw the concert ticket on her refrigerator. I know it's circumstantial, but the evidence seems pretty convincing to me. I don't know exactly how it went down, but I really believe they are in this together, and it's very likely they are involved romantically."

"Well, if that's the case, we need to find some proof," added Mick.

Mia continued, "We can try to get a search warrant but that would tip them off. Right now, they think we're considering this an accident and nothing more. But if we don't do something, this thing will die on the vine."

"It's not likely we can even get a warrant based on what we have now," Keller replied, adding, "even if we could and it shows there's a relationship between the two, it doesn't prove anything. They'll both lawyer up, and we're screwed."

Mia refused to back down. "They're amateurs. They'll trip up, Jack. My bet is that Sullivan will crack first. She's probably not the one who cooked this whole thing up. I'm guessing this was all Lennox's idea."

"Lennox is up to his eyeballs in this without a doubt; it just seems a stretch that Sullivan is involved," Keller explained. "There's a distinct likelihood that when she hit Lombard that morning, he was already dead, and last time I checked, hitting a dead guy with your car is not a fucking crime."

A big part of Mick McCallister's job was protecting his boss, and Jack Keller knew it. "We've got to step very carefully here. If we don't play this just right, we could create one hell of a shit storm for the sheriff."

"Okay, okay," Mick said. "Maybe a search warrant isn't the best approach right now, but we might be able to get authorization for a wiretap. We tap Lennox and Sullivan's phones for any communication between them. We can do it covertly and they are none the wiser, that's a big advantage over a warrant."

"A wiretap is getting harder and harder to get these days. Good luck with that, Captain," Keller said.

"I'll call the DA. I'll outline what we know so far and see if he thinks we have a shot. He'll know which judge might throw us a bone. I'll let you know."

The captain stood up and the meeting was over.

Back in the bullpen, Keller unlocked the top drawer of his desk and took out his burner phone.

SEVENTEEN

"Hey, Mick, how are you doing?"

"I'm doing great, Dave, how are things in your shop?"

"Busy as usual, but that's okay. What can I do for you?"

Dave Baxter was in his second four-year term as the Rocklin County District Attorney. He had narrowly won re-election three years earlier when he fought off a challenge from an opponent who had made millions suing drug companies in huge class action lawsuits. The fight had been a nasty one and left Baxter very wary of anything that could damage his public reputation. Mick knew it and thought it could help in his efforts in securing the DA's assistance in getting the wiretap.

"I've got a case that my people are working that at first appeared to be a relatively straight forward fatal traffic collision, but now we're pretty convinced it was more than that. I'm looking for some help in securing a wiretap."

"Okay, Mick, what have you got?"

The captain outlined the case.

"So, you want me to try to convince a judge to authorize a wiretap based on a concert ticket? Is that what you're asking me, Mick?"

"With all due respect, Dave, I believe the case makes a lot of sense. The physical evidence doesn't add up to an accident—clearly this was more than that. Someone killed our victim, and in all likelihood he was killed somewhere else altogether. The primary suspect is his business partner who certainly had plenty of financial motive to kill him or have him killed. There's a likelihood that the woman who was involved in the accident has a romantic relationship with the primary suspect. And believe me, from what I've been told, the woman looks like some kind of movie star. A real head turner."

Mick continued, slightly lowering his voice. "And there's something else. I can see this case making a huge splash in the media. All those national news shows—they are going to be lining up for this one. This case has all the elements the public loves. It could put us on the map, but I just want to make sure it comes out well, for all of us."

"Yeah, you're right, Mick. This thing has sex, money, murder... the whole shebang. Okay, I'll talk to Judge Green—he's probably our best bet. I'll call him when we finish here, and I'll let you know what he says. Is that fair, Mick?"

"That's more than fair."

After he hung up, Mick texted Mia.

"Can u come by my office?"

"Come on in, and close the door behind you."

Mick got right down to business. "In our meeting today, I definitely picked up on that vibe from Keller. I'm starting to think it's more than just Keller being Keller—there's something going on."

"He sure gave me hell for my field trip to Big Pine the other day," Mia added. "He was clearly upset with me for doing that without him, but I just chalked it up to his personality. But he seems to be going out of his way to deflect attention from Sullivan, and that concerns me."

"The strategy is pretty straight forward. I mean, any investigator would likely be thinking the same way. But he doesn't seem to be fully on board. He even hedged on the wiretap."

"Do you think he could be drinking again?" asked Mia.

"Possible, let's keep an eye on him."

"Okay, Captain."

"Thanks, Mia."

"Are you free tonight?" Mick asked. "I could make us something for dinner at my place. It won't be as good as your cooking, but I can manage something."

"The last time you cooked me dinner it was grilled cheese and fruit cocktail from a can."

"I've got a fresh loaf of bread and a new can opener. How about seven?"

EIGHTEEN

Keller left work after the meeting and headed to Rosebud. The enormity of the task ahead weighed heavily on Keller's mind as he walked quickly towards Lisa's apartment. He knew he had a chance to amend for his sins, to make things right and by doing so, gain the love and support of the little girl he had lost nearly thirty years earlier. He wanted to make good. Yet there was so much that could go wrong.

Lisa let him in and offered coffee. She had been through the wringer and it showed. "I'm so scared," she confessed. "I don't know what to do."

"That's why I'm here. I need you to do exactly as I say. Lisa, it's very important we're on the same page. The next few days will be critical."

Lisa gazed blankly at her coffee. She couldn't quite fathom the mess her life had become.

"They're going to ask a judge for permission to tap your phones," he explained. "Your home phone, work phone, and your cell will all be hot. We need to have a strategy for this. There are a couple of ways we can go, but first let me ask, have you had any contact with Scott Lennox since we met at the café?"

"No, he said we shouldn't talk until things blow over and the money's in the bank."

"Okay, good. I need you to stay off the phone unless it's for work or routine business. We can't control what Lennox does, but if he doesn't call, the wiretap won't yield a thing."

"But what if he does call?"

"Try not to answer any call until you know exactly who it is. If Lennox does reach out and leaves a message, we'll have to deal with that as it comes. You and I only communicate on the burner phones, no matter what."

"Okay." She began to see just how much her father was risking.

"Now, we need to talk long term. First, your relationship with Scott." Lisa looked down, ashamed.

Keller glanced around the kitchen, and his eyes fell on the refrigerator. It had helped him discover his lost daughter and given Serrano deep suspicions about Lisa's relationship with Lennox. Those suspicions could land her in prison.

"Look, Lisa, if the department cracks this case, both you and Scott are going to be held accountable. The way I see it, he'll be charged with first-degree murder, and because he did it for financial gain and because it was pre-meditated, it qualifies for the death penalty. You were an accomplice, and that would probably get you a ten-year sentence. I'm not saying this to upset you or scare you; I just want to be straight with you so you can make the best decisions from this point forward. What we do now will set the wheels in motion and determine what's going to happen to you. There are no easy answers, no easy outs. I can break down the consequences of whatever direction you choose, but ultimately the decision is yours. Do you understand what I'm telling you?"

Lisa nodded as the tears welled up in her eyes.

"Do you love him enough to stick by him, even if that means you both go to prison? And remember his term could very likely be life— or worse. Or do you want to cut your losses and let him go? If you go to the authorities now, before they come after you, you will be in a position to offer them something, essentially turning states evidence against Scott. In return, you would likely get some break on your sentence, maybe 3-5 years."

"What if I run? What if I leave the country and never return? How hard will they look for me? I mean, it's Scott they want, right?"

"They will want both of you. This story is a juicy one. It has all the elements the media likes, and they will run it to death. And not just locally, it will likely go national. Ever heard of Nancy Stein on cable TV? This is the kind of thing she likes to beat into the ground night after night. I'm not saying this to scare you; I just want you to know what you're looking at. If this gets the media attention I think it will, then the RCSO and the DA will be more determined than ever to catch you. They don't want to look bad and if you 'escape,' so to speak, it won't look good for the sheriff or the DA."

"What if I change my identity and get a new life? I really don't have anything else to keep me here without Scott. Mom is dead, and I have no other family. I mean, why not run?"

"Well, that's an option. But do you really want to be on the run all your life?"

Neither spoke. Keller was surprised at her strength and resolve. The time was right for him to press the issue.

"You said Scott planned on taking the insurance money and start a new life with you. That was part of the plan I assume, that he'd divorce his wife and marry you?"

Lisa nodded.

"Well, as I told you the other day, the policy was for $2 million, not $500,000. Now, that could mean a lot of things, so don't jump to any conclusions about his motive for lying to you."

"I know," she said. "And if he lied about the money maybe he never was going to leave his wife. He used me to kill his partner, and now I'm worried I could be next. I wish I could tell them everything I know and hang his ass for good. But he's not worth going to prison for. You don't think he'd come after me, do you?"

"I won't let that happen," Keller said.

"I think I should take my chances and disappear."

It could work, Keller thought. But Lisa would need help.

NINETEEN

Mia arrived at Mick's a few minutes after seven. As she pulled up the gravel driveway, the memories and emotions came rushing back. She loved this house and the man inside.

Mia drove around to the back and saw the garage door was open for her arrival. A collection of wildflowers in a vase was sitting on the workbench inside. She pulled her car into the garage, picked up the vase of the flowers, and headed toward the house. Mick saw her coming up the walk and opened the door as she stepped up onto the porch.

"They're beautiful. Thank you so much, Mick."

Mick gave her a big smile and took her hand.

"You're welcome. I'm hoping the flowers make up for dinner."

They went through the den and into the kitchen.

"The place looks great, Mick."

"Thanks, I've done a few things since you were here last. I put in some hardwood floors upstairs, and I put in an oversized shower in the master bedroom. Room for two," he said with a smile.

"Aren't you handy?"

"Can I get you a glass of wine? I've got a really good Pinot if you're interested."

"That would be great, thanks."

Mick walked to the wine rack and pulled out a bottle of Parker Creek, a wine from a local winery.

"I found this at a wine tasting a few months back. Hope you like it."

Mick popped the cork and poured two glasses. He handed one to Mia and lifted the other in a toast.

"To the honorable Judge Don Green, who has authorized a wiretap for us on the Lombard case."

"Great news! So the DA agreed with the strategy?"

"He took a little convincing, but it worked. We need to get one of our electronic surveillance guys with the DA's people to get everything set up, but we should have things in place within the next couple days."

"So, if the wiretaps work, and we catch Sullivan and Lennox communicating, do you think that will give us enough to arrest and file on them both?" asked Mia.

"It depends on the conversations. If they talk about the murder, we're good. If they communicate but don't directly implicate themselves, then we'd need to see what the DA thinks. Personally, I think we'd have enough, but you know how cautious prosecutors are—they want it to be airtight before they file, especially in a case like this with all the potential media attention. Think about it—this case has everything. We'll have news media satellite trucks parked up and down the streets."

As they moved to the living room toward the large wood-burning fireplace, Mia worried about the possible fallout if the case went sideways. She couldn't let that happen—not for George Lombard, not for the department and most importantly, not for Mick. If they couldn't make a case, it could cost Mick the election. On the other hand, if Lennox and Sullivan were brought to justice, Mick could ride it to victory. The George Lombard murder case was rapidly becoming a pressure cooker, and Keller was a wild card.

"I'm still concerned about Keller."

"Look, maybe we're over thinking this whole thing," Mick offered. I did a pretty in depth background on him and while the drinking was obviously a concern, there was nothing in his history that suggested he ever screwed with a case."

"Yeah, well, Lisa Sullivan is awfully pretty. I just hope he's not somehow involved with her. Crazier things have happened."

"Really? You get that vibe from him?" he asked.

"Maybe."

"God, I don't even want to think about what that could do to the case and the department and reputations of all involved. It would be a pretty shitty way for Sheriff Connelly to wrap up an otherwise exemplary career with RCSO."

Mia answered, "Well, some women can be pretty conniving when they need to be."

"Geez, he's like thirty years older than she is."

"Oh yeah, well that would never happen. An old man pursuing a beautiful young woman," Mia replied sarcastically. Then smiled and added, "I mean, look at us. You are *way* older than me, and we both know I'm just after your money."

"Um, we are all of two years apart, young lady. And as far as my millions go—if you can find it, you can have it."

"Forget the millions. Where's that grilled cheese you promised me?"

"Bad news. Turns out my Velveeta expired. So you're stuck with a little antipasto, lasagna, and fresh sourdough."

"No fruit cocktail?"

"Maybe for desert," he answered.

"I'm very impressed, Mick. When did you learn to make lasagna?"

"When I picked it up at Ferraro's on the way home."

"Very clever, McCallister. Let's eat, I'm starved."

TWENTY

The bright sunshine beamed through the windows as the snow melted outside the Serrano house. Chuck was sitting down to breakfast. He loved Mia's "Denver Scramble."

"Dad, you don't have to do this if you are uncomfortable with it. I don't mean to put you on the spot."

"I don't mind, Mia. If I can be of help to you in the investigation, I'm happy to do it."

"Okay, well let's leave as soon as we finish breakfast. I told Mick I'd be in a few minutes late today."

"Sounds good to me."

Mia cleared the breakfast dishes and thought about her next move. She didn't like involving her father in her work life, but she knew it was the safest way to determine what exactly Keller was up to. Sometimes, she thought, extreme measures were needed to get the job done. What she and her father were about to do was not technically illegal, but it was certainly pushing the envelope. She had weighed the unwritten rule of supporting your partner against her fear that Keller might be playing fast and loose with the rules. It certainly wouldn't be the first time an investigator fell for a pretty suspect, but she'd be damned if she was going to let him muck up this investigation.

She also felt a little guilty for not telling Mick. But, if things went bad, the blame needed to all fall on her, no one else. There was no way she would let this affect his career and his future run for sheriff.

"Are you ready, Dad?"

"Yep, let's go."

The two climbed into Mia's car and drove to the address she had found on the Internet. The business was in an industrial area just east of Denver in a row of nondescript buildings. The sign on the front of the shop was small; it was clearly a destination people sought out, rather than a place people just happened upon.

"Good to go, Dad?"

"Yep, I'm ready."

"Do you have the cash I gave you?"

"Got it, no worries. I'll be fine, Mia."

Chuck climbed out of the car and paused momentarily before he closed the door.

He peered back in at Mia, gave her a big smile and said, "This is kind of fun."

Keller stopped at the Mountain Pacific Bank in Castle Springs on his lunch hour. The teller gave him $9,900 in crisp one hundred dollar bills. Under federal law, all withdrawals over ten thousand dollars must be reported to the government. The teller had handled count-less transactions for $9,900 in her career and even many in which the customer had withdrawn $9,999. So many, in fact, she'd stopped wondering what sort of illegal activity was afoot. After all, she wasn't a cop, she just worked in a bank.

The wiretap, reluctantly authorized by Judge Green, took three days to put into place. His reluctance was evident in the restrictions that came with the tap. The order covered the home, work, and cell phones belonging to Scott Lennox and the cell and home phone for Lisa Sullivan. The judge couldn't see the justification for a wiretap on Lisa's work phone. That was a line at Mercy Hospital where she worked as a licensed vocational nurse and dozens of people typically used the phone during the course of the workday. The judge felt it would be too much of an intrusion on people unrelated to the case. The order limited surveillance to ten days.

A team of six deputies was assigned the task of monitoring all calls coming and going on the five lines authorized under the wiretap order. The team would break into two groups of three, each working a twelve-hour shift. The Electronic Surveillance Unit, or "ESU" as it was known, operated from a remote undercover location a few miles from RCSO headquarters. It was tedious work, but it was their best bet to gather evidence that Sullivan and Lennox conspired to kill George Lombard for financial gain.

Under the judge's order, the RCSO was allowed to listen to the first thirty seconds of any and all phone calls that came in or went out on any of the five lines. If conversations weren't related to the case, deputies were required to end their surveillance.

Chuck was amazed at how simple the technology was to use. The small store Mia had taken him to reminded him of the old Radio Hut he often visited as a boy. One of Chuck's many childhood hobbies was building am radios, using nothing but a soldering iron and a Radio Hut kit. Now, for less than $150, he had a fully functional satellite GPS tracking system in his hands. Free software downloaded to his computer and phone would allow him to integrate the data from the GPS device onto a map. Chuck thought back to his early days with WellRock, when the company would contract with the federal government to provide similar technology. That technology was far less efficient, yet cost millions. Times had certainly changed.

From his workbench in the basement Chuck heard Mia come home from work. The frantic scraping of Sasha's claws on the hardwood floor was a dead giveaway.

"I'm down here, Mia!" he called out.

A minute later, Mia made her way downstairs.

"Hey, Dad, how's it going?" Mia asked.

"Getting the software loaded and just double checking everything to make sure it's good to go."

"Okay, Mr. Rocket Scientist, show me how this thing works."

"It's an interactive GPS. We control the unit and receive data through SMS, or text messages," he said, showing her the phone. The GPS is in this unit. It gets attached to the car with this magnetic case," Chuck said, pointing to two small black boxes on the table. "I access it by calling a number and entering the device code. The unit then sends me back the location as a text message."

"Wow. So you have to keep calling it?"

"Yes, but I did a little research and was able to find a program online to automate the process. With the phone connected to the computer, I can get coordinates every fifteen seconds. Then I use simple plotting software to interpret the data, which displays here on the map," he explained, pointing to the computer.

"Holy cow, Dad. You rigged up all this?"

"Yeah, it was nothing, really. Here, let me show you. Take the GPS and go outside and walk down the street a bit. Then come back."

"Okay, come on Sasha, we're going for a walk."

Mia grabbed the device and headed off. She returned a few minutes later, and Chuck generated the report.

"Here's a map of the neighborhood, and this red line here," Chuck said pointing at the screen, "shows just exactly where you've been. You can obviously go much farther away than the neighborhood. I can have the map reflect the greater Denver area, or even the whole state of Colorado. There are really no limits as to where we can track him. And it's accurate within ten feet!"

"This is terrific, Dad. Okay, let's talk about the next part of the plan."

"I've got that figured out, too. Keller and I have never met, so I just need to get the tracking device on his car. From there, I can monitor his every move, and if he goes anywhere near Lisa Sullivan's home or work, we'll know. Once it's in place, I can follow him—"

"Whoa, hold on there, Dad. I didn't say anything about you following Keller. I just wanted a record of his travels that I could use to confront him with if and when the time comes."

"I know that, Mia. But I've been thinking about it. Isn't it better if we know what he's really up to?"

"No, Dad," she said, now concerned about how deep he was getting into her scheme. "I don't think we need that much. This isn't for court. You can track him from here, period."

Chuck tried to hide his disappointment. "Well, okay. I just thought..."

"I know, Dad, and I appreciate it. But let's figure out how to get the device on his car and see what the tracking software tells us. You've done an amazing job."

"Did you get his home address?"

"I've got it upstairs. He lives up in a duplex in Castle Pines. I know he drives a black Ford F-150 truck, and I'm thinking if you go out there in the early morning you should be able to plant the thing, provided he doesn't have a garage."

"I can go tomorrow morning. I'll just get up a couple hours early."

"Okay, that'll work, Dad."

She knew she was breaking all kinds of rules by tracking Keller and especially for getting her dad involved. But Mia also knew Jack Keller was up to something. She knew it in her bones.

TWENTY-ONE

Chuck tossed and turned most of the night and was staring at his alarm clock as it went off at 2:30 a.m. He dressed quickly, made himself a cup of strong, black coffee, and was soon on his way. The weather was clear but cold, and there was no snow on the ground. No snow meant no footprints.

Castle Pines was a short ten-minute drive from the house. He thought about the plan as he entered I-25 and headed north. While he understood her concerns, Chuck was disappointed Mia had put her foot down on his plan to follow Keller. He really wouldn't be in any danger, he reasoned. Keller wasn't a criminal after all, he was a cop. As Chuck saw it, the worst-case scenario would be that Keller figures out he's being followed and he confronts him. He'd have no idea he was Mia's father, and Chuck would talk his way out of it. No harm, no foul.

Looking down at the map on his phone, he found Keller's duplex. Chuck caught a break; there was no garage and parked in front of the place was a black Ford F-150 truck.

Chuck pulled the GPS from his pocket and searched the back of the truck for a flat surface that could accommodate the device. Just below the bumper he found a good spot, and he maneuvered the GPS until he felt the magnet click tightly against the metal.

He pulled away knowing the difficult part was over. After a short drive, Chuck pulled over to test the system. It worked perfectly. "Not bad for an old man."

Back in his basement, Chuck set up the cell phone and laptop on the TV tray next to his lounge chair. He reclined, proud of his accomplishment and excited to see if the red dot moved at all on the screen. Keller, however, wouldn't be up for a few hours.

Mia rose early and immediately went in to check on her father. His bed was empty, but she quickly found him in the basement sound asleep. She leaned over and kissed her him gently on the top of the head.

"Oh, hi, Mia," he replied, rubbing his eyes. "I was just checking on Keller. He's still parked in front of his house."

"Yeah, I can see that. Everything went okay?"

"Oh, yeah, like clockwork, Mia. No problem at all."

"Okay, that's great, Dad. Thanks again for all your help. Now we sit tight and monitor his movements from here. That's understood, right?"

"Yep, I got it. Just tracking him, that's all."

"Okay, I'm going to get some coffee, then run off to work. I've got an early meeting with the assistant DA on some traffic cases. I may run errands after work, so I might be a little late coming home. Do you need anything?"

"No, I'm good, Mia. I think I'll just hang out here this morning. I may go on a hike later today if the weather holds."

"Okay, Dad, thanks again. Have fun and be careful."

As Mia headed off, Chuck stared at the laptop. The red dot hadn't moved, but it was still early and Keller most likely hadn't left for work. As he was considering rebooting the devices to be sure everything was in working order, Sasha interrupted. Seeking some attention and a warm bed, she hopped up into Chuck's lap and nuzzled up to him. Chuck glanced at his watch, then looked back at the computer screen.

"Whoa, Sasha, we've got liftoff," Chuck said. The dog didn't seem the least bit interested. The red dot began moving, slowly at first, then at a much faster clip. He reached over to the computer and expanded the map view. He watched as Keller entered I-25 and headed south, exiting at Avenue F in Castle Springs. A few minutes later, the red dot came to a stop and Chuck reached forward to zoom in on the location.

Sasha, frustrated at the lack of attention, jumped down from the chair and headed up the stairs to find a more suitable spot. "Hmm, that's just a half mile from here," Chuck said softly to himself. He opened a new tab in the browser to check the address. It was St. Joseph's Catholic Church.

Chuck searched the church website and saw that daily Mass was celebrated at 7:30. Chuck glanced at his watch. What harm would it do if he stopped by the church? Chuck quickly ran up the stairs, grabbed his jacket and his car keys, and was out the door before he could talk himself out of it.

St. Joseph's was a relatively new church in Castle Springs, but the parish itself had been there since the 1960s. The area had grown over the decades, and the new building was able to accommodate the hundreds of families that attended services on weekends. Morning masses weren't so crowded. There were only a dozen or so cars in the lot when Chuck pulled up and Keller's truck was among them.

Chuck parked on the opposite side of the lot, where he had a good line of sight. Mass let out at 8:05, but the black truck remained. By 8:15 just two vehicles were in the lot: Keller's and one other. Chuck started to worry he was more exposed than he should be. But just as he was considering a move, two men appeared and headed in his direction. One wore a dark wool trench coat, the other a ski jacket. Chuck slumped down in the front seat.

Peering over the dashboard, Chuck could see the man with the trench coat was older. He had no idea what Keller looked like, but it didn't take long to figure it out. As the younger man turned, Chuck saw the priest collar. Their conversation was animated and the men were arguing.

The pair parted without a handshake and Keller climbed into his truck. Chuck ignored his daughter's orders and followed behind. He reasoned that Keller was probably headed back to the I-25, and that happened to be Chuck's way home. But Keller didn't go straight to the I-25, he stopped at Mountain Pacific Bank. Unable to resist, Chuck turned into the lot as well and found a parking spot as far from Keller as possible.

What was Keller up to at the bank? Why was he arguing with a priest? He realized there could be very reasonable explanations, but how could he be sure?

Keller came out the door just as Chuck was coming around the corner. Suddenly he was eye to eye with the investigator. Chuck gave a quick nod in Keller's direction as the two passed one other. Not wanting to generate suspicion, he continued into the bank. Chuck walked over to the new accounts area and took a seat. His heart was racing.

"Can I help you, sir?" asked the young man. "Are you interested in opening an account?"

"Oh, no, thank you. I'm fine. Just waiting for someone. Thanks, though."

Chuck figured he'd had enough excitement for one day. He'd track Jack Keller from the safety of his basement, at least for now.

TWENTY-TWO

"Sergeant Rainey, Captain McCallister calling. What, if anything, is happening with our wiretap operation? I need some good news."

"I wish I had some good news for you. Lennox is busy selling ice. Lisa Sullivan got a reminder from her dentist that she's due for her annual cleaning, otherwise there's zip on her. Sorry, I know it's not what you're after, Captain."

"No kidding," Mick said. The wiretap order was only good for another three days. "Well, I need something, Brett, and I need it soon. I don't want this case to slip away."

"I feel your pain, Captain, but I can only tell you what they say. I can't make 'em say it, you know? If it was up to me, I'd call them both myself for you."

"Yeah, I know. This one's a pain in my ass."

"If anything breaks, you'll be the first one I call, day or night."

"All right, Brett, thanks. And tell your guys I really appreciate the efforts with this one. I know it's like watching paint drying down there. What you guys do for these taps would send me off the deep end."

"Will do, Cap."

Mick dialed Mark Archer in RCSO Media Relations.

"Hey Mark, it's Mick. Can you come over to my office?'

"Sure, I can be there in ten."

Lieutenant Archer was the spokesperson for the department and liason to the media. Essentially, Archer was the 'front man' for the RCSO. He was the face and the voice of the department, maybe more so than the sheriff himself. The rule of thumb in law enforcement was if there was good news, the sheriff did the interviews. If it was bad news, which was more often the case, it would be Archer.

It was a thankless job, but Archer managed to do it without making many enemies. He had been the RCSO spokesperson for more than a decade and had handled reporters on cases ranging from the routine to the downright sensational. Mick knew Archer had solid relationships with reporters from Colorado Springs to Denver.

One of the perks of the spokesperson position was reporting directly to the sheriff. Archer didn't have to go through an undersheriff or captain; if he needed something he simply walked into Connelly's office and asked for it. His number one rule was to keep the sheriff personally informed. He never wanted Connelly to open the newspaper or turn on the TV and see something about the RCSO that he didn't already know. Connelly hated surprises and Archer did his best to make sure there weren't any.

Archer was well aware Sheriff Connelly was about to retire. He also knew Mick McCallister was on the short list of candidates with a decent chance of being elected.

The captain had also called Mia to the office. She arrived before Archer and immediately sensed his frustration.

"Have a seat, Mia."

"Uh oh."

"I just spoke with Brett Rainey in ESU."

"And?"

"Nothing. Beyond nothing, and we're seven days into this tap. Three days left and then we're out of time."

Mark Archer knocked as he stuck his head in. "Captain? You rang?"

"Come on in, Mark. You know Investigator Serrano."

"Sure, hey, Mia."

"Hi, Mark. How's the training going?" she asked. Mark Archer was a triathlete. Tall and lanky, he spent evenings and weekends training and it showed. His dark hair and good looks made him appear far younger than his fifty-two years.

"All good, thanks."

Mick jumped in. "Mark, do you remember a fatal TC we had a few weeks back—out on Highway 46?"

"No, don't think I did a press release on that one."

"Have a seat, and you might want to take some notes. We thought initially that it was an accident, but the evidence points to something else, and we're shifting gears."

"Like what?" Archer asked, intrigued.

"Our victim was a 56-year-old guy named George Lombard, a Castle Springs resident and part owner of an ice company here in town. Initially, it appeared Mr. Lombard had been hunting and was struck and killed by a car traveling on a remote section of Highway 46. Inspector Serrano was the first investigator on scene. The deeper we dug, the more it began looking like a homicide—with insurance money as the motive. So now Keller and Serrano are running the investigation together."

"What's the policy worth?"

"Two million to his business partner," Mia told him.

Mick continued as Archer took notes. "That business partner is a guy named Scott Lennox. Together they owned Lennox Ice Company. We think he orchestrated the accident for the insurance payout. The theory goes that Mr. Lennox, who is married, is having an affair with a young woman named Lisa Sullivan. The same Lisa Sullivan that reported she struck our victim on Highway 46."

"Damn, the media will eat this one up," Archer predicted.

"Like white on rice, but we've gotta make the case," McCallister cautioned. "What we've done is set up a wiretap on both. If we can get them conspiring on tape and then break one or the other in interrogation, we'll be good."

"What can I do to help?"

"We're seven days into a ten-day tap, and we've got zilch. No contact whatsoever. We're running out of time and we need you to turn up the heat. They may be thinking they're in the clear and are just waiting for the insurance check to land in the mailbox. What I'd like to do is get something in the paper—say we are re-opening the case following some new leads and we think this may not have been an accident. Something that will make them think their plan is unraveling. Something to put the fear of God into them."

"So they read the article, freak out, one calls the other to make sure they have their bases covered. You snag them with the tap," Archer said.

"That's the plan. Investigator Serrano here will be happy to brief you in more detail. But we don't have a lot of time, Mark. It's already Friday—if possible we'd like to see it in the Sunday paper. Any later and our tap will be exhausted."

"I can make it happen."

"Outstanding. Thanks for the help, Mark."

"I'll send you my bill," Archer teased. "I need to make some calls, but Mia, can we touch base before you leave tonight?"

"I'll come by your office."

"Perfect. Cap, I'll call you when I know something," Archer promised as he left the office.

"Sure hope it works," Mia said. There was a lot riding on this.

"I got an idea," Mick told her. "How about you and I steal away for a nice discreet dinner somewhere tomorrow night?"

"Wow. A big Saturday night date. Haven't had one of those in a while. What do you have in mind, Mister?"

"Mia, we're at work, it's Captain Mister, if you don't mind," he teased. "I don't know yet, let me think about it, and I'll surprise you. Does that work?"

"Works for me."

"Pick you up tomorrow at seven?"

"Sounds good. Meantime, I'm gonna pull my case file for Mark."

Archer knew just where to start. The Front Range News-Press was the area's primary newspaper and their website was the go-to regional news source online. He'd call his good friend Anita Sanchez, the paper's top reporter.

Sanchez had been around the news business longer than Mark Archer had been at RCSO. They shared a solid professional relationship and had become good friends, a friendship that had paid dividends on both sides. Archer and the RCSO got a fair shake in the News-Press, and Sanchez sometimes got tipped early on the best stories coming out of the department, courtesy of Mark Archer.

Mia was able to provide Mark with all the relevant details of the case. From there, the two formulated the core story and ran it by the captain for approval. Once McCallister had signed off, Archer called Anita Sanchez and told her what he needed. In exchange for an exclusive story, Anita would make sure the story about the Lombard investigation would make the Sunday edition, above the fold.

TWENTY-THREE

Mia spent the better part of twenty four hours trying to decide what to wear on her dinner date with Mick. The fact that he wanted to surprise her was romantic, but it complicated the fashion call. Ultimately, she selected a black mini dress she'd picked up at a Denver boutique a few months earlier for 70% off. It was a dress that screamed sexy, emphasizing all of her curves.

A few minutes after seven, the doorbell rang. Sasha went nuts, and Chuck answered the door. He welcomed Mick inside and offered him a drink.

"Only if you join me."

"If you insist," Chuck replied with a wink as he reached up for the bottle of high-end French vodka in the cupboard.

"Still a vodka drinker, I assume?" asked Chuck, holding out the bottle for Mick to see.

"Yep, or a good Pinot Noir when the mood strikes."

"Well, let's go with the clear stuff tonight," Chuck suggested.

Just as Chuck poured a couple of healthy shots of vodka, Mia came in and gave Mick a kiss on the cheek.

"Easy with that stuff boys," Mia teased.

"Wow, Mia. You look like a million bucks!"

"Thank you. You look quite handsome yourself."

It was rare to see Mick out of uniform, and the tailored navy suit and light blue shirt made him look more like a New York bond trader than a sheriff's captain.

"How 'bout a small one for you, Mia?" her father offered.

"No, thanks, I'm fine. I need to keep my wits about me tonight. You never know what this guy has planned. Whatever it is, it's a surprise. He wouldn't tell me a thing."

"I'll take good care of her, Chuck, no need to wait up."

"All right, you two have fun," Chuck called out as they headed for the door. Mick had taken just a sip of his vodka. Chuck would make sure it didn't go to waste.

Outside, Mick proudly opened the door to his new BMW X5.

"What's this, McCallister? A new ride?"

"Yeah, just a little something I picked up this morning. It was time for something new. My old car had over 150,000 miles. Looks like I made the right call. You and that dress look perfect in it."

"Very nice. Congratulations."

"Thanks."

"Okay, Mister, where are we heading?" asked Mia.

"You'll see soon enough."

"I'm guessing your place?"

"Nope, I've actually had painters over all day, and it was all I could do not to get high from the paint fumes. It really stinks."

"You poor man."

Mick navigated the I-25 on ramp and headed north.

"North huh? I guess that means Santa Fe is out," joked Mia.

"Yes, good deduction, Investigator."

Mia sat back and enjoyed the ride. Things were never strained with Mick, they fit perfectly, she thought. No need to fill every minute with conversation, they were just comfortable being together.

Thirty minutes later, Mick exited at 16th Street in downtown Denver.

"So we're not going up to Cheyenne, either?" Mia teased. "Just where are you taking me?"

"You'll see soon enough, young lady. Remember, patience is a virtue."

"Yeah, I hate that."

Mick reached over and took Mia's hand. Tonight was special for both of them. Mia squeezed his long fingers. "I'm glad you drive an automatic."

A few quick turns and Mick was pulling into the parking structure of a forty-story, high-end condominium complex adjacent to Denver's 16th Street Mall.

"Oh my God, you bought me a place!"

Mick chuckled again. "Man, you are full of yourself tonight."

"Just in a good mood, that's all. There's no place I'd rather be, ya know?"

Mick quickly found a parking space and they headed to the elevator.

"You're killing me, McCallister. Where the heck are you taking me?"

"Almost there."

Mick pushed the button for the fortieth floor. Within seconds the doors opened and the two stepped into a long hallway.

"This way," Mick said, leading. When they came to a door marked 4007, Mick stopped and reached into his pocket for a key.

"What's going on, McCallister?" Mia wondered out loud. Mick ignored her, opened the door and they stepped inside. It was the most beautiful place she had ever seen.

"Oh my Lord," Mia said as she looked quickly around the expansive open floor plan.

She walked over to the living room and looked out the floor-to-ceiling window. The view was spectacular; the lights of the greater Denver area twinkled everywhere she looked. She turned to Mick, "This place is unbelievable, but what are we doing here?"

"Having dinner."

"Um, does the owner of this place know we're here? Or are we breaking and entering?"

"It's my brother's condo. He's out of town for the weekend, and he asked me if I'd check on the place for him. So, that's what we're doing—checking on the place for him."

Mia remembered that Mick had a younger brother, but they'd never met.

"If I may ask… What does your brother do for a living? Rob banks?"

Mick smiled. "Close. He's an investment banker. Hit it big a few years ago and bought this place. Paid almost $3 million for it, but it comes with pool privileges. At least that's what he always tells me when I give him a hard time about it."

"The place is incredible. I can't get over the view."

"Yeah, it's pretty spectacular. Let me make you a drink, and I'll show you the rest of the place."

Mia nodded at Mick and looked back at the view from the living room window.

"You can see Coors Field. It's right there, off to the left."

"During the summer, Steven will just walk the five blocks and go to a lot of the games. Although, you can see some of the action on the field from the window."

"Wow, what a life."

"Yeah, he's really done well for himself. I'm proud of him," Mick said without a hint of jealousy in his voice.

"Where is he this weekend?"

"He and his wife, Jennie, are skiing up at Aspen."

"Of course… Where else could they be?" Mia chuckled.

Mick came over to Mia at the window and handed her a glass of chardonnay. Mick was sticking with vodka.

"So we've checked on the place, made sure there are no burglars or mass murderers here, so where to next?"

The doorbell rang. "Uh oh, are we expecting company?"

Mick didn't say anything but turned to answer the door as Mia stayed by the window, enjoying the view. Moments later, a man with a large, wheeled cooler and a satchel arrived.

"Mia, I'd like you to meet Chef Andre. He'll be making us dinner this evening."

"Hello, nice to meet you, Andre."

"The pleasure is all mine."

Andre nodded at the two of them and disappeared into the kitchen.

Mia looked at Mick. "You are full of surprises tonight."

"This guy makes a fruit cocktail that you won't believe," Mick teased.

"I'll take that, a glass of chardonnay, this view, and you—and I'll never need another thing as long as I live."

Mick smiled, leaned in, and kissed Mia gently on the lips.

"I can deliver all of the above—with the exception of the view, of course."

"I can live with that."

They kissed again. Andre walked in and interrupted the moment.

"Oh, my apologies. I was just going to ask you about the time frame for dinner. When would you like things to be ready?"

"An hour or so would work well. That is, if that works for you, Mia."

"That would be perfect, thanks."

"Very well, then. Dinner will be served at nine o'clock. Again, my apologies for the intrusion."

"Quite all right, Andre. No worries."

He turned back to Mia. "Let me give you the rest of the tour."

Mick walked her through the condo. The rest of it was just as spectacular as the living room. Views of the city from all three bedrooms, marble throughout the bathrooms, a fully equipped workout room— the place had everything.

Mick and Mia spent the time before dinner enjoying the view and talking about anything and everything. This was not an evening for a lot of RCSO talk; this night was theirs.

The hour went by quickly, and at nine o'clock Andre came into the living room and announced that dinner was served. The dinner table was set up close to the window, offering a different view than the vantage point from the living room. The view was just as amazing but looked due west.

The food was both beautifully presented and delicious. The entrée was Mia's favorite—lightly grilled scallops and mushroom risotto.

"Oh my God, Mick. These scallops just melt in your mouth."

"Glad you like them."

"Thanks for remembering they are my favorite."

"How could I forget? You order them everywhere we go!"

They both laughed and enjoyed the rest of dinner. It was nearly eleven when Andre came into the living room where Mick and Mia were enjoying a cognac.

"I just wanted to let you know that everything is finished up in the kitchen, and if there is nothing else, I will be on my way."

"I think we're fine, Andre. Outstanding job with dinner," Mick replied.

"Yes, it was fantastic," added Mia.

"It was my pleasure. I will let myself out. Have a wonderful evening."

They enjoyed another cognac and relaxed on the big sofa. The conversation flowed effortlessly from the beautiful condo to travel. As the night grew long, Mick got focused. "I think we should talk about us."

Mia took the lead, "It's been wonderful being with you again these past few weeks. I didn't realize how much I missed you, and I feel like the connection between us is as strong as ever. I hope you feel the same. I really believe we have a future together, and I think you believe that, too."

"Absolutely," Mick said, holding her tightly.

"I think we belong together, Mick, but I don't want to do anything that could jeopardize your future with the department. I think you're going to be a great sheriff, and the last thing I want is to put you in the position of having to publicly explain your relationship with a subordinate. It could damage your campaign and I just can't have that."

"Then I won't run," Mick said firmly. "It's not worth it. You're more important than the job."

Mia felt her limbs go weak. It took a few moments to take it all in.

She shifted her position on the sofa, leaned in, and kissed him. A kiss that told Mick exactly how she felt. It was long, deep, and intimate.

She stopped and held his face in her hands. "I want you to know I feel the same way. You're more important than any job, too. But if we're going to be together, we need to do what's right for both of us. I want you to run. I want you to win. I know there's a way we can work this out."

"Mia, I'm perfectly happy where I am."

"You're running, McCallister, and that's all there is to it. We'll talk about the details later."

They kissed.

"Now let's get out of this dump and go back to my place."

TWENTY-FOUR

S cott Lennox poured himself a cup of coffee and slipped the Sunday edition of the News-Press from the plastic wrapper. The article, above the fold on the front page, hit him like a two-by-four upside the head.

RCSO to Reopen Investigation into Fatal Accident
By NP Staff Reporter Anita Sanchez

A seemingly routine traffic death last November 29th on Highway 46 may not be so routine after all. The Front Range News-Press has learned that police have re-opened the case involving the death of 56-year-old Castle Springs resident George Lombard. The accident occurred at 5:29 a.m. when Lombard crossed the highway and was struck by a car driven by 32-year-old Lisa Sullivan of Rosebud. It is believed that Mr. Lombard was on an early morning deer hunt at the time.

Mark Archer, spokesperson for the RCSO, wouldn't elaborate on what new evidence had been uncovered during their investigation but did say the case had "taken a new turn" and that investigators were taking a fresh look at the incident.

"We investigate all accidents, fatal and otherwise, occurring within our jurisdiction. In this case, we have recently uncovered some evidence that led us to believe that Mr. Lombard's death may not have been accidental

as originally believed," said Archer.

Archer declined to elaborate any further on the case, citing that to do so could compromise the investigation.

Scott put down the newspaper, and struggled to breathe. Panicked, he picked up the phone and called Lisa Sullivan at her apartment. He was breaking a rule he'd ordered them both to follow, but this was an emergency. The phone rang twice and went to voicemail.

"Hey, it's me. Look, I don't mean to scare you, but there's an article in today's newspaper that says the police don't think Lombard's death was an accident. They say they're re-opening the case. We need to talk, but I don't want to do it on the phone and I can't get away from my wife until later. Meet me at noon today at the Bean Crazy coffee house in Castle Springs off Petal Highway. We need to meet up and get our story right. See you in a few hours… I love you."

Chuck nursed his second cup of coffee as he watched the laptop and cell phone on the table in front of him. It had been a boring weekend. Keller left home only once, and that was for Saturday evening mass.

Chuck considered taking a hike or running some errands. His interest in espionage was waning and his legs were getting stiff in the moist basement air. As he prepared to pack up, the red dot on the computer shifted. Keller was on the move. He watched closely as the dot approached I-25 and headed south toward Castle Springs.

His rationale was simple. He was going to run errands anyway, so why not just bring the gear and see what Keller was up to? Besides, Chuck figured the government had given him top secret clearance back in the day, he had the chops for basic surveillance.

From his SUV, Chuck followed the dot to the SaveCo supermarket parking lot. "Who does their grocery shopping at seven on a Sunday morning?" he grumbled.

Nearly thirty minutes passed with no sign of the investigator. His imagination wandered. Maybe Keller was meeting with Sullivan in the store. It would be clever to connect in such a public pace. Chuck was cold and tired of waiting. He decided to go inside for a cup of coffee and a look-see.

Armed with a fresh coffee, Chuck roamed the aisles. He rounded the end cap from canned goods and spotted Keller in the toiletry section. His heart skipped a beat. Their eyes locked briefly over the distance, but Keller simply looked away. Chuck was certain Keller wouldn't know who he was anyway, so there was no real danger. Still, with no sign of Lisa Sullivan, he thought it best to head back to the car.

Back in his SUV, the morning sun made it uncomfortably warm. Chuck rolled down the window, toyed with the cell phone and considered pulling the plug on his little surveillance operation. Police work, he thought, wasn't all it was cracked up to be.

Chuck felt the grip on his jacket before his mind could process the sight of the arm coming through the open window. The grip was tight and the speed of it all took the wind out of him.

Jack Keller.

"Wanna tell me why the hell you've been following me, Old Man?"

The investigator was far stronger than Chuck had imagined. His heart raced and he uttered a few incoherent sounds as his mind tried to catch up.

"I'm waiting for an answer," Keller demanded. He loosened his grip. "Talk to me."

"I don't know what you're talking about."

Keller let go and leaned into the window, resting his arm on the door. To a passerby, it appeared as though two friends were having a conversation.

"Well, that's one hell of a coincidence. St. Joseph's Church, the bank, and now SaveCo? What's your name, Old Man?"

"This is some kind of mistake. I don't…"

"Don't screw with me. Give me your wallet."

Chuck hesitated.

"Your wallet, Old Man! Let's see some ID."

Reluctantly, Chuck pulled the wallet from his back pocket and opened it for Keller. The investigator studied it closely.

"Well, Charles, you wanna tell me why you've been following me around? You got an axe to grind with me? Did I arrest you for something? Pop your grandson? What's your problem?"

Chuck saw an opening. "You arrested my son a few years back. It was a bogus charge, but it stuck, in no small thanks to you, and he went to prison for three years. You ruined his life. You trumped up those charges against him. You're a dirty cop, and I wanted to catch you doing something illegal so I could turn you in. Payback."

"What was his name, and what did I pop him for?"

"Ruben, Ruben Serrano. You accused him of robbery. He did three years because of you. He had a wife and son, but he lost them and it's your fault."

"I don't remember ever arresting any Ruben Serrano, and I've got a pretty good memory."

"Well, he sure as hell remembers you." Chuck was gaining confidence in his story. Keller at least was listening to what he was saying.

"Reuben Serrano, huh? Where did he do his time?"

Chuck and Mia talked about a lot of cases handled by the RCSO. He knew nothing about the state prison system, so he tried the only name he could remember.

"La Vista. He was in La Vista."

"Okay, Old Man, give me your ID again."

Chuck complied.

"You live here in Castle Springs, Mr. Serrano?"

"Yes, I do. I live with my daughter," he told him, instantly regretting it.

"Here's what we're gonna do," Keller told him. "You're going to give me your keys. I'm going to step over there and make a call. If you come back clean, you can go."

Chuck handed over the keys and Keller stepped away from the SUV. Chuck struggled to listen but couldn't make out the words. He could only see Keller's silhouette in the rear view mirror looking at his license and talking on the phone.

"Hey, Nikki, it's Jack Keller. Look, I need a favor. I'm supposed to meet up with Mia Serrano this morning on a case. I've misplaced her home address and she's not answering her cell. Can you look it up for me? Sure, thanks, I'll hold."

Keller returned to the SUV and handed Chuck his ID. "Okay Old Man, you're clean."

A wave of relief washed over Chuck. "Listen, I'm sorry, I made a mistake."

"You any relation to Mia Serrano of the Rocklin County Sheriff's Office?"

"Mia Serrano? No, I don't know anyone by that name. There are a lot of Serranos. No relation to anyone named Mia."

"That's funny," Keller said, snatching Chuck by the jacket again. "Since you fucking live with her."

TWENTY-FIVE

Chuck stood helplessly beside the SUV as Keller pulled out the laptop and cell and set them on the hood. The investigator tinkered with the electronics, chuckled and shook his head in disbelief.

"Gee, Charles, pretty high tech for a guy your age."

Keller locked up the SUV and slammed the door. He poked Chuck in the chest with his index finger. "Listen, Charles, and understand me. I'm a law enforcement officer, and I don't appreciate being stalked. There are laws against this sort of thing."

Chuck never seriously considered the consequences of getting caught. He was suddenly terrified of what this could mean for Mia, and possibly Mick.

"I'm hoping there's a damn good explanation for this, so you and I are going make a little run over to your house so I can hear it. And make no mistake—if you want to play games or think you're going to fuck with me, you can sit your ass in a holding cell until we sort it out in front of a judge. Got it?"

Terrified, Chuck reluctantly agreed.

"We'll take my truck," Keller added.

It took the veteran investigator only a few seconds to find the GPS tracker Chuck had mounted under the vehicle.

"Listen, I didn't…," Chuck pleaded.

"Shut up, Charles," Keller barked. "Get in the damn truck."

Mia woke with her head on Mick's chest. The night had been wonderful. They made love and fell asleep together in a warm embrace.

Mick began to rustle. "Hey, good looking," he whispered.

"Good morning," she said, squeezing him tightly. "I wish we could stay right here all day."

"I'm good with that," Mick said, smiling. "Although, I could go for a cup of coffee. Think your dad is downstairs?"

"No, I heard him go out awhile ago. He likes to take hikes on Sunday mornings. Why, you worried about the walk of shame?"

"Ha," Mick scoffed.

"Dad loves you. He'll be thrilled you're here."

As they approached the house, Chuck was filled with dread. How could he possibly explain himself to Mia? His stupidity could damage not only her career but her relationship with Mick.

Keller saw Serrano's unmarked RCSO car in the driveway.

"Does Mia keep her personal car in the garage? Keller asked.

"Yes, most of the time."

"Any idea if she's home right now?"

"Not really. On Sundays she sometimes does the shopping or runs errands. She didn't tell me anything about her plans for today."

"We'll find out soon enough."

Keller parked the truck fifty yards or so from the house, around a little bend in the street. If Mia was out running errands, Keller didn't want her seeing his truck when she got back.

At the door, Sasha was there instantly to greet Chuck, but her wagging tail turned quickly into an angry bark once she saw Keller.

"It's okay, Sasha, it's okay." Chuck picked up the dog and Sasha relented. But she didn't take her eyes off the stranger.

"I hear water running," Keller observed.

"That must be Mia," Chuck said.

"Okay, then we wait. Got a comfortable place to sit in this place?"

Chuck led Keller into the living room. They each took a seat, with Keller on the sofa and Chuck on the recliner across from him.

"So, why were you following me, Charles? Can you at least tell me that?"

Chuck didn't respond.

"I take it Reuben isn't here. Too bad, I would have liked to hear about the hard time he did at La Vista for the robbery conviction. You made a mistake on that one, Charles. La Vista houses women and transgendered inmates. So your imaginary son is a tranny, Charles?"

More silence.

"You gotta have a plan, Charles, and amateurs never do. I've been a cop for over thirty-five years, and I always have a plan. I've had lots of threats, so I'm always watching my back and I don't miss much. I didn't miss you at St. Joseph's the other morning or at the bank. Hell, you almost knocked me over. Then this morning at the SaveCo, you pop up again—and I'd had enough, so I gave you a little surprise. I wish I had a picture of the look on your face when I reached in through your window. Priceless. Never take your eye off your mark, Charles. That was your big mistake… allowing me to get the drop on you."

"I'll remember that," Chuck said, giving Keller an icy stare.

Keller chuckled. "Well, good. Then this whole episode hasn't been a waste for you, Charles. See, you learned something."

There was movement upstairs.

"Okay, Charles, it's show time. Sounds like Mia's coming down," whispered Keller.

Chuck fidgeted in his seat, dreading Mia's reaction.

Fresh from the shower, Mick was dying for a cup of coffee. Mia had told him Chuck was gone, so he didn't bother to get dressed just to run to the kitchen.

Had the sunlight reflecting through the front window not caught his eye, Mick probably wouldn't have even noticed the two men in the living room. But it did. Mick stood before his lead investigator and his girlfriend's father wearing only a towel.

"Mia!" Mick called out loudly. "You might want to come down here." No one spoke.

"Coming!" Mia said as she came down the stairs. "Mick, your phone was just buzz—"

She stopped cold in her bathrobe holding her boss's cell phone. Mia was utterly confused.

"C'mon in, everybody," Keller bellowed, sarcastically. "This is turning into quite a busy Sunday morning for all of us! Mia, I had the unexpected pleasure of meeting your father this morning at the supermarket. And apparently that was just the first surprise of the day. May I suggest we all take a seat?"

"What the hell is going on here?" Mia asked.

"I think your dad has been watching a few too many cop shows. I caught him following me today, and earlier this week, for that matter. His skills are a bit unpolished, but he's got potential. Just before you two made your appearance, I was asking Charles why he was so interested in an old investigator like me. Perhaps you can shed some light on this?" Keller asked, his gaze locked on Mia.

Just as Mia started to respond, Mick's phone rang loudly and began vibrating. He glanced down at the caller ID, "I've gotta take this; it's Brett Rainey from ESU."

Mick turned away, his free hand holding the towel in place.

"Hey, Brett, what's up? When, and what was said? So the article did the trick, huh? That's terrific!"

Keller's focus shifted immediately. The call was probably trouble for Lisa. As he contemplated the consequences, his burner phone began vibrating. He quickly reached into his pocket and hit the mute button. Jack knew who was calling.

"When are they supposed to meet?" Mick asked Rainey.

Mia and Keller could only watch and imagine what exactly was going down. Chuck just wanted to sneak down to the basement and escape.

"Well, they want to keep their stories straight. But look, the timing couldn't be better. The wiretap was set to expire tomorrow. We're gonna need arrest warrants, fast."

Keller's phone vibrated again, this time signaling a text message. Lisa needed help. He wanted out of there, fast.

"If you could send the transcript of the warrant to the DA's office and the warrant team, that would be a big help. Arresting officers will be Keller and Serrano. No, that's okay," Mick said, looking around the room, "I'll brief them myself."

It was awkward for all.

"Thanks again for all the hard work on this, Brett, and thank your ESU guys for me. Right, see ya," Mick said as he switched off the call.

"What gives, Captain?" Keller asked.

"Jack, I'm sorry I didn't have you up to speed on this, but I had Archer run a story in this morning's paper in hopes of rattling Lennox and Sullivan. Looks like it worked. Lennox left a message on Sullivan's voicemail a few minutes ago. He set up a meeting for them to get their story straight. They are meeting today at noon at the Bean Crazy on Petal Highway."

"I thought I was the lead investigator on this case, Captain," Keller said angrily.

"Look, Jack, now is not the time," Mick shot back.

"Clearly," Keller snapped.

"Look, Investigator, I need you and Investigator Serrano to coordinate the takedown team on this. We've only got a few hours to make this happen. Present evidence notwithstanding, we're professionals. So here's what we're going to do: we'll stage at the department's storage warehouse in the industrial center around the corner from the Bean Crazy coffee shop. We all know the location; we've used it for training. I'll get Archer on board, and I need both of you ready to do the interrogation after the bust."

Mick glanced at his phone.

"It's just past 8:30. We can discuss what happened here another time. Right now it's time to go to work. Any questions?"

"No," said Mia.

"On it," said Keller. "May I be excused then?" he added.

"Yes, Investigator, you may be excused," Mick responded, annoyed. Sometimes Keller's snide attitude really pissed him off.

"Thank you, Captain. Good morning, all," Keller shot back as he headed out, closing the door firmly behind him.

Mia turned to Chuck, "Damn it, Dad! What—"

Mick interrupted, "Mia. Not now."

Chuck seized the opportunity, "Yeah, Mia, you guys go to work. I'll be here with Sasha."

TWENTY-SIX

Keller had very little time to make things happen. Unless he moved quickly, Lisa might be arrested and held to answer for her role in the murder of George Lombard. But he was only able to pick up bits and pieces from McCallister's call.

Lisa's text read, "Scott called, I didn't answer, but he left a message. What do I do? Pls call."

Keller was dialing his burner phone even before he made it to the truck.

"Hello?" Lisa said, shaken.

"What did he say on the message?"

"He said there was an article in the paper this morning and that the cops were reopening the investigation. He said we needed to meet to get our stories straight. He wants me to meet him at noon. I'm so scared."

"Where are you right now?"

"I'm at home."

"Okay, Lisa, I need you to listen carefully. One way or another you can't stay there. I need you to pack. One bag only. Meet me at Tamale Jack's near your house, you know the place, right?"

"Yes."

"Meet me there in thirty minutes."

"Uh, okay."

"Lisa, everything's going to be all right. We'll work it out. I'll take care of you."

"I'll be there in half an hour," she said.

Jack stewed with each passing mile as he headed south on I-25. An old man had followed him, his captain was apparently screwing his partner, and somebody planted an article about his case without consulting him.

The article pissed him off the most. It was a clear sign he wasn't trusted at RCSO. Where did that come from? Serrano? McCallister? Were they conspiring against him? Could they know more about Lisa than they let on? And why the hell was Serrano's father following him?

McCallister was back in his office twenty minutes after dispatching Keller and Mia. He had begun planning on the way to the office. Keller and Mia would take the lead. He'd need another four undercover cars with eight undercover deputies. The captain doubted Lennox and Sullivan had the potential to become violent when confronted, but it was a public place on a Sunday afternoon and he wasn't going to take any chances. The UC cars would be strategically placed—two in the parking lot of Bean Crazy and the other two parked out on Petal Highway, pointing in opposite directions and ready to initiate a pursuit in the unlikely event Lennox and Sullivan decided to run. Uniformed deputies working the beat would be alerted and be ready to assist if it turned into an actual pursuit. McCallister was confident there was no way Lennox and Sullivan would elude capture.

Mick called Mark Archer so he could alert Anita Sanchez at the News-Press to the takedown. It was payback for the article that put things in motion. She wouldn't get the story before anyone else, but the tip would allow her to prepare and be first online with details. Most media outlets only had inexperienced, skeleton crews on weekends, giving Sanchez an even bigger advantage.

Next, McCallister dialed Sheriff Connelly. He hoped the boss hadn't decided to sleep late. Mick never liked waking him up, but he was confident this was a call the sheriff wouldn't mind taking.

"Sheriff, it's Captain McCallister. We got a break in the Lombard case..."

When she got to the office, Mia began reviewing the murder book. She knew the case inside and out, but by refreshing her memory of every detail, she'd be ready for the interrogations. Any suspect can refuse to answer questions, but most choose to talk. It's often the best opportunity for investigators to catch a perp in a lie, so every detail mattered.

Mia had trouble concentrating after the bizarre scene that had played out in her living room. Why would her dad follow Keller after she'd specifically told him not to?

Keller wasn't likely to let it go. Mia thought it might be best just to come clean and tell him why she had him followed and why she was suspicious. No cop is above the law.

It was a little before ten, less than two hours before the takedown. There was enough time to talk with Keller before the bust. She picked up the phone to set a meeting. After all, he probably had a few things to say to her, too.

TWENTY-SEVEN

Tamale Jack's in Rosebud was a hot spot during the week, but on weekends the place was mostly deserted. It was far from fancy; food was ordered and picked up from the same counter. The morning special was a chorizo and egg burrito.

"What can I get you?"

"Iced tea and a Diet Coke," he replied.

"Chips and salsa?" the high school-aged counter girl offered.

"For breakfast? Uh, sure," Jack smirked.

Keller took his tray to a table along a side wall, keeping a safe distance from the other customers; namely an elderly couple that looked close to finishing their meal. He took a long draw from his Diet Coke while getting a good look at the old man across the restaurant. Elderly gentlemen were on Keller's radar this morning, and he amusingly hoped to himself that Charles Serrano hadn't enlisted a team of senior citizens in some AARP chat room to follow him around the state.

Lisa arrived and came right to the table. They hugged. It was evident she had been crying.

"Look, we don't have a lot of time. We need to talk things through and lay out a plan of action from this point forward."

Lisa agreed.

He leaned in close to her. "Just so you know, Scott will be arrested this afternoon when he shows up at the coffee place."

Lisa was torn. While she wasn't willing to go down with him for this crime, she had loved Scott Lennox, or at least loved the man she thought he was and had planned to spend the rest of her life with him. All that was gone now.

"I still can't believe he lied to me about the insurance money. I wonder now if he ever really planned to leave his wife. I mean, I think he did love me, but maybe he got cold feet. He knew I would keep the secret. I couldn't go to the police and tell them what happened; he knew I was in too deep. Maybe he planned to give me part of the $500,000 to shut me up, then stay with his wife and have the rest of the life insurance money."

"I think that's a very likely scenario. It happens, Lisa, don't beat yourself up over it. One way or another, your relationship with Scott is over. It can't be anything but over, unless you want to go down with him. Listen carefully to me, you really need to be sure about the next step because there's no going back. If you run, you'll be running for good. They aren't going to forget about you. It's a sexy case and the media will eat it up. But even when they lose interest, from time to time, the story will resurface. Your picture will be everywhere, at least everywhere within the U.S. That's why Mexico could be your best bet, and I have a place there."

"I've thought it through a thousand times. Mom is dead. I don't have any close friends. The only person in my life now is the father I never knew."

"Yeah," Keller said, sad for his daughter and sorry for all the years lost.

"I didn't mean it like that."

"It's okay," Jack said, trying to reassure her.

"I love that we have a relationship now. And I hope that can continue even if I am on the run. Will those phones that we use still work in Mexico?"

"Yes, they'll work."

"I just can't go to prison. I'd rather die. Do you really think I can have a life in Mexico?"

"Yes, I do. Is that what you want?"

"I think so."

Keller continued, "I'll do everything possible to help you with whatever decision you make, but at this point you don't have a lot of options, and I think Mexico is your best bet."

"I want to go," she said sternly, nodding for emphasis.

"Okay, then we'll make it happen for you. Now, this is important. No matter what, don't use your cards. No ATM withdrawals, no debit cards, no credit cards. Everything in cash." Keller pulled a thick envelope from his jacket. "This will get you started."

Keller checked to make sure no one was looking as Lisa thumbed through the contents. "Oh my God," she said. "How much is this?"

"Twenty thousand. Be careful with it."

"I can't take this…"

"Please, you're my daughter."

"You're risking so much by helping me."

Jack shook his head. "Don't worry about me; let's just get you into Mexico. We've only got half an hour or so before I need to leave to get back to Castle Springs for the arrest. Let me outline what you need to do, step by step, to get out of the country and what you need to do once you're in Mexico. You have to do exactly what I say."

Jack laid out the plan in detail as Lisa committed it to memory. There was no room for error, he reminded her.

"C'mon," her father told her. "It's time to go."

TWENTY-EIGHT

Keller drove back to Castle Springs, alone with his thoughts. It was hard to leave Lisa, but if she followed his instructions, she'd at least make it out of the country.

Then there was Serrano's phone call. Why did she want to meet before the takedown? What was her angle? Fuck her, he thought.

Jack had just left his daughter and already wondered where she was.

Mia arrived for their meeting a few minutes early. Soon, Keller pulled in. Why, she wondered, was he driving his own truck instead of his unmarked department car?

He drove up next to her so their cars were positioned driver's door to driver's door. With their windows open, the two were face-to-face a few feet apart. The weather had turned cold and a stiff breeze was coming from the west. This would be an uncomfortable conversation on many levels.

"You called this meeting, Serrano, so spill it."

Mia took a deep breath, "Jack, I have great respect for you as an investigator, but I have something to say, and I'm just going to say it."

Jack braced himself. "Geez, Mia, then go ahead and say it."

"The reason we, I mean my dad, put the GPS on your car... Well, I had some concerns that you were helping Lisa Sullivan. If you're having an affair with her and are trying to keep her from being arrested... I mean, c'mon, Jack, do you really want to jeopardize your career for some woman? I thought you were a better man than that."

Keller broke out in laughter. So that was it? She thought he was screwing Lisa Sullivan? God, if she only knew, he thought to himself.

"Wow, Mia," Keller replied, struggling to get the words out. "I don't know what to say. Except that I can assure you that I am not sleeping with Lisa Sullivan. There is no romantic, sexual, or deviant relationship between me and our suspect. For God's sake, Mia. That's why you had your father tail me? I guess I should take it as a compliment, but seriously... You thought I was screwing her?"

His reaction caught Mia off guard.

"You were so protective of her," Mia replied defensively. "Every time I brought up her possible involvement in the case you found a reason to shoot it down. You climbed up my ass for looking for her sister in Big Pine, and you made it pretty clear to me and the captain that you thought Lennox acted alone in the murder."

"You could have just asked me straight out, Mia. Look, I've been doing this for a long time, and I know how to investigate a fucking murder. I'm not trying to disparage you or the captain, but I just have more experience than you guys. You've got a lot of potential as an investigator, or at least I thought you did until now. But I'm twenty, almost thirty years of homicides, rapes, and robberies ahead of you. I follow my hunches because they're usually right."

"So, I have your word," Mia said, trying to retain some dignity, "that you aren't involved romantically with Lisa Sullivan?"

"With God as my witness, I have never laid a hand on that woman, and I never would. Maybe if she had an aunt I might..." he added jokingly.

Mia looked long and hard at Keller. She was a pretty good judge of people, and she believed Keller's response was genuine. But she wasn't fully convinced that Keller was being totally honest with her. It was an intuitive sense telling her to be cautious. But with the arrests of Lennox and Sullivan about to go down, she let him off the hook.

"All right, Jack, I'll take you at your word. And I'm sorry about the GPS tracker. I was out of bounds, and I apologize."

"Ya think? I'd be a little more pissed off if I wasn't so flattered you thought I was banging Lisa Sullivan. Now, if you don't mind, can we go to work?"

"Okay."

"Oh, and I promise not to cop a feel when we bust her today. But if she's all worked up and tries to put the moves on me, I'm counting on you, partner, to keep me safe," he teased.

"You know, you really are an asshole, Jack," she shot back.

Keller smiled and gave Mia a little nod as he rolled up the window and pulled away.

By 11:30, the RCSO team was assembled for the takedown of Scott Lennox and Lisa Sullivan.

The route Lisa Sullivan was taking out of Colorado would put her in New Mexico by late afternoon and Arizona before she would need to stop for the night. Keller repeatedly told Lisa to drive carefully and obey all traffic laws. He was hoping her car wouldn't make the state's "hot list" before she was able to cross the New Mexico state line, but regardless, it was critical she didn't draw any attention from law enforcement.

"Hey everybody, let's get this thing done," Captain McCallister shouted to the RCSO personnel gathered in the industrial park just east of Petal Highway.

"You've seen the pictures of our two subjects. Our intel says Scott Lennox and Lisa Sullivan plan to meet today at noon at Bean Crazy

Coffee. Neither of our subjects have a criminal history so we don't expect any problems with the takedown today, but keep in mind these two are wanted in connection to a homicide, so take no chances. Scott Lennox is our primary. The girlfriend, Lisa Sullivan, is the accomplice."

"Our leads today are Investigators Jack Keller and Mia Serrano. They will be watching from across the street during the takedown. Both our subjects know these two investigators, so we can't have them in the line of sight for obvious reasons. Robert Garcia and Doug Saint, I want you in the coffee shop. Once they're in custody, Keller and Serrano will Mirandize them, and then they'll be transported separately to the station. We want to keep the two apart from each other so they won't have a chance to talk, understood?"

There were nods all around.

"The location, Bean Crazy, is almost always busy. There will likely be many customers. So we wait for them to leave the coffee shop and make the arrest in the parking lot. I want every effort made to take these two into custody before they get to their vehicles and have a chance to leave the area. We sure as hell don't need a pursuit that puts the public in danger. Everybody got it?"

The team was in agreement. As takedowns went, this was pretty basic.

At 11:45, everyone drove the few blocks to Bean Crazy and took up their assigned positions. Jack and Mia took Mia's unmarked car and parked a hundred yards away. From there they would have a clear view of the shop, but were far enough away to avoid detection.

At precisely 11:50, Saint and Garcia walked into the shop together. Mick was right, it was busy with about two dozen customers inside. Once Saint and Garcia were in position, he came in, got coffee and a newspaper, and took a seat by the window.

Two cars took their positions in the Bean Crazy lot and two others were out on Petal Highway as directed.

At 11:59, Scott Lennox pulled in. Once inside, he scanned the room for Lisa Sullivan, didn't see her and took a seat at one of the few empty tables. Mick was just ten feet away. Garcia and Saint were on the opposite side near the exit door. Lennox looked around toward the parking lot every few seconds for Lisa. He shifted nervously in his chair and repeatedly glanced at his watch. By 12:05, there was still no sign of her.

By 12:15, both McCallister and Lennox were growing concerned. Mick remained patient; his people wouldn't make a move until Lennox did. And so they waited.

Finally, at 12:40, a perplexed Scott Lennox stood to leave. Mick nodded to his men, and they casually followed the target outside. Mick was close behind.

"On the ground! On the ground!"

As perps often do, Lennox hesitated, prompting two deputies to help him to the ground, quickly and forcefully.

"What the fuck is this?!"

Seconds later, Mia and Jack pulled up, coming to a quick stop next to Lennox's car. He was cuffed and yanked to his feet.

"This is ridiculous. Who the hell…?"

"Mr. Lennox," McCallister said. "I think you've met Investigators Keller and Serrano."

Keller turned to Mia, giving her the honor.

"Scott Lennox, you are under arrest for the murder of George Lombard. You have the right to remain silent. Anything you say can and will be used against you in a court of law. You have the right to an attorney. If you cannot afford an attorney, one will be provided for you. Do you understand the rights I have just read to you?"

"What the fuck are you talking about? This is some kind of mistake. I had nothing to do with…"

Mick cued the deputies and they placed him in the back of Saint's unmarked car. Garcia sat in the back with him, and the car sped away. The arrest of Scott Lennox had taken less than three minutes.

"Where the hell is Sullivan?" McCallister asked, looking at Keller and Mia.

Keller shrugged, but hoped she was out of state by now.

Lisa was filled with relief as she crossed the border into New Mexico but couldn't help but wonder if she'd ever see her home again. She guessed Scott was in custody by now, facing a murder charge. She envisioned him in jail. On one hand, she was sad for the loss of what they had once had, the plans they had made together, and the love she thought they had shared. But at the same time, she felt some perverse pleasure knowing Scott would pay for what he did. After all, he lied to her and was never going to leave his wife. He lied about the insurance, and he used her to help him kill a man.

TWENTY-NINE

The group gathered around a conference table in the Investigations Bureau. While Mick was pleased they'd scooped up Lennox, he was none too happy the other key suspect was still at large.

"I want Lisa Sullivan," Mick said firmly. Mia gave Keller a quick glance across the table. He looked as surprised as anyone that Sullivan had been a no-show.

"We've got Lennox, and he's the bigger fish in this thing, but we need to find the woman. And we need to find her fast. The press is going to get wind of this, and they're going to start asking questions."

The captain turned to Mark Archer.

"Mark, how much does Sanchez at the News-Press know about this case? Did you tell her we were looking for two people in connection to the murder?"

"I didn't give her a lot of specifics about the case, but I did indicate that we believed a conspiracy was behind the homicide. She's not stupid. She can draw her own conclusions when she learns we arrested only one person today. She'll definitely be asking me about it, but I'm not sure what exactly she will put in her article."

Mick responded, "Well, we can go one of two ways on this. We can just play up the arrest of Lennox today, not mention a conspiracy, and just let people believe we picked him up for Lombard's murder. People won't naturally assume he had help. We will eventually have to come clean about it, though, and when we do there will be some finger pointing asking why we didn't say any of this at the time of Lennox's arrest."

Archer interjected, "Yeah, but we can always say we kept it quiet for the good of the investigation, that outlining the motive at these very early stages would have compromised the case. We do it all the time in homicide cases. Then, when we do find her, we tell the press that the investigation led us to another person we believe participated in the killing of Lombard."

The captain answered, "That's true or we can just lay it all out there. We do have one in custody, and we can say that we don't believe he acted alone, and his accomplice in this murder is Lisa Sullivan. And then we plaster her picture all over the state of Colorado. She'll be hotter than the bottom of my laptop. Some alert citizen will spot her and call it in. You know the press—her picture will spread like wildfire."

Mick looked across the table. "Mia, Jack, I'd like to hear your thoughts."

Keller looked at Mia and nodded, giving her the floor.

"I think we should go public with Sullivan. I say we put her picture on the friggin Nancy Stein cable show. We tell the story, let people know what she did. She shouldn't skate on this; she was an accomplice in the murder. The faster we get on it, the better chance we have of picking her up. That's my two cents. But I'd really like to hear what Jack thinks."

Mia fixed her stare on Keller.

"Well, I think we need to have a little perspective here. And with all due respect to my partner here, Sullivan's not Jack the Ripper; she's a goddamn nurse from Rosebud, Colorado."

He continued, "Before we worry about the newspaper or TV, maybe we ought to do some basic police work and go find Lisa Sullivan. Jesus Christ, everybody's assuming just because she didn't meet Lennox for a cup of coffee, she's armed to the teeth and hopping a bus to Canada. C'mon people, we don't even know if she ever heard the message from Scott Lennox! Has anyone here called the hospital where she works?

Who knows, maybe she's reading the Sunday paper in her apartment right now, for Christ's sake, or skiing down the fucking slopes at Vail!"

Keller had a point, and everyone knew it.

"Now, let's just say we look everywhere and she doesn't turn up. I think the captain had it right with the first scenario. It's probably best that we keep the whole Sullivan thing quiet for now and focus the attention on the arrest of Lennox. We can do a lot in the way of searching for Sullivan without alerting the public. We all know most of the time, the public's help is a bigger pain in the ass than it's worth. If we release her picture and say we are offering a reward, we'll get hundreds of damn leads on her, with half of those telling us she's hanging out with Elvis down at Mister Mountain Donuts. And let's say she is on the run; its not like she's had tactical evasion training with the CIA. We'll zero in on her the first time she uses her fucking Macy's card."

Mick considered the reward. Under RCSO policy, he could offer up to $25,000 for information leading to the arrest and conviction of Sullivan. But Jack was right—a reward was a double-edged sword. Bounty hunters and nut cases would often emerge when money was on the table. There was also the issue of having RCSO staff monitor a tip-line twenty-four hours a day. He thought it best to hold off for now.

Mick addressed the group. "All right, listen up. We need to call the DA's office and get a search warrant for Sullivan's apartment, and get one for Lennox's home and business while we're at it. We need to see what kind of evidence we can dig up. I'll call in additional resources. We need to send a team to the hospital, toss her place in Rosebud, and raid Mister Mountain fucking Donuts if that's what it takes."

He looked at his watch. "We will schedule a press conference for 7 tonight. That gives us about six hours to scoop her up. If she's not in custody by then we go public."

He turned to his lead investigators. "Keller, Serrano, I need you two for the interrogation, so get ready for Lennox. Mark, come down to my office so we can brief the sheriff."

"Will do, Captain."

Mia turned to Mick, "Captain, when you call in for additional people, can you tell whoever is going to search Sullivan's apartment that they need to grab that concert ticket off her refrigerator? We have to bag it."

Archer called Anita Sanchez to give her an advance on the story. He didn't say anything about Lisa Sullivan, as he hoped she would be in custody by the time the press conference got underway.

Keller went outside for some privacy and a clear cell signal. Lisa picked up after two rings.

"Hey."

"Where are you? Out of Colorado, I hope?"

"Yeah, I crossed into New Mexico a while ago. I'm going to go as far as I can tonight before I find a motel to get some sleep."

"Okay, good to hear. You doing okay?"

"I'm okay."

She paused then asked, "Did Scott get arrested?"

"Yeah, he did. He's in custody. I'm going to question him in a few minutes. I don't think he'll have much to say. Look, I need to fill you in on what's going to happen next. The department will be—"

"Shit!" Lisa exclaimed. "There's a state trooper behind me, and he just put on his flashers. He's coming up behind me. Oh God, oh God…"

"Stay cool. They don't know you're wanted. Hang up and call me back when you can!" responded Jack.

The phone went dead.

RCSO hadn't issued any alerts on Lisa, but they would likely be statewide by nightfall. However, if she got a ticket, it would be big trouble. Her license plate and driver's license would pop up immediately in any kind of data search, and RCSO would know she had been pulled over in New Mexico. "That's the last thing I need," Jack thought to himself.

"Where have you been, Jack?" Mia asked as he walked into the conference room. "We need to get in there and interview Lennox, like, right now."

"Sorry. Are we good on the warrants?"

"The warrant team is staging near her apartment in Rosebud. Deputies already poked around the hospital, and we know she's not there, so they're focusing on the residence. The other team is getting ready to hit Lennox Ice and his house."

"Good," Keller said. "You ready for Lennox?"

"Yup."

"Me too, let's go hammer his ass."

Mick was peering at Lennox through two-way glass when Keller and Mia walked into the observation area where Mick was standing. All three could see Lennox through the glass, sitting in a chair and looking despondent.

"Everything set?" Mick asked his investigators.

Both Mia and Keller nodded.

"Look at him, almost makes you feel sorry for the prick," said Keller sarcastically.

"How do you want to play this, Jack?" asked Mia.

"I'll start. Give me some room and you can jump in when you think it's appropriate. I don't see him confessing to anything, at least not now. Let's just lay the groundwork and try to establish a rapport. I think that's more likely to happen with you, Mia. I'm guessing he's a sucker for a good looking woman."

"Do you want to bring up Sullivan?" she asked.

"Not now. The less he knows about what we know, the better. Let's see what he has to say about Lombard's death and see if we can trip him up."

Jack opened the door, walked in confidently, and took a chair opposite Lennox. Mia took the chair next to Jack. Lennox looked up but didn't speak.

Keller started, "Can we get you anything? A glass of water, a soda, anything at all?"

Lennox shook his head.

"Okay, well if you change your mind just let us know. Listen, Scott, we just want to get this whole thing cleared up."

"This is crazy," Lennox told them, pleading.

Mia spoke, "Scott, we are going to read you your Miranda rights. I know they were read to you earlier when you were arrested, but we're going to read them to you again now. And as you can see, we're tape recording our conversation with you as well, just for the record."

No response from Lennox.

Mia read him his rights, and Jack started in with the questions.

With Lisa Sullivan still on the loose at 7 pm, the RCSO proceeded with the press conference. Mark Archer stood before the dozen or so reporters gathered in the RCSO downstairs conference room testing the mic levels. A podium was set up at the front of the room with the backdrop of the Rocklin County Seal on the wall directly behind it. The TV crews had set up lights pointing towards the front of the room and a small stack of microphones lay along the top of the podium. Anita Sanchez was in the front row.

Archer began, "Ladies and gentlemen, we'd like to get started now. First off, thank you all for coming out on such short notice. Does everybody have a copy of the press release?"

Archer continued, "This afternoon, the RCSO arrested 46-year-old Scott Lennox for the November murder of 56-year-old George Lombard. Both men are Castle Springs residents. The details of the murder and the arrest of Mr. Lennox this afternoon are all outlined in the press release. As I'm sure you all know, I'm not in a position this evening to answer specific questions about the homicide or the investigation that led to the arrest of Lennox. We can't do or say anything that could possibly compromise the integrity of the case. The only details we can offer to you this evening are what we've covered in the release. If any of you need the content of the release said aloud by either me or Captain McCallister for the purpose of on-camera TV or radio interviews, we'd be happy to do that at the conclusion of this press conference. Having said all that, there is something we need your help with this evening. At this time, I'd like to ask Captain Mick McCallister to come up and talk about that."

Mick stepped up to the bank of microphones and looked out at the reporters.

"As Lieutenant Archer indicated, we need your help this evening. We do not believe that the individual arrested today, Scott Lennox, acted alone in carrying out this homicide. We are seeking a second individual we believe played a role in the murder of Mr. Lombard."

He held up a color, eight by ten copy of a Sullivan photo they pulled from the Internet.

"That second individual is Lisa Sullivan, 32 years old, of Rosebud. At this point, I can't elaborate on her exact involvement, but we consider her a suspect and are seeking the public's help in getting her into custody. We have copies of this photo for you to take with you this evening, and we have them in electronic format as well. Again, anything you can do to get her photo out to the public would be greatly appreciated."

"Is the RCSO offering a reward for her capture?" asked a young female TV reporter.

"No, not at this time," he responded.

Mick knew the story would get plenty of attention based on the sensationalism of the case and the photo of Sullivan. Even still, Mick knew interest would quickly wane without an arrest. If Sullivan was still at large after a couple of days he would need to shift gears. Offering a reward when the interest had faded would get the story back on the on the front page. "Give it legs," as the reporters liked to say.

After a few more questions, the formal conference ended. Both Mick and Mark Archer spent another thirty minutes doing TV and radio interviews.

The media event gave Keller another chance to sneak out.

"Lisa, what happened?"

"You won't believe this. A trooper pulled me over for talking on my cell phone. God, if he only knew," she said with a nervous laugh.

Keller was relieved, but still concerned.

"Shit, that's not a good thing, Lisa. That ticket will go into the system and—"

"I said he pulled me over. I didn't say he gave me a ticket. He was cute, and I flirted with him. We talked for almost fifteen minutes. He was super nice, said he'd let me off with a warning, just this once."

Still not good, Keller thought. Clearly she had made an impression. If he saw her picture on the news, the trooper would certainly remember her. All Jack could do was hope the news story didn't make it to the television stations in Santa Fe or Albuquerque any time soon. He didn't share his concerns with Lisa; she had enough to worry about.

"Okay, well, keep on driving. Go as far as you can tonight; get into Arizona if you can."

"I will. I'll call you when I get to a motel."

"Okay, if I don't answer, I'll call you back as soon as I can."

THIRTY

Kit Bumgartner was sitting in her apartment in Golden with her husband Ralph, watching the credits roll at the end of an old episode of *American Gladiators*, when the ten o'clock news came on.

"Turn it to Channel 40. They've got reruns of *Roseanne*. I don't want to watch the news, hon, it's too depressing," she said.

Ralph nodded toward his wife and looked for the remote control to change the channel.

"What the hell did you do with the remote?" he snapped at his wife.

"You had it last. It wasn't me that wanted to watch *American Gladiators*. I hate that shit."

Kit glanced over at the TV as Ralph slipped his hand into the cushions of his lounge chair for the remote.

"Oh my…"

"Found it!" he exclaimed as he turned. "What is it, Kit? You look like you've seen a ghost."

"Shhhh, quiet. I want to hear this."

Ralph turned his attention to what Kit was staring at on the screen.

"Oh my God," Kit replied, staring in disbelief as Lisa Sullivan's picture flashed on the screen, followed by footage showing an industrial plant with a sign identifying it as the Lennox Ice Company.

"Police say Sullivan was part of a murder plot hatched by the owner of this Castle Springs ice company, 46-year-old Scott Lennox, who is in custody at the Rocklin County Jail tonight. Sources familiar with the case say it was Lennox who recruited Sullivan to help carry out the crime. Lisa Sullivan is described as five feet six inches tall, 130 pounds, with blonde hair and blue eyes. Police say they served a search warrant on Sullivan's Rosebud home a few hours ago and are in the process of gathering evidence there now. Police believe that Lisa Sullivan is on the run tonight."

"Oh my God," Kit said again, in shock.

Anchorwoman Kate Kitchens continued the story with a large graphic displaying the RCSO phone number.

"Lord Almighty," Kit said as the anchorwoman moved on to the next story.

Ralph muted the TV.

"What is it, Kit?" he asked.

"I know that woman they just showed on the news. She was in the café."

"Come on, Kit, you get a lot of people coming through that place."

"Yeah, but I'm sure I waited on her. She was with some old guy. Looked to me like he was breaking it off with her. I know that's her, look how pretty she is. I remember thinking she could do so much better than that old fart. I remember it because she threw her iced tea on him. He just sat there with it drippin' down his face."

"Geez, Kit, you gotta call it in," Ralph urged.

Kit paused and thought for a moment.

"Did they say anything about a reward?"

"No, I don't think so. They just want people to call it in if they see her. Kit, what are you gonna do?"

"I dunno… I wanna think about it."

After eighteen years of marriage, Ralph knew Kit did things in her own good time.

It was after ten by the time an exhausted Jack Keller left the station and headed home.

He was frustrated, but not surprised, that the Lennox interrogation went nowhere. While he hadn't lawyered up, he did clam up. Other than a few nods, an occasional grunt and a series of denials, Lennox was pretty much non-responsive. Jack had even tried to antagonize him in an effort to get him to lose his composure and start talking, but Lennox didn't fall for it. But Keller still had a lot of tricks up his sleeve when it came to interrogating suspects, and he'd barely had time to scratch the surface. He looked forward to having another run at him after Lennox spent a night in jail. Keller knew that a night spent with hardcore gang-bangers, rapists, and meth dealers could change a man. Lennox was a softie and likely wouldn't get a whole lot of sleep. If a lawyer didn't enter the picture soon, Keller felt confident that he would get something from Lennox the next day when he and Mia questioned him again.

As Jack took the exit off I-25, his burner phone went off.

"Hey, where are you now?"

"I made it to Arizona. I'm at a motel off the interstate. I'm beat."

"Okay, good. You paid cash for the room, right?"

"Just like you told me. Other than money for gas and a quick bite to eat, it's all I've spent. And like you said, I won't use a credit card or ATM."

"Okay, sorry to keep bringing it up, but one little mistake and we're in deep—"

"I know."

Keller was relieved Lisa had made it safely out of Colorado and was now two states away. He hadn't seen the news, but doubted the Lennox story ran anywhere outside the Denver area, at least not yet.

"So where are you in Arizona?"

"A place called Winslow."

Keller remembered the lyrics of the old Eagles song, 'Well, I'm standing on a corner in Winslow, Arizona. Such a fine sight to see...'

"Winslow, like the Eagles song," he said fondly.

"Huh?" she asked, puzzled.

"Take It Easy," he said, referring to the song title.

"Um, okay, I will," she replied, now thoroughly confused.

"Never mind," Jack replied, reminded of the generation gap. "Give me a call tomorrow morning when you leave. You should be there by tomorrow night. I'm very proud of you."

"I will. And I just want to thank you again for everything."

"Get some rest. I'll talk to you then," he said, trying not to tear up.

THIRTY-ONE

"**C**an u come by my office when u get in?"

Mia got Mick's text as she arrived at RCSO the next morning. It was early, and it had been a long and difficult night. After the interrogation, Mia had driven to Rosebud where the warrant team was searching Sullivan's apartment.

By the time she finally returned home, it was well past midnight and her father was waiting up. Chuck felt awful about the confrontation with Keller, and he didn't want to go to bed without apologizing to his daughter for all the trouble he had caused. She accepted his apology, but not before giving him a good lecture. She knew she couldn't stay angry with her dad for very long. Once they patched things up, Chuck told Mia what he saw while tailing Keller, including the somewhat agitated exchange between Keller and the priest at the church. While it did seem odd on the surface, it was far from sinister.

It was after two in the morning before Mia finally got to sleep. The nightmare returned, this time with a new twist. Vivid hues spiraled downward, sucking Mia into a kaleidoscope of color before exploding out in a river of red—blood red. Mia was caught in the current and struggled to find a way out, reaching for something to pull her out of the abyss. She awoke with a start, sweaty and anxious but with the lingering feeling that she was close to that one piece of the puzzle that would blow open the case.

Jack and Lisa—was there a connection?

By 6:00, she decided to get an early start to the day by prepping for the second interrogation with Lennox.

Back at her cubicle, she dropped her briefcase on the desk and, armed with an extra large latte, headed toward the captain's office. It was going to be a day for caffeine.

She poked her head in.

"Hey there."

"Hey, Mia, come on in and close the door. You're here early."

Mia smiled and responded, "I could say the same about you."

"I was pretty keyed up after yesterday. Got home and tried to sleep but didn't have much luck. I gave up at 4:30, hit the gym, and came in. What's your excuse?"

"About the same as yours, minus the gym."

Mia had already briefed Mick about Sullivan's apartment. The search team seized the usual stuff, including her computer, but there was nothing found that pointed directly to her involvement in Lombard's murder. However, the concert ticket from the refrigerator was gone. Mia wasn't sure what to make of that.

She also told him that the search team deployed to Lennox's house had similar results; they searched his computer but uncovered nothing that amounted to a "smoking gun" linking Lennox to the homicide. She also gave Mick a quick briefing on the interrogation.

"I'm hoping we can get something out of him this morning before he can lawyer up," she told the captain hopefully.

"We have to get Lisa Sullivan," Mick said flatly. "She's the lynchpin. Without her, it's all circumstantial, and we'll have to take first degree murder off the table. Best we'd do in that scenario is manslaughter, and even that's no slam dunk.

Mia understood. "Right now, things don't look very good. Sullivan is on the loose, and Lennox has clammed up. And I still don't have a good feeling about Keller."

"Well, now that you mention Keller," replied Mick.

"Oh God," Mia muttered, dreading this conversation.

"As I recall from the events of yesterday morning, Keller claimed your dad had been following him. Is that…"

"Listen… what he… I thought…" Exasperated, she let out a long breath.

"Is it true?"

"Yes," she confessed.

"What in the hell was he…" Mick started, then stopped and asked a side question. "How old is Chuck?"

"72."

"What was your 72-year-old father doing following Rocklin County's most experienced investigator?"

Mia took a deep breath.

"I shared some of my concerns with him. You know, about Keller possibly being involved romantically with Sullivan."

"Which—" Mick tried to jump in.

"Was a mistake," Mia continued. "I shouldn't be talking about cases with my father, but I did. So my dad, wanting to help me, decided to follow him." Mia purposely left out the GPS tracking device. Mick was stressed enough.

"Keller said Chuck followed him to a supermarket?"

"And… a few other places. Keller was apparently onto him by the time they got to the market. That's where Keller cornered him and started asking him questions. He quickly figured things out, got pissed, and made Dad take him to the house to confront me. And apparently that's right about the time you came down in your… your…"

"My towel? Look, you're going to have to resolve this with Jack," Mick said.

"I already did. We talked before the Lennox takedown yesterday. We met, and he basically bitched me out."

"What about us? Did that come up?"

"No. There wasn't time."

"Well, he obviously knows. We'll have to see how that plays out."

"He didn't say anything to me about it, but again, we didn't have a lot of time. He just swore up and down he wasn't involved with Lisa Sullivan. He actually laughed at the suggestion."

"So, are you off the Keller/Sullivan love connection now?" he asked.

"Uh. Not completely."

"Jesus, Mia."

"I'm an investigator, too, Captain. What—I can't have a hunch?"

Mick gazed at her. Even at the crack of dawn with no sleep, she was beautiful. "You know what my problem is?" he asked.

"What?"

"I'm in love with you."

"And that's a problem?"

"No, it's great, but it does complicate things a bit."

"I love you too, Mick. And as soon as this case is closed, I will get a transfer back to patrol, and we can be together. And as far as your run for sheriff, like I said the other night, I think you should do it. Don't pass on your dreams for me. You'll make a great sheriff after the people of Rocklin County vote you into office."

"You'd do that for me?"

"Of course, I would. If it means we can be together, then I'm happy to do it."

"Mia, I don't know what to say."

"No need to say anything."

"Well, I'm hoping we can find a way to keep you where you are. But it's early yet. Still, speaking of running for sheriff, I do need to start the process. Set up a campaign, raise money, set a strategy."

"What can I do to help?"

"We need to put together a campaign team of people who would be interested in supporting me."

"Okay, I will give that some serious thought, Mr. Sheriff."

"I like the sound of that, but let's not get ahead of ourselves."

"You're going to win, Mick. And I will do everything I can to help."

"Thanks, Mia. As far as Keller goes, there's nothing we can do about it now, so we'll play it as it comes."

"Dad feels awful. Just so you know."

"I'm sure he does."

Mia wanted to give him a hug, but thought better of it. It was still early, and it didn't appear anyone was around, but she didn't want to take any chances. Mick could sense what she was thinking.

"I'd better get to work," Mia replied as she walked towards the door.

"Yeah, me too."

Once back in her office, Mia sent off a quick email to Keller asking what time he wanted to meet and have another go at Lennox.

Keller snatched the burner phone as it vibrated on the kitchen table. "Hey," he said.

"Good morning." Lisa sounded tired.

"How'd you sleep?"

"Not great, but I'm ready to hit the road and wanted to check in with you before I get going. I wouldn't want to get a ticket for talking on my cell while driving."

Keller chuckled. "Well, it seems you are pretty good at charming New Mexico state troopers."

"Yeah, but I'm in Arizona now, so all bets are off," she joked.

"Somehow I don't think that would matter much."

"How long do you think it will take me to get there?"

"Probably about five hours, give or take. He's going to meet you at three this afternoon, so you've got plenty of time. I'll call him again to confirm. Once I do, I'll get you the final details."

"So, is my picture on the news?"

"Yep, you are officially a wanted woman."

"Is it at least a decent photo?" she asked with a tired, forced laugh.

"Yeah, we got one from your hospital's newsletter on the Internet. Great job on the United Way campaign, by the way," he added.

Lisa laughed. "Thank you."

"It's all going to work out, Lisa. You just have to trust me."

"I do trust you. I just can't believe how much my life has changed over the past couple of months. And I need to wrap my head around the fact that my life will never be the same. There's no going back."

Keller didn't know what to say. Lisa sensed that and said, "Talk to you in a little while, then."

"Okay," he said. "Talk to you then."

The line went dead.

"I love you," he whispered into the phone.

THIRTY-TWO

"**H**ey, Lennox, wake up. You've got a visitor."

Waking up wasn't much of a problem. Scott Lennox hadn't really slept. It had been a rough night.

The guard led him down a long corridor towards visitation. Inside, there was a row of seats separated by partitions, each with its own telephone.

Laura Lennox couldn't have looked more out of place. If the designer clothes, bag, sunglasses, heels, or fragrance didn't give her away, the pricey jewelry and perfectly placed Botox did. Laura Lennox was the definition of "high-maintenance." In social circles, they called her the "Ice Queen," for both her revenue stream and lack of emotion. The visit was clearly a painful one for her. Not so much out of concern for her husband, but for the humiliation. She sat down gingerly, fearing she might stick to something.

"Hello, Scott," she seethed.

"Hello, Laura."

She peered through the glass at her husband with utter disdain.

Scott put his head down and wept.

"You tell me you have to run some errand, then disappear all day. The police came to the house, Scott! I thought you were dead in some accident. They tell me you're in jail and they have a search warrant. They went through our house, Scott. Strange people rifled through my things. They tossed everything onto the floor. Goddammit Scott, it was so humiliating! And our son, what do I tell him? Everyone we know saw the news. It's on the front page of the fucking paper, people are calling the house. What in the name of Christ am I supposed to tell them?"

"Laura, I am so sorry. This is a nightmare, and I feel like I'm drowning. My life is spinning out of control. I am so, so sorry."

"You're sorry? That's all you have to say to me?"

"I can't talk about it here. I need an attorney, and I need one now. They questioned me last night, and I'm pretty sure they are coming back today to do it all again. I need help, Laura."

Laura stared at her husband through the glass. He was a pathetic figure, but was he guilty of murder? Did it really matter?

"Who the fuck is Lisa Sullivan?"

Scott hesitated.

"Answer my question or I'm walking out of here, and they can fry your ass as far as I'm concerned."

It would all come out anyway. He took a deep breath, looked directly through the glass into Laura's eyes.

"I was having an affair with her. It was just sex, nothing more. It's over; it's been over for quite some time. I don't know what made me do it. It's just… after Sam left for college, I don't know, things changed. I did something stupid, and for that I am truly, truly sorry. Please forgive me. I'm begging you. You have to help me."

Laura Lennox sat stoically across from her husband. She didn't respond; she just let his words wash over her. At least he admitted the affair. She had known things weren't right between her and her husband, but she chalked it up to the long hours he spent at the ice company. Now his business partner was dead, and the police were saying Scott and this woman did it.

She had a decision to make. Throw in the towel on her husband of more than twenty years or do what she could to save him. Laura wondered if he could really be a killer. You never know what people are capable of, even ones you shared your life with for more than two decades.

She thought of their son, Sam, away at college, in tears on the phone with her late last night after seeing the news reports on television. He was devastated.

Laura could walk away or stand by her man. The choice came down to one factor: what was best for Laura Lennox—socially and financially.

"You're going to need a lawyer."

Scott's head dropped down and the tears began again.

"I'll make some calls."

"Thank you, Laura, thank you."

Repulsed by the spineless man sitting before her, she hung up the phone and walked out, head held high.

"You ready to roll?" Mia asked as she poked her head into the bullpen.

"Yeah," Keller said. "Let's go pay Mr. Lennox a visit."

Keller and Mia walked across the Justice Center compound to the jail where Lennox had spent the night in lockup and took the stairs down to the interrogation section. They went through security and checked in with the sergeant on duty.

"Okay, I'll have him brought up. Busy morning for your boy."

"What do you mean?" asked Mia.

"Some woman came in to see him. She was a piece of work, too. Don't get many high-society types in here. You just missed her."

Mia looked at Keller, "You think he got a lawyer already?"

The sergeant overheard the question, "She didn't strike me as the lawyer type, but I'll check the logs." A minute later the sergeant had the answer.

"Yep, the visitor was a Laura Lennox. Must be your boy's better half, I'm guessing?"

"That she is," answered Keller.

"Well, that might explain why she was so pissed. The guard said she was cold as ice and ripped your boy a new one. Hell hath no fury, huh?" the sergeant added with a chuckle.

"Maybe we should just hand him over to her. Speedy justice," Keller joked.

"That'd save me a lot of trouble. We'll bring him back down and let you know when he's ready to go."

"You want to take the lead again, Jack?" Mia asked.

"Yeah, maybe he'll be a little more open with us after a night on the cot. And we might look pretty good in comparison to a visit from the missus this morning."

Lennox was escorted into Interview Room 2. He wore a standard issue RCSO jumpsuit and "belly cuffs" that kept his hands at his side on a chain wrapped around his waist. The sergeant notified Keller and Mia their perp was ready.

The investigators eyed Lennox through the one-way glass in a dark hallway adjacent to the interview room. He looked beaten and despondent, head down, staring at his chains.

"Good morning, Scott, hope you slept well," Keller said as they entered. Keller was armed with a cup of coffee and a file folder.

Lennox didn't budge.

"Investigator Serrano and I wanted to chat with you a little more this morning and see if we can clear this mess up."

"Don't bother, I'm getting a lawyer."

The investigators eyed one another. They didn't have much time, if any.

Keller spoke, "Well, that's certainly your right, Scott. You know, we're just trying to help you clear this thing up, but when that lawyer comes in here, well it ain't gonna be about helping you. He's gonna see just how many hours he can bill. Next thing you know, he owns himself an ice company."

"I'm not talking until I see my attorney."

"Well, okay. But seems like a shame, I was really hoping we could work somethin' out with the DA given the fact that your partner was about to croak anyway."

Lennox looked confused. He wanted to ignore Keller, but he was having trouble concentrating. Keller turned to Mia.

Mia sat down close to Lennox and used the same tone she used when trying to help her troubled high school students at Columbine. "Look Scott, the autopsy showed Mr. Lombard had cancer. Pancreatic cancer that had metastasized throughout his body. So you see, you basically killed a dead man. We think if you can do the right thing here, we can get the DA to work with us and help you."

"You're not gonna play me," Lennox said weakly, fidgeting with the chains around his waist.

"It's the truth," Keller said sympathetically.

He opened his file and tossed down a picture from the autopsy. "See for yourself. That cancer shit was eating him up."

"He's right, Scott," Mia told him. "And look, we know your wife was in here earlier. If I were her, I'd get the best lawyer I could find and tell him to take apart Lennox Ice, get me every dime possible, and make sure you rot in a cell along with your girlfriend."

Lennox rocked slightly back and forth in his chair.

"But there's a way through this without losing everything. Don't you think you should just take some time and see what we can do for you before some big shot lawyer comes in here and starts taking everything you've ever worked for?"

No response from Scott Lennox.

"Listen to her, Scott," Keller said. "She's making a lot of sense."

Mia jumped back in, "After all, we know Lisa Sullivan is culpable in all this. You sure as hell don't want her coming in here, cutting some deal that puts it all on you. Whose idea was it, anyway? Was it hers?"

Jack realized he needed to take back control of the interrogation before Mia gave Lennox the idea of pinning the entire murder on Lisa. Lennox rolled his head back, looked at the ceiling and took a deep breath.

"Scott," Keller said. "We know—"

"I have nothing to say without my attorney. So fuck off and leave me alone!"

Keller and Mia looked at one another. Keller shrugged and nodded toward the door.

"Okay, Scott, if that's the way you want it. Too bad, we could have helped you," Keller told him sadly. "Your buddy was close to checking out, that cancer is a bitch. All that money… two million big ones would have been in your bank account by spring. If you change your mind, give us a call, but the clock is running. Tick tock."

Keller grabbed the autopsy photo as they left. The inspectors stopped for a view through the two-way glass.

"Shit, I was hoping he'd end up with a public defender, but I'm guessing Mrs. Lennox may spring for a real, honest-to-goodness defense attorney," Jack said.

"I thought I had a chance there," replied Mia.

"Don't stress it. He wasn't going to talk. But that angle with the wife, that was good. I'm impressed," Keller said.

"Thanks, Jack."

"No shit, Serrano. That was really good. I wanted to confess myself," he told her. Keller had seen perps turn on less, and Serrano was very convincing. He was also grateful Lennox didn't bite when she'd brought up Lisa. That could have turned everything on its head. Jack knew the high-priced attorney would try to blame Lisa but that would take time, and he could use that time to make sure she was far away and safe.

Keller and Serrano were blinded by the sunlight as they emerged from the jail building. "I have a contact over in the courthouse that may know Lennox's wife," Keller offered. "I'm gonna run over there and see what I can find out. Sounds like she'll be running the show. Might give us some insight."

"When do you want to brief the captain?" Mia asked.

"Give me an hour."

THIRTY-THREE

Jack headed across the quad toward the courthouse where he pulled out the burner phone. "I thought I'd check in. Where are you?"

"At a Deal-Mart, just outside Flagstaff. I bought another phone like you told me. It was expensive but comes with 750 minutes. I'll text you the new number after we finish."

"Great, and I'll pick one up here and get you that new number as well. So, you're getting close. Roberto will meet you at three o'clock at the gas station off Highway 85 at exit 39. He'll handle everything from there, including taking you to the storage place. I've already called ahead and made the arrangements, so the manager knows you're coming. It should be simple and quick."

"Okay, do you want me to call you when I meet Roberto? Or call when everything is done?"

"Just call me when everything is done, unless there are any problems. But Roberto will take good care of you. You can trust him."

"Okay, I better get going. I'll call you when I'm there."

"Talk to you then."

Captain McCallister was looking over the Denver area newspapers, checking the Lennox/Sullivan coverage. Pretty good coverage overall, but it went both ways. Big news coverage brought lots of attention and with it an expectation from the public that Lisa Sullivan would be captured. The pressure was on, and Mick was feeling very uneasy.

The phone rang, breaking his concentration.

"Hey, Mick, thought I'd check in."

"Geez, Mia, you're already back from your interview with Lennox? That can't be good."

"Yeah, we just finished. Lennox is lawyering up. Oh, and guess who we're pretty sure sprung for the attorney?"

"Well, if I had to guess, I'd probably say his old lady?"

"Bingo. Can you believe that? He pulls this crap, and the jilted wife comes to his rescue. If he were my husband and he did that, he'd rot in hell."

"Duly noted," Mick responded with a chuckle.

"You said you wanted to see us after. Keller and I can come up in a few."

Keller began. "So when we get there the sergeant on duty tells us Lennox has already had an early morning visitor—none other than Mrs. Lennox. And the guard said she was beyond pissed. She must have worked him over pretty good because by the time they bring our boy into the interview room, he doesn't look good. So I poured it on and told him about Lombard's cancer. You could tell it messed up his mind. And Serrano gave him something else to think about that was pretty good."

"Oh yeah?" Mick asked.

"I just told him maybe his wife wasn't paying the lawyer to get him off but to help her take every dime she could out of his business and then let him hang for his sins."

"It was nicely played," Keller added.

"Not sure it did any good," replied Mia.

"It was impressive, Serrano. You planted a seed. You never know."

"Okay, well I need to brief the sheriff," Mick told them. "I also need to call the DA and find out how he wants to play this thing. Although without Lisa Sullivan, we haven't given him a lot of options. And he's not going to be very happy about it."

Keller was direct. "Captain, arresting Lennox yesterday was the right call. We all wanted them both, but you had to grab Lennox while you had him in the cross hairs. He could have disappeared, and we'd be far worse off than we are now."

"I know. It is what it is. But thanks for that."

Mick briefed the sheriff then made the call to DA Dave Baxter.

"Hey, Mick, hope you've got some good news for me on this Lombard case. That woman could make us look like fools if you can't bring her in."

"I wish I did. She's still loose, and Lennox has lawyered up."

"Can't say I'm too surprised about Lennox. You know who's taking the case?"

"Not sure yet. Looks like his wife is bringing someone in. Love knows no bounds."

"No kidding. I'll do some checking around and see if I can find out. Now what can you tell me about Lisa Sullivan?"

"Not much. The picture we released to the media generated a handful of calls, but so far nothing has panned out; unless you believe she's serving up Grand Slam breakfasts at the Denny's in Lone Tree. That's one of the things I wanted to talk to you about. I'm thinking maybe we should offer a reward. I'm authorized to go to $25,000, but I held off, worried it would be a distraction. But her face is in all the papers and on TV, and we're getting very little. The money could trigger something with someone, and at the very least it will get another round of media interest going and keep her picture out there. I'm thinking maybe tomorrow we offer the money, that is, of course, if nothing breaks between now and then."

"Might not hurt, Mick. We have to get her into custody, pronto. I don't have to tell you the clock's ticking. We've got 72 hours to file, which means Wednesday, and I don't have shit to show a judge right now."

"Yeah, I know."

"If we have to cut him loose it'll look like we've failed on two fronts—Sullivan's escape and Lennox walking. Either one of those is bad enough, but both is a double whammy. This is turning into a god-damn tire fire and we've got an election coming up, Mick."

Mick wasn't sure if Baxter was talking about his own re-election efforts or Mick's possible run for sheriff, but either way he was right.

Keller laid an old road map across his desk. The computer would have been easier, but computers leave a trail. His finger traced Lisa's path, and he guessed she was an hour or two from Phoenix by now. He'd feel much better once she made the connection with Roberto.

Michelle, an investigations clerk, stuck her head in his office.

"Jack, you had a visitor while you were out."

"Yeah, who was it?"

"It was a priest. He left his card," she said, handing it over. "He said it was important that he talk to you."

"Okay, thanks."

Jack knew who it was without looking at the card. He didn't have time for Father Jon right now.

Archer put a call into Anita Sanchez at the News-Press.

"Hey, Mark, got any news for me on Lisa Sullivan?"

"Geez, Anita, don't I get a hello, Mark, how ya doing?"

"Oh, sorry. Hello, Mark, how ya doing? Got any news for me about Lisa Sullivan?"

Archer chuckled, "Just this, RCSO will be putting up a $25,000 reward for information leading to the arrest and conviction of Lisa Sullivan, effective tomorrow, provided of course we don't scoop her up between now and then. If we go with the reward can you get us back on the front page with that?"

"Sure, I can do that. Anybody else know?"

"Not yet, I'm giving you a head start 'cause I'm such a nice guy."

"So, what's the deal with this woman? You guys were pretty vague yesterday with the press release and the news conference. I understand she's an accomplice, but how exactly did things go down?"

"Anita, you are asking for way too much. I can't give you all that right now. When the time comes, I'll see what I can do. But I may need some help in exchange."

"Okay, Archer, play your little game," she chided. "Send me what you've got on the reward, and I'll get you some play."

THIRTY-FOUR

After driving through Phoenix, Lisa Sullivan merged from Interstate 10 onto Highway 85. The highway sign read 119 miles to Lukeville, the border town where she hoped to cross quietly into Mexico.

Lisa was surprised at the beautiful landscape of the Arizona desert. She found the scenery mesmerizing and strangely relaxing. She knew it wouldn't last, but for the moment she allowed herself to melt into the solitude of the drive.

At 2:45, Lisa took exit 39 and found the gas station where she was to meet Roberto. She didn't know what he looked like, but Jack told her not to worry, Roberto would be making the contact. She pulled into the station, parked and looked around the lot, but didn't notice anything or anyone unusual.

A few minutes later, a short Hispanic man in his mid-thirties approached. He motioned for her to roll down the window.

"Hello. You must be Lisa, no?"

"Yes, I am. And you must be Roberto?"

"My friends, they call me Frito."

"Okay, Frito," she replied. "So what now?"

"There is storage place just down the road. You follow me. I'm in Toyota pickup, okay?"

"Sure, I can do that."

Lisa followed Frito down to a storage yard. The worn, beat up sign out front read, *Lotsa Storage*. The office was a trailer.

They both parked near the trailer and Frito walked to Lisa's car.

"My friend Jack said you have a package for me."

"Oh right," Lisa said, digging in her purse. Jack had given her a small box when they said goodbye. "Here it is."

Frito opened the box and took out a wrapped stack of twenty dollar bills. Lisa was confused.

"What is that for?" she asked him.

"You wait here, señorita," he said and disappeared into the trailer.

The peace she felt on the road earlier was now gone, replaced with anxiety. Yesterday morning she had been sitting in her apartment in Rosebud, Colorado, and now she was in Arizona, in a place she had never heard of, waiting on a guy named Frito.

After a few minutes, Frito motioned for her to come inside. The office was small and cramped. Two scary men sat behind desks and spoke Spanish to Frito. One of the men stared at her, and Lisa was afraid something very bad was about to happen. The older of the men walked to an old metal cabinet and opened the door. She held her breath, fully expecting him to pull out a gun.

Instead, he pulled out a Polaroid camera.

"Is okay, Miss Lisa. These men, they help us with ID to get you across the border," he assured her. The men suddenly understood and wailed in laughter. She laughed along uncomfortably, feeling the fool.

Frito explained the men had friends at the border office. They had digital files of identities that could be encoded onto cards with computers. The identities were apparently leased by these men from someone with access to the border control computers, then sub-leased to customers like Lisa. Her passport card would be good for one trip across the border.

They took a headshot with the Polaroid and presented Lisa with a perfectly forged US passport card. The price was $1000 or a stack of twenty dollar bills.

Once outside, she and Frito parked her car in an aisle among dozens of other vehicles, most covered in a layer of desert sand. *Lotsa Storage* was apparently a full service business. She climbed into Frito's pickup, and within minutes they were headed south to the border.

"So how long will it take to get there?" Lisa said, changing the subject.

"We take about one hour to Gringo Pass. That's where we cross over. From there, about one more hour."

"There's a place called Gringo Pass?"

"Lukeville—that's the real name, but we say Gringo Pass because Americans come through there," he said with a big smile. He gave her a tourist card to fill out. It was actually a piece of paper for anyone entering Mexico. Lisa matched the information from her passport card to the lines on the form. For the next two hours, Lisa would be Stephanie Clark of Chandler, Arizona.

THIRTY-FIVE

"Hey, Mark… It's Anita. Thought I'd give you a heads up. The News Press just received a fax from the law firm of Pabst, Kramer, and Solomon in Dallas, Texas informing us that none other than Mr. Branch Kramer will be defending your boy Scott Lennox. You should read this thing, it's over the top. It goes on to say that he will be meeting with his client today at 5:15 at the RCSO jail in Castle Springs."

"Can you fax that to me, Anita?"

"Sure, no problem. I especially like the fact that he's timing his arrival at the jail to meet with Lennox at five fifteen… Gee, you think that will get any live news coverage from the Denver TV stations? What a transparent piece of shit."

"Fax it to me."

"It's on the way."

Archer immediately called Captain McCallister.

Satellite and microwave TV trucks began arriving at the Rocklin County Jail just after 4:00. After consulting the sheriff and DA, McCallister and Archer decided it was best not to give Lennox's attorney any ammunition. They would allow Kramer his show and only counter with a news release on the new $25,000 reward for information on Lisa Sullivan.

"Squeeze in people, the show is about to begin," McCallister said as Keller, Serrano, and Archer shuffled into his office a little before five o'clock. It was a tight fit, but they all managed to find a spot in view of the TV in the corner.

"Famed defense attorney Branch Kramer is in Colorado tonight to defend a Castle Springs man on murder charges," the anchor said. "46-year-old Scott Lennox was arrested over the weekend in connection with the death of his business partner, 56-year-old George Lombard, also of Castle Springs. You're looking live at the scene outside the Rocklin County Jail Complex where we're expecting Kramer to address the media in just a few minutes. Once that happens we will bring it to you live."

The anchors moved on to other stories for the time being.

Archer broke down what they were seeing. "Branch Kramer is the definitive media whore. He announces his arrival for 5:15, and since Denver stations have to spend all that money to send their satellite trucks down here he knows he'll get play at the top of the news, too. He'll do a little song and dance and promise to come back and talk to reporters again after he meets with his client. That'll get him a plug at the end of the five o'clock and another teaser at the top of the six. Then, he'll come out of the jail and do a longer bit between 6:10 and 6:15, which they'll cover live. He'll get another mention at the end of the six and a full wrap up for the ten o'clock news. If this were a public defender, this story gets 30-45 seconds, tops. The guy is a righteous blowhard, but he knows how to play the game."

"So why aren't we out there trying to diffuse this character a bit?" Mia asked.

"Branch Kramer would love nothing better than to engage us on the steps of the jail. That kind of story could play for a couple days. It's better to let him have his little moment. If we were out there and got a little testy with him then that drama becomes the story. We don't want that, so if we ignore Kramer and his antics, the media will pretty much have to use what we've put out today, which is the reward. So essentially, they'll have to put up her picture and our tip line number—it's all they've got from us. We'll actually get more play on the reward that we might have without Mr. Kramer."

"We good on the phone bank?" Mick asked.

"We scraped together six staffers and deputies to go 24/7, in eight hour shifts, at least for the first 48 hours. Most of the meaningful calls tend to come in early," answered Keller.

"Jack, Mia, after this little circus plays out, why don't you two go down and sit on the phone lines for a bit?" Mick asked. "See what, if anything, pops."

They nodded in agreement.

Back from a commercial break, the anchors tossed back to the live picture from Castle Springs. "Continuing coverage," they called it.

A reporter stood among the crowd, likely recruited by Kramer staffers. "Rob and Erin, Branch Kramer arrived moments ago here at the Rocklin County jail where he plans to meet with his client, Scott Lennox. As we've reported, Lennox was arrested in connection with the murder of his business partner, found dead on a rural county road in November. Kramer is making his way up the steps now, in his trademark western suit and cowboy hat. I've been told that Kramer will make a statement."

"Well, there's a shocker," Mia said to the TV as Kramer squeezed behind a stand of microphones.

"Your presence is a testament to our thirst for justice in Rocklin County and the great state of Colorado. And I am here to see that justice is carried out for Mr. Scott Lennox. I can tell you that when I learned the details of this case, I was shocked and saddened, outraged really, by what has transpired here. An upstanding member of the community has been railroaded on trumped-up charges based on weak circumstantial evidence, all due to the political ambitions of the district attorney and the Rocklin County Sheriff's Department. The case against Scott Lennox is a sham. But this case is about more than Scott Lennox. This is about bureaucratic power run amok. It's about those bureaucrats running roughshod over the rights of hard working Americans in an effort to disguise their own inequities. And I am here to demand freedom for Scott Lennox and every person unjustly accused."

The crowd clapped and hooted their support. "Right now, I'm going to meet with my client, Scott Lennox, and I promise to brief you again shortly. Thank you again for your support, and God bless America."

The camera pulled back to the reporter as Branch Kramer turned toward the jail. "There you have it. Legendary defense attorney Branch Kramer characterizing the murder case against Castle Springs businessman Scott Lennox as a 'sham.'"

"He went from famed to legendary in like ten minutes," Jack said.

"Meantime, the Rocklin County Sheriff's Office has yet to arrest a second suspect wanted in connection with this case and a short time ago announced a $25,000 reward for information leading to the arrest and conviction of 32-year-old Lisa Sullivan of Rosebud. They ask if you have any information on her whereabouts to call the tip line on your screen. We're live in Castle Springs. Rob and Erin, back to you."

Mick clicked off the TV. "Listen people, we've got to get Lisa Sullivan in custody or this guy's going to turn us into a laughingstock. Get down to the phones and keep me posted."

THIRTY-SIX

Frito's truck inched forward as they approached the Lukeville border crossing. The line of cars stretched at least 300 yards and it took close to an hour to reach the front. There were three gates and he edged the truck toward the one marked, "Nothing to Declare."

At the gate, Frito nodded to the guards and the men shared a knowing glance. Both guards were intimidating and wore sidearms. As the taller of the guards talked with Frito, the other walked to the passenger door. She handed over the passport and tourist cards as the guard angled for a better look.

The guard paid little attention to her documents and instead focused on her chest. After what seemed like an eternity to Lisa, he handed them back. "Umberto, está bien!"

The other guard waved them through and Frito put the truck into gear and quickly pulled away. Lisa exhaled and they both burst into laughter.

"I'm not sure why I'm laughing, my God, I was terrified! I thought he was about to climb in the truck with me."

"You did good, Miss Lisa. No worries now, we will be there soon," he promised.

Lisa smiled and sat back a little in the seat, trying her best to relax.

"So, how did you get the name Frito? I'm guessing that's not the name your mother gave you."

"When I was little there was Fritos; you know, the chips. They had the Frito Bandito in their ads and I used to act like him, all crazy. My friends thought it was funny, and everyone calls me Frito."

"Well, I'm going to call you Roberto. Is that okay with you?" Lisa said with a smile.

"Sí, señorita, sí," he replied with a smile.

"So, tell me about Rocky Point?"

"Puerto Peñasco. The gringos call it Rocky Point. It is on the Sea of Cortez. Very beautiful."

"How long have you lived there, Roberto?"

"All my life. I work at one of the big hotels. I fix things; they break, I fix."

"Are you married?"

"Yes, Juanita is my wife, and we have four children."

"Wow, big family. What does your wife do?"

"She cleans rooms at the Grand Sonoran. She works very hard and gets good tips from the American tourists."

"Where do you live?"

"Just outside of town. Costs much to live in Puerto Peñasco. My truck gets me and Juanita to our jobs."

"What about your kids?"

"We have two boys and two girls. The boys are twelve and six, and our girls are nine and seven."

"Where do they go to school?"

"Only the boys go to school. The girls stay home and help with sewing and other work. My Juanita also works for Americans who have homes here, doing odd jobs, and the girls help her."

An hour later, Lisa was able to see the ocean in the distance. They must finally be getting close to town, she guessed. She was taken aback by what Roberto had told her. The boys go to school, and the girls stay home and help the family eke out a living. What kind of a chance would they ever have at a better life?

"We are close, Miss Lisa. If you look towards the ocean, you can see a beach with many condominiums. Our friend Jack owns one of them, and that's where you will stay. It's very nice there; you will like it very much."

The Sea of Cortez shimmered in the distance. Roberto was right; it was beautiful. She could understand why Americans would come here.

"Jack asked me to get you a new passport with a different name. Do you know what you want your new name to be?"

She hadn't thought about a new identity, but it made sense. She couldn't be Lisa Sullivan anymore.

"I haven't even thought about it. When do you need a name from me, Roberto?"

"Jack said as soon as possible."

"Okay, then I will get you a name. Once I get settled into the condo, how will I contact you?"

"Jack gave me your cell number so I can call you and I will give you my number. But I come by each day to check on you and see how you are doing."

A minute later, they were driving along a sliver of road winding down to the beach. Down below, Lisa could see clusters of white condominiums standing three stories tall. Roberto slowed the truck and pulled onto a long stretch of private road that served as access to a dozen or more of the condos. He pulled into the driveway of a large unit that sat directly on the beach and parked in a space marked 2B.

"Welcome home, Miss Lisa."

The condo was large, sparsely furnished but tasteful. There were two bedrooms and two baths, along with a living room with high ceilings and a huge picture window looking out onto the beach at the breaking surf. It was a gorgeous setting, and Lisa found herself excited at the prospect of this place as her new home. The kitchen was a bit dated, but the bedrooms and bathrooms were spacious. The master bedroom had a king size bed and a veranda that looked out onto the beach. Her dad had done well with this place, she thought.

"I got you some food and put it in the refrigerator and cabinets. You need more, I can get it tomorrow."

"Thank you so much, Roberto. You are very kind to do all this for me."

"No problema, señorita."

The doorbell rang. Lisa was startled.

"Is okay, Miss Lisa. Just someone to help you. Mr. Jack said it would be good."

Frito opened the door and a pretty, middle aged woman equipped with a large tackle box came inside. "This is Berta," he said. "She is my sister and the best hair stylist in Puerto Peñasco."

"Nice to meet you," Lisa said.

"Muy bonita," Berta said as she gave Lisa the once over. "Sí, muy bonita."

Berta led her to a chair at the table. "I give you new look," she announced as she tossed a drape over Lisa and fastened it behind her neck. "You no worry, I make you muy more beautiful. I give you color, too."

She had trusted Frito with her life. He and her father had done everything they'd promised. So, she would trust Berta as well.

Two hours later the makeover was complete.

Frito looked at Lisa and hardly recognized the person standing before him. Berta had given her a medium length bob-style that looked fresh and casual. The vibrant, light brown color had a reddish tint that gave her a relaxed, cosmopolitan look. It was a big change from the long, straight, dirty blond style she'd worn for years. Berta had indeed made her beautiful.

"Muy bonita... Sí, señorita Lisa?" Berta asked.

"Oh, yes, sí, sí, thank you so much. It's beautiful! Gracias!"

Lisa went to her purse, drew out a hundred dollar bill, and offered it to Berta.

Berta's eyes got big when she saw the cash. She thanked Lisa profusely and packed up. Frito saw her to the door.

When Frito returned Lisa turned to him and said, "Jack told me to pay you for your help today. He said that I was to pay you $500, is that correct?"

"Yes, ma'am."

Lisa counted out ten one hundred dollar bills and handed them to Roberto.

"Oh, señorita, this is too much."

"Nonsense. Roberto, you've been exceptionally kind to me today. Please, take the extra money and help your family. I insist."

Frito stuffed the cash deep into his front pocket.

"I thank you. You are very kind, Miss Lisa."

"It's nothing, Roberto. Thanks for being my very first friend in… Puerto Peñasco, is that how you say it?"

"Sí, señorita. Your Spanish is good."

"Well, it's bound to get even better. Thank you again."

"De nada. You call me if you need things—day or night."

After Roberto left the condo, Lisa slumped down onto the sofa in the living room, exhausted. The life she had in Colorado was now gone. The father she never knew was keeping her out of jail. She was alone in a place far away from everything she knew.

Keller and Mia left Mick's office and headed downstairs to the makeshift phone bank that had been assembled in a conference room.

"I'll meet you down there in a minute," Keller told his partner. "Gotta hit the men's room."

Keller peeled off and headed toward the clerical offices on the second floor. The area was all but abandoned after five o'clock, and he knew the men's room would be empty.

Inside, he checked the stalls and pulled out his burner phone. Lisa should be in Mexico by now, he thought. He dialed her new cell number.

"Hey."

"Well, how's Mexico? Everything go all right?"

"Mexico is beautiful, and your place is great. I'm just trying to get my bearings."

"So everything went well with Frito? Any problems at the border?" Jack asked.

"Not really, we got stopped by the guards but after a minute or two they let us in. Roberto has been great. I really like him. He's been a huge help to me."

"Roberto?'

"Yes, that's Frito's given name, and I'm going to be calling him that."

"Oh, okay. Did his sister show up?"

"Yes she did, and she was amazing. You'll hardly recognize me."

"Well, that's the goal. Look, I hope to get down there soon. But I have to wait for the right time. I hope you understand."

"I understand, I just wish you could be here. What's going on there?"

"Lennox lawyered up, he's not talking."

"Wow, that didn't take long."

"And his lawyer's a big shot. Branch Kramer. Ever heard of him?"

"Wait, is he that cowboy that's always on the cable shows?"

"He's the one."

"Wow. How did…"

"From what we understand, his wife hired him."

"Seriously?"

"That's what they say. Oh, and listen… they put out a $25,000 reward on you."

There was no easy way to say it.

"Oh my God."

"With this Branch Kramer character involved, this story could grow and your picture could end up everywhere. So we need to get you a new ID ASAP. You're going to need a new name."

"Roberto and I are working on it," she assured him. "What if Scott and his new attorney decide to lay the whole thing on me? What if they say I killed Lombard so Scott would leave his wife and run away with me and all the money. What happens then?"

"They won't play that card. At least not yet. Their best strategy, in my opinion, is for Scott to clam up and make the prosecution prove its case. It's working so far. There's not enough physical evidence, so as I see it, the only way Scott goes down for this is if you testify against him. The prosecution needs you. They'll want you to turn state's evidence—in other words, testify and tell what happened. If you did that then Scott would almost certainly go down, and you'd be offered a deal of some sort in exchange for your testimony. So, the last thing the defense wants is for you to be found. As long as you are in the wind, I think they are pretty safe. And they know it."

"Just thinking about it makes my head hurt."

"Let's just get you settled in and take things as they come. Even though you're in Mexico, you still need to keep a low profile, especially now."

"Okay, I will. So we'll talk tomorrow, then?"

"Absolutely. Now, get some rest."

The calls from the five o'clock news generated mostly sightings of Lisa in and around the town of Rosebud. People reported seeing Lisa Sullivan at the grocery store, gas station, dry cleaners and the gym. There were a few calls putting her as far away as Longmont and Pueblo, but they weren't strong leads. All would have to be checked out, regardless.

Branch Kramer made another appearance in the six o'clock news and stations again showed Lisa's picture and mentioned the reward. It too generated calls. The operators were told to hand over anything remotely promising to Mia or Keller.

Ralph Bumgartner just about ripped Kit's arm off as she arrived home from her shift at the Mountain View Café.

"C'mon, Kit, you gotta see this. That Castle Springs murder fella's got some fancy lawyer, and the sheriff is puttin' up a $25,000 reward for that lady you seen. Here sit down, he'll be back on in a minute."

The picture of Lisa Sullivan was back on the TV screen moments later, and Kit was more certain than ever Lisa Sullivan was the woman she'd seen at the café.

"That's her all right," Kit said.

"Kit, that's $25,000. That's the brand new RV tent trailer we want and enough to take it all over the country. You gotta call. Here, I wrote the number down for you."

"Okay, Ralphie, I hear you, just bring me the phone."

"I got it right here," Ralph said, handing Kit the wireless handset.

Kit dialed and waited as the call went through.

"Hello, I'm calling about the missing woman you're looking for. I think I seen her, and I thought I'd call it in… Well, how do y'all pay that reward anyway? I told you I seen her at my work… at the Mountain Cafe off I-70… Okay, I'll hold."

Belinda turned to Jack and Mia, "I have a lady on the line who she says she saw Sullivan a few weeks ago at a cafe off I-70 near the ski resorts. Who wants to take it?"

"I'll take it," Keller said.

He took the phone from the clerk. "This is Investigator Keller, how can I help you?"

Jack listened for a few moments, then turned to Mia and rolled his eyes.

"Well, the sheriff's department is offering $25,000 for information that leads to the arrest and conviction of Lisa Sullivan. I'm not sure what else I can tell you about it… Like I said, there has to be an arrest and conviction—assuming, of course, your tip is the one that leads us to her, then you'd get paid… Tell me where you saw her."

Keller swallowed hard. The woman's voice confirmed his fear—it was the waitress who gave him the attitude.

"Um, okay, when was this? And you're sure it was Lisa Sullivan?" Keller asked.

After several seconds, Keller lowered his voice and continued, "Have you told anyone else about this?"

"You told Ralphie? Who's Ralphie?"

Keller turned away from the others sitting at the phone bank. "No, ma'am, you don't need to call anyone else. But I will give you another number, and if you think of anything else, you can call me directly. Now can you give me your contact information?"

Keller offered Kit Baumgartner his private cell number. He jotted down her name and contact information and promised to investigate. He thanked Kit for the assistance and handed the receiver back to the clerk. Keller then waited for Mia to get off another call.

"Well?" he asked her.

"A big nothing. You?"

"Same," Jack said, trying to look disappointed.

THIRTY-SEVEN

After morning mass, Jack went to the sacristy to see Father John.

"Good morning, Jack. Guess you heard I came by your office?"

"Yep."

"Would you like to come back to the rectory for a cup of coffee?"

"Sure, we can do that."

Keller followed the priest across the side parking lot and into the rectory.

Keller started. "So, your visit yesterday to my office… It was just a social one?"

"Hardly, Jack, and I have no doubt you know what's on my mind."

"Actually, I haven't a clue."

"I saw the news about the arrest of the man in the murder case. I also saw the news about the woman they're searching for."

"Did you want to report a sighting, Padre?"

"Jack, don't be a smart ass. My concern is about the conversation we had a couple weeks ago on Castle Trail. You told me about a struggle you were having about a daughter you had recently come to know. How she was in trouble and you felt an obligation to help her."

"I remember."

"You said you were willing to risk your career for her, and you asked me if somehow you helping her could be justified given the mistakes you had made with her early in her life."

"Yeah, I remember that too, but—"

"So, is this woman on the run your daughter?"

He would have been a great cop, Jack thought.

"Like I said, Father, it's not a big deal."

"You aren't answering my question. I need to know, is the woman they're looking for your daughter?"

Jack looked down at his coffee cup on the table. Then he spoke, "Let me ask you something, Father, just a hypothetical question. Do you mind?"

"Go ahead."

"If you and I talk about something, something private, isn't that, like, protected? Isn't what a priest hears from a parishioner held in confidence? Doesn't the priest have an obligation to keep quiet about it?"

"I think you are mistaking an ordinary conversation a priest might have with someone with what is said in the confessional. Clearly, anything said under the sacrament of reconciliation is held in the strictest confidence. Neither the police nor the courts can order that conversation be disclosed. I guess it could be compared to the attorney-client privilege. But something that is disclosed in the course of an ordinary conversation, like the one we are having right now, is not protected."

"It seems to me that's a pretty fine line. I mean, who's to say what you interpret as ordinary conversation, as you put it, isn't something much larger in the mind of the person who is saying it. I mean, you hear stuff all day long from people; it's your job. Just another day at the office. But for the ordinary person, the conversation they are having with their priest is huge, and they in fact wouldn't have said the things they said if they thought there was any risk of the priest going public with what was said. Make sense?"

"You are making a lot of assumptions here, Jack. When the conversation starts out with 'Father, I need to confess something' or 'Father, it's been six months since my last confession, these are my sins…' that falls under the confessional rule. When things are discussed in the normal course of conversation, then that is obviously something different. I think there's a pretty clear delineation between those two scenarios."

Jack shook his head. "I disagree. If someone is sharing with you things that could never be shared with anyone else, and they are asking not only for guidance, but really for permission and ultimately forgiveness, then that clearly falls under your confession rule."

They were at a standstill.

Father Jon leaned forward. "Jack, I think you know the right thing to do. Please, don't put me in an awkward position."

"That almost sounds like a threat, Father."

"I have a moral obligation to do what is right. This is a very difficult situation."

"So, what are you going to do, Padre?"

"For the time being, I'm going to pray on it, Jack. I'm going to pray really hard for guidance."

Jack stood and walked to the door. Father Jon didn't see him out.

Jack was livid. The priest was playing a very dangerous game. If Father Jon came forward and revealed their earlier conversation on Castle Trail, everything would come apart. The focus of the investigation would shift to him, and he'd be forced to tell what he knew about Lisa. If he told authorities about his role in Lisa's escape, then she would certainly be captured and charged as an accomplice to murder and likely for evading arrest. Under that scenario his daughter could be looking at a sentence of 20 years or more.

He was also growing increasingly concerned about Branch Kramer and the media attention he brought to the case. Kramer knew there would be a phalanx of reporters following his every move, and those reporters would spread the story far and wide. That meant a story that wouldn't normally get much play outside Colorado could easily become national or even international news. The last thing he needed was for Lisa's picture to be shown on CNN and the other networks, especially the ones that reached into Mexico.

On her first full day as a Puerto Peñasco resident, Lisa took a long, leisurely walk on the beach. She headed south from the condo past high-end resorts, shops, and restaurants. Before long she found herself inside a small boutique along the boardwalk; the colorful beachwear had lured her inside.

"Welcome to Summer Fling, can I help you?"

The saleswoman had a bright, friendly smile and a deep Puerto Peñasco tan.

"Well, I just arrived in town, and I think I need to pick up a few things if I'm going to blend in around here. I love your shop, it's so colorful."

"We just got in a new shipment, and I've got some things that would be perfect for you. Let me slip in the back and bring out a few thing for you to see. Do you mind?"

"Oh, that would be great, thanks."

What if she asks me my name? Lisa thought. Should she give her name as Lisa or should she make something up? Her father had told her she needed to come up with a new name but she hadn't decided on anything. What name should she pick, knowing it was quite possible she'd spend the rest of her life with it?

"I think these should fit you. There are a couple of sundresses, some shorts, and a few tops. Oh, and I included a couple of swimsuits. If you want to try the stuff on, the dressing room is over there. I'm Sarah, just holler if you need another size or color."

"Thanks so much. I will do that."

Lisa took the clothes and walked back to the dressing room while Sarah helped another customer. She tried on each outfit and loved them all. Why not, she thought, I need a new wardrobe to go with my new life. She gathered up the clothes and walked up to the front counter.

"You have great taste, Sarah," said Lisa with a smile.

"Can I wrap them up for you, then?"

"Yep, I'll take them all."

"Great, will that be cash or charge?"

Suddenly, Lisa realized she had no money.

"Oh, my gosh. I am so embarrassed. I totally forgot my wallet. I was really just on a walk along the beach and didn't plan to do any shopping this morning. I'm sorry, Sarah, can you put these aside for me, and I'll come back and pay you then?"

"Of course, don't worry about it! It happens all the time. What name should I put on the bag in case I'm not here when you return?"

It came to her in a flash. "Natalie. Natalie Summers."

"Great. I hope to see you when you come back in. It was nice meeting you, Natalie."

"It was great meeting you as well, Sarah. Thanks again for all the help."

Natalie Summers walked out of the shop and back onto the beach on the beautiful shore of the Sea of Cortez.

McCallister got the call he was dreading from the DA.

"Anything new on Sullivan?"

"Not much, Dave. We've had some calls into the station reporting sightings, but you know how that goes. Nothing significant."

"Well, if nothing breaks in the next twenty-four hours, we're going to have to cut him loose. Without something from the woman, we don't have enough to hold him."

"I know. When she didn't show on Sunday I had to make the call on Lennox. I'm sorry about the flack. It was my call, and I take responsibility."

"Look, Mick, you did the right thing. When you have them in your sights, you grab 'em. But we'll take a hit and that asshole Kramer will fan the flames. On the bright side, it will send that blowhard back to Dallas and the press will move on to the next story. But when you do get Sullivan, we'll need a rock solid case. We can't get burned on this twice."

The waves crashed onto the beach and echoed through the condo. Inside, Lisa pondered her new life. She had walked into the dress shop totally unprepared. Now, she had a name, but no background. She had to fill in the rest of the puzzle.

Lisa realized the farther she strayed from her real life, the more likely she'd get tripped up. So, she would still be a nurse. She'd say she'd come to Puerto Peñasco for an extended vacation. But why? Escaping a broken marriage, maybe? A big inheritance came her way? Maybe she won the lotto? There were lots of options, but which would bring the least amount of scrutiny? And where was she from? She knew she should stay clear of her Colorado past, but St. Louis had been her home for the first few years of her life, until her father had walked out... maybe that would work. What about her age and her birthday? Should she change those as well? So much to consider, she thought.

There was a knock at the door. It was Frito.

"Hi, Roberto, thanks for coming over."

"No hay problema, Miss Lisa."

"I did a dumb thing this morning. I went for a walk down the beach and ended up in a little dress shop. I find a bunch of stuff and I go to pay for it and like an idiot I realize I didn't bring my wallet. The girl in the shop was super nice, and she put my stuff aside. So, I need to stop there so I can pay for my stuff. Do you mind?"

"De nada, I take you anywhere you want to go."

"And maybe on the way back we could stop at a market so I can pick up a few things. Oh, and I need to find an English/Spanish translation book. I've got to start getting comfortable with the language, at least some of the common words and phrases."

"Sí, comprendo."

As they drove down the streets of Puerto Peñasco, the sounds and smells wafted through Roberto's old truck. The little town was colorful and vibrant and Lisa was taken by its charm. Her first order of business was the dress shop. Sarah was still there.

"Hey, you're back! I've got your things up front."

"Okay, great. I felt like such a dope this morning, but I saw this place… Well, let's just say I have a real weakness for cute clothes, and your place is full of them."

Sarah chuckled as she tallied the bill.

"That'll be $279.45 US dollars."

Lisa paid with three crisp, new $100 bills.

"So, where are you staying in town?"

"In a condo on the beach a couple of miles north of here. It's a friend's place."

"Sounds nice. Hey listen, I've got some friends, co-workers really, and we're having a little party tomorrow night. Just casual, nothing too serious, probably be 15-20 of us. It's a nice group of people. If you're not doing anything, it would be great to have you come by. Just stop in for a drink or whatever…"

The question caught Lisa off guard.

"Um, you know, that sounds great. How nice of you to invite me."

"Here, I'll jot down the address. It should be close to where you're staying. Hope to see you tomorrow night, then."

"How fun, I'm looking forward to it. Thanks again for everything."

After leaving Summer Fling, she and Roberto made a quick stop at a local market to pick up some groceries. As luck would have it, the little market also had a translation book.

Mia and Keller shuffled into Mick's office after spending most of the day chasing down tips in and around Rosebud.

"We ran down every legit sighting we had, Captain," Mia said.

"All for shit," added Keller.

"Have a seat," Mick said.

The two investigators fell into the chairs, exhausted.

"Serrano has managed to put together a nice profile of our suspect's comings and goings," Keller said.

Mia went from her notes. "It's your typical serial criminal profile," she said sarcastically. "She gets a non-fat latte with one sweetener at a coffee place on Ashford in Rosebud just about every weekday, gets her nursing uniforms dry-cleaned at the QuikClean, which is next to the SaveCo where she buys her groceries. She takes an occasional yoga class at Rosebud Fitness but isn't a regular and doesn't bring her own mat."

"Great," said the Captain, "just more of nothing."

"Yeah, I figured we'd hold off on the FBI profiler," added Keller.

"We were able to talk with a couple nurses she worked with at the hospital. And we found the gal she was with when she met Scott Lennox."

"And?" asked Mick.

"Zoe Lieto, RN. They're not that close, they just like the same music. Zoe vaguely remembers some guys behind them at the concert and a beer being spilled but doesn't recall Scott Lennox because..."

"This should be good," Mick replied.

"She was drunk, 'totally wasted,' in her words, as she was most nights back then, due to a messy divorce, her family history of alcoholism, and a million other reasons she went on and on about."

"The good news, Captain," Keller interjected. "Is that Zoe's now in a twelve-step program."

"Well, I'm so glad to hear that," Mick replied sarcastically. "But it leaves us with nothing to hold Scott Lennox with. I just got off the phone with Baxter, and we're going to have to cut him loose."

"I'm sorry, Captain," Keller said.

"Me, too," added Mia.

"We'll take a hit from his high-priced mouthpiece, but Lennox could get sloppy if he thinks he's in the clear. I want to keep a close eye on him."

Jack Keller's apartment was sparsely decorated but served him well. Just after 5 o'clock, the voice of a cable news anchor echoed in the living room as Jack scraped the last remnants of mashed potato from a microwavable tray. He wished he was in Mexico watching the sunset with Lisa and reached for the burner phone.

"Hey, how's the Mexican sunset?"

"Absolutely beautiful."

"It always is. And how was your first full day in Puerto Peñasco?"

"It's been nice. I took a long walk on the beach this morning, bought some new clothes, picked up some groceries, and now Roberto and I are back at the condo getting stuff put away."

"Wow, you've been productive."

"Yeah, I'm getting settled in. Oh, and I chose a new name for myself."

"Really? Tell me about it."

"I found this really cute dress shop today, and it just struck me. The name of the shop is Summer Fling, so that's my new last name, Summers."

"And how about a first name?"

"I'm now Natalie. Natalie Summers."

"Natalie, huh? I like it… Oh, wait a minute, I think I get it," he responded, chuckling out loud.

"Oh really? What do you get?"

"Why you picked Natalie."

"Okay, tell me then."

"You were born on Christmas day. Natalie is the English form of the Italian word for Christmas, like Buon Natale."

"I'm impressed, Investigator Keller! It seemed the right thing to do—go back to the day of my birth when you were in my life. And now you've made my new life happen."

"Thanks, Natalie. That's very sweet."

"Wow, that sounds weird. It'll take some time to get used to a new name."

"Well, you will. Just use Natalie for everything from now on, get in the habit so there are no slip-ups. I'll call you Natalie as well. And tell Roberto, too."

"Okay, what else does Roberto need to get my ID and passports made up?"

"Just give Roberto the name and he'll take care of the rest. When the passport comes, memorize everything on it."

"So, what's going on with the case?" asked Natalie, shifting subjects.

"Well, it doesn't appear anyone saw you leaving town, which is good. It's a great mystery around here how you could have just vanished into thin air. We've had some typical bogus calls; one had you working as a waitress at Denny's in Lone Tree."

"How about Scott? What's going on there?"

"Well, I told you yesterday he lawyered up. Tomorrow we hit the 72-hour mark, so he'll either have to be charged with Lombard's murder or be released."

"Any chance he'll be charged?"

"Nope. The only way it can work for the DA right now is with your testimony and that's not going to happen. So he'll walk out of jail tomorrow. But that doesn't mean he's totally free; it just means that he's free to go for now. He can be rearrested and recharged at any time, assuming there's sufficient evidence. But like I said, without your testimony, I don't see that happening. They really thought you and Scott would meet at the coffee place the other day, and they'd arrest you both together. But even then they'd only have a case if you agreed to testify."

"So, in essence, Scott is a free man because of me. Because I ran he can go back to his wife."

"Yeah, pretty much. But you need to look forward. It's pointless to worry about the past. Believe me, it does no good," Jack said as he thought about his own past. Natalie went silent.

187

"You still there?"

"Yeah, I'm here. It's just really hard, that's all."

"I know it is."

"So when will I get to see you?"

"Depends on when things cool off up here. But pretty soon I think."

"Okay, I'm looking forward to it."

"Me too, Natalie, me too."

THIRTY-EIGHT

The turbo-prop private plane landed just after eleven the next morning at an airport outside Castle Springs. Two SUV limousines were parked there, ready to take Branch Kramer and his entourage directly to the steps of the RCSO jail. He had timed his arrival to coincide with Scott Lennox's release, which was conveniently scheduled for when several Denver television stations were in the middle of their live, midday newscasts. He was prepared to claim another Branch Kramer victory for another "innocent client."

Archer, Keller, and Mia met up with Mick in his office to watch it play out on the news. Welcome to the Branch Kramer Show, Part Two," Mick told them.

"He'll hit us pretty hard, but this will be it," Archer explained. "So we take our medicine and move on."

"Okay, here we go," Mick said, turning up the volume.

"...Brian Banks is live at the scene. Brian, what can you tell us?"

"Tiffany, we're expecting the arrival of Branch Kramer at any moment now. Kramer has returned to Colorado today to coordinate the release of his client, Castle Springs businessman Scott Lennox, arrested over the weekend in connection with the murder of his business partner, George Lombard. Sources say RCSO investigators were unable to gather enough evidence to formally charge Lennox within the 72 hours the law allows."

The camera began to jostle and people behind the reporter were moving about quickly.

"Okay, Branch Kramer has arrived and is now headed up the steps to say a few words."

The scene was rapidly deteriorating into the circus-like environment that many in the news business call a "media gang bang."

"Okay, it looks like he's going to be a little bit out of our frame, so bear with me—this is live TV. We need to move to get him back in our shot. Jim, bring the camera around to the other side if you will… Bear with us, folks, as we maneuver a bit to bring you the best possible coverage."

As an eager Brian Banks and his videographer moved quickly towards Branch Kramer, other news crews also began jostling for position. There was a lot of shoving, which prompted a rival Denver reporter to give Banks' cameraman a hard elbow to the ribs. The cameraman lurched forward, bringing his camera down hard and fast into Branch Kramer's mouth. The impact knocked out both of Kramer's front teeth and sent a stream of bright red blood from his mouth onto his crisp $300 white shirt.

"There appears to be a scuffle of some sort, uhh…," the anchorwoman said as the chaotic scene unfolded on live TV.

A bloody Branch Kramer lashed out at the cameraman, "You fucking idiot!"

"Uh, oh my, we apologize for that," muttered the helpless anchor as the scene continued to play out. The cameraman was able to regain the shot, though drops of blood on the lens marred the view. Branch Kramer quickly descended the steps with a handkerchief to his mouth, climbed back into the limo and, like a secret service detail whisking away a president, was gone in seconds.

Howls of laughter filled Mick's office. "You know, you don't hear 'fucking idiot' enough on live TV," mused Keller.

"It was more like 'futhing idiot,' really. You just don't realize how important those front teeth are until you lose them," Mia added.

They sat in the captain's office and enjoyed the moment again and again, thanks to the DVR.

The scene would also play out thousands of times on TV and social media. The story of Scott Lennox's release took a back seat to Branch Kramer's bloody mouth. As did any mention of the search for Lisa Sullivan.

Lisa, now Natalie, wasn't much of a TV viewer back in Rosebud but decided to check out what the cable lineup had to offer at the condo. As she flipped through the channels, she found CNN and was startled when she saw Branch Kramer's picture on the screen. Her stomach turned sour.

"Famed defense attorney Branch Kramer is recovering tonight after suffering injuries he sustained during a live news conference in the town of Castle Springs, Colorado. The Dallas based attorney, known for his bigger than life persona, was in Colorado securing the release of a client from the local jail when reporters apparently got a little carried away. This is how the scene played out on live TV."

Natalie gasped in disbelief. The story was about Scott's release from jail but instead focused on his lawyer and his bloody encounter with the media. She braced herself, fearing she'd see her picture, but it never appeared.

After several days of drama and stress, Mia readily agreed to Mick's dinner invitation. He would buy and she would cook at his place.

By 6:30, Mia was at work at the stove and Mick was digging around in the cabinet.

"I think we could use one of these," he said, holding up a bottle of Pinot Noir.

"You read my mind."

Mia opened the refrigerator. "How old are these green beans?"

"I don't know, a month maybe."

"Eww, green on top, fuzzy gray on the bottom. That's disgusting. You bought steaks and potatoes but no vegetables? You need vegetables to be big and strong, Mick."

"I think there's broccoli in the freezer."

"Ah, you mean the box of melted cheese with three pieces of green stuff?"

"Tastes better that way."

"I give up. Cheesy broccoli it is," she said as Mick surprised her with a kiss and handed over a glass of pinot.

"Mmm. That's a nice pairing. Especially after the last three days."

They were interrupted by Mick's cell phone. The DA was calling.

"Hey, Dave. You see the show Kramer put on today?"

"You bet I did. Made my week. That little accident took away his chance to crucify us on live television."

"Yeah, no kidding," Mick said.

"I don't want to ruin the moment, but the media will get back on track before long."

"I know."

"That's what I called about. Mick, I don't think I need to remind you how important it is we have a good outcome on this case. I'm up for re-election, and the word on the street is that you are running for sheriff. Let me know what I can do to help when the time comes for you to declare."

"I will do that, and I certainly appreciate your support. It means a lot."

"Now, do you need anything at all from my office to help in the search for the woman? If it's a staffing issue, I can provide you with some of my investigators."

"No, I think we're good for right now, but I appreciate it."

"We can offer her a deal for her testimony, but only if we find her.

I'm not trying to beat a dead horse here; I just want to make sure we're on the same page. We both have a lot to gain and a lot to lose."

"We're on the same page, and we'll find her. I appreciate your support, and I'll keep you posted on Sullivan and my candidacy."

"Very good. I don't know about you, but I'm planning on fixing myself a drink and watching the clip of Kramer losing his teeth again. They tell me it's already got 300,000 hits on YouTube."

"I'm with you, Dave. Thanks."

Mick hung up, turned to Mia, and offered a toast.

"Actually, I'm way ahead you."

The 'beep, beep, beep,' of the microwave echoed through Keller's duplex. Armed with an old potholder, Jack dropped the tray on the kitchen table.

Jack didn't say grace out loud before meals at restaurants or at work, but he always did at home. He made the sign of the cross and whispered "Bless us, O Lord, and these, Thy gifts, which we are about to receive from Thy bounty, through Christ, our Lord. Amen."

That night's bountiful gifts included, as they did most nights Keller ate at home, a Salisbury steak patty, some corn, and mashed potatoes. He peeled back the plastic and watched the steam billow from the tray. For a good sized man, it wasn't much of a meal, but Jack had a dozen more if he was still hungry.

As the Salisbury steak cooled, he popped open his personal laptop and studied a map. It showed Castle Springs on the top right and Puerto Peñasco at the bottom left. Keller couldn't wait to cover the distance and see his daughter again. He was confident that Natalie was safe for the time being, but he knew the search for his daughter wouldn't end anytime soon, and as a wanted suspect, she'd never be out of danger.

Jack's worries took away his appetite. He dumped the rest of the

Salisbury steak in the trash and reached for his burner phone. He wanted to fill her in on the bloody drama outside the courthouse, unaware she'd already seen it. Mostly, he just wanted to hear her voice. But she didn't pick up, so Keller left a message.

"I miss you," he said as he ended the call.

Jack stretched out on the sofa and quickly faded off to sleep.

"Wow, you're amazing. How do you cook these steaks perfectly, every time?" Mick asked Mia.

"Sheer brilliance."

After dinner, they agreed not to talk about work and just relax in front of the TV. The plan was a good one, but proved impossible. During every commercial break, teasers for the ten o'clock news showed video clips of a bloody Branch Kramer battling with reporters. It was like zoo animals turning on their keeper, they joked.

Finally, Mick suggested they go to bed.

"To sleep?" Mia asked playfully.

Mick answered quickly, "I'm open to suggestions."

Mick followed Mia up the stairs, one step behind but with his hand placed protectively at the base of her spine. As they arrived at the top, she turned and kissed him passionately. Unwilling to let go, they moved toward the bedroom until Mick finally scooped her up and carried Mia to the bed. Their lips met again, and they quickly undressed each other. Before long he lowered his body onto hers, and they began to move, in rhythm, as one.

THIRTY-NINE

Natalie needed to take her mind off of what she'd seen on CNN, so she took Sarah up on her offer. The party was just a few blocks from the condo, and she walked the short distance in just a few minutes.

The house was unmistakable. It was the largest and most beautiful home she had seen in her short time in Puerto Peñasco. As she approached, the sounds of laughter and festive music poured from an open doorway. Natalie stepped into the foyer. The home had an open floor plan, and she could see a living room, dining area, and kitchen— all tastefully decorated in an elegant, Mediterranean design.

"Hola, señorita. Are you here for the party?"

The woman was dressed in all white and carried a plate of hors d'oeuvres.

"Yes, I am. Sarah invited me. Do I have the right place?"

"Sí, señorita. The guests are out back on the beach. Please, join them. May I bring you something to drink?"

"Yes, thank you. Chardonnay, if you have any."

"Of course, I will bring it to you on the beach."

Natalie walked through the living room toward the voices. Not wanting to look like a party crasher, she quickly surveyed the guests, looking for Sarah. Aside from Roberto and Berta, she was the only other person Natalie knew in Puerto Peñasco.

"Natalie! So glad you made it!"

Sarah rushed in from the beach.

"You look beautiful. And I love the dress."

"Oh, thanks. I got it at a terrific little shop in town."

Sarah laughed and led Natalie by the arm.

"Come on, I'll introduce you."

"I can't stay long… I just thought I'd drop by for a few minutes."

"I think you'll like my friends. I told them you were new in town. I hope you don't mind."

The surf crashed in the distance as the beach glittered from the moonlight amid the fire-lit torches and beach chairs.

"Take off your shoes."

Natalie slipped out of her sandals and left them on the patio. Sarah grabbed her hand and pulled her toward the small crowd.

"Hey, everybody!" Sarah called out as they approached the group. "This is the friend I was telling you about. Natalie's new in town, so be nice to her!"

Natalie was welcomed by the group of nearly twenty. It was an even mix of men and women, all gracious and friendly. The server arrived with her wine and Natalie raised her glass to the crowd.

"Thank you all for the warm welcome, it's nice to be here."

The others raised their glasses in unison. As Natalie and Sarah stood and chatted, another young woman joined them.

"Hi, I'm Alyssa."

They shook hands. "Nice to meet you."

"When did you get in town?"

"Just a few days ago. It's my first visit to Puerto Peñasco, and I can't believe how beautiful it is."

"We all call it our hidden gem. Everybody knows about Cabo and Cancun, but not many people know about this place. But word is getting out, and it's growing quickly."

"I'll bet," Natalie said. "So, do you live here or are you on vacation?"

"I live here. I left L.A. and came down two years ago. It's the perfect place for a new start," Alyssa told her.

If she only knew, Natalie thought.

"I kind of escaped from a bad relationship and needed a new start," Alyssa said. "I had been here a few years back on vacation, and I remembered it. I thought, why not? The place just has a great vibe."

Natalie agreed. "You know, I got that sense right away as well. I went for a walk yesterday along the beach, and I couldn't believe how many people greeted me."

"Yeah, that's the beauty of this place."

Sarah joined in. "Alyssa works in the jewelry store next door to Summer Fling."

"Oh, okay. Is that how you met, working next to one another?"

"Well, sort of," Sarah explained. "But really, most of the people here work in some capacity for Peter. He owns a lot of the businesses in town. So we all know each other that way. He has these get-togethers maybe once a month. He likes to have a cohesive group of employees."

"Works for me," said Alyssa, raising her glass.

"In fact, this is Peter's house," said Sarah.

"One of his houses... Oh, and did I mention he is hot?" Alyssa added, smiling.

"It's a gorgeous house."

Sarah gave Natalie a brief history on Peter. "He came down here from the states, like, twenty years ago and just saw the potential in this little fishing town. He loved the beauty of the place and started buying up little businesses, one by one. His family had some money and financed him in the beginning and then things just took off. Now he's the biggest landowner in Puerto Peñasco and owns more than forty businesses, including the Marbella."

"The Marbella?" asked Natalie.

"Boy, you are new in town," responded Alyssa. "The Marbella is Puerto Peñasco's only five-star resort—very ritzy, very exclusive. It's where the rich and famous come and hang out when they truly want privacy and don't want the crowds and craziness of some of the other Mexican resort towns. The Marbella caters to people who just want to do nothing but enjoy the ocean and each other."

"That sounds incredible but not exactly a place I could ever afford."

"I've only stayed there a handful of times myself," Sarah replied. "But I go there a lot for work. I haul half the store up to the Marbella when someone wants to shop but doesn't want to leave the privacy of the resort. At first I thought it was crazy, taking all those outfits up there, because it's such a hassle. But these women buy almost everything I bring in their size, and since I work on commission, well, it pays the rent."

Natalie shook her head. "Not exactly a world I'm familiar with…"

"So, where are you from Natalie? We didn't have much chance to talk yesterday at the store."

"I'm from St. Louis. You?"

"I'm from Seattle, originally," Sarah told her. "I went to school at Arizona State in Tempe and that's how I discovered this place. On spring break, a bunch of us would haul down here and go a little crazy. It was close and getting across the boarder in those days was easy."

"I went through there a few days ago. I thought the guard was going to get in the car with me."

Sarah understood all too well. "Imagine the guards when they saw six college girls on spring break pulling up to the border all crammed into a '91 Honda Civic."

Both Natalie and Alyssa laughed at the thought.

"Bet you guys were something to see," replied Alyssa.

"Oh, yeah. Girls on a mission. Those were the days. After graduation from ASU, I tried to find a job in Phoenix, but the economy had tanked and there was nothing out there. I needed a little getaway, you know, to clear my head, and so I came down here. That was five years ago, and I'm still here."

"You never went back to Phoenix or home to Seattle?" asked Natalie.

"Not really. I had a friend bring my stuff down from Phoenix—it wasn't much. And I was never that close to my family, although, when my mother died, I did go back for the service."

"Oh, I'm sorry, Sarah."

"Thanks, but like I said I was never really that close to my family. It was kind of a messed up situation."

"So, are you a Mexican citizen now? I mean, how does that work? How does someone stay here and work?"

"There are ways to do it, legal ways. A lot of the people who work in Peter's businesses are Americans like me and are here long-term."

"Well, who knows? Maybe I'll join you."

"Everyone, dinner is served," the woman in all white called from the patio.

"Let's go," Sarah said to Natalie.

"Dinner? It's after ten."

"Get used to it. It's a little bit like Europe here, everything is later. The good thing is that dinner is usually a light meal, or we'd all weigh 300 pounds."

The group quickly came in from the beach and filed into the dining room. The table was large, beautifully set, and brimming with food.

"This is a light dinner?" whispered Natalie to Sarah.

"Yeah, look at what it is. Fish, fresh fruit, all healthy stuff."

"Okay. But first I need to use the restroom. Can you point me in the right direction?"

"Sure, it's right past the living room, second door on the left."

Natalie excused herself and made her way across the living room, down a hallway, and into the bathroom. A few minutes later she emerged and bumped into a man who was the epitome of tall, dark, and handsome.

"Oh, I'm so sorry. Please, excuse me," she said quickly.

"That's quite all right, Miss...?"

Natalie looked up and into the eyes of the most handsome man she'd ever seen. She hesitated, feeling her face flush and her heartbeat quicken.

The man smiled and extended his hand. "I don't believe we've met. I'm Peter Donnelly."

"Oh, I'm sorry, hello. I'm Natalie. Natalie Summers."

"Well, I'm very pleased to meet you, Natalie." His eyes held her focus, and his hand held hers a beat longer than courtesy would require. "Are you hungry? Let's have some dinner and get acquainted."

"Yes," Natalie squeaked. She was light-headed as he led her to the dining room. All eyes were on the couple when they arrived at the table. Peter pulled out the chair next to his, and Natalie took a seat.

Dinner was full of easy conversation among friends. As the wine flowed, the volume elevated, and Peter routinely leaned in close to speak with Natalie, his lips often lightly brushing the side of her cheek. Natalie was watching her alcohol intake, and although she had consumed only two glasses of wine, she felt completely intoxicated by the company of Peter Donnelly.

After dinner, the party moved back to the beach, but Natalie and Peter lingered on the patio.

"This is so beautiful."

"Yes, it is," he answered, looking directly into Natalie's eyes.

She was entering dangerous territory, on so many levels.

It was late morning before Natalie crawled out of bed. The stress and strain of the past week drained her energy, and she needed the rest. Feeling refreshed, she walked to the living room and opened the sliding glass doors. The breeze poured in with the salty scent of the sea. She lay on the couch enjoying the view from a distance. Natalie couldn't stop thinking about Peter Donnelly.

Handsome, sexy, smart—he was everything Scott was not. Her thoughts drifted back to Colorado. *How did I ever fall for him? I completely screwed up my life and for what? A lying cheater who never even loved me?* It was a conversation she had with herself many times over the past few weeks. She never came up with a good answer and knew she probably never would.

Natalie turned her thoughts back to Peter. She closed her eyes and imagined his arms around her, his breath on her neck, the comforting cadence of his voice. He was sexy, but she knew this was something more. In just one evening, this man had gotten under her skin.

After a shower and a quick breakfast of fresh fruit, Natalie headed off for Summer Fling. She wanted to thank Sarah for the party invite and see if she might know of any job openings around town. She still had more than $18,000 left from the money Jack had given her but knew that wouldn't last forever. If she was going to make Puerto Peñasco her home, she would need to earn her own money.

As she walked along the beach, Natalie came to an older section of town just southeast from the condo. The buildings weren't new and modern like Summer Fling and the other high-end shops, but Natalie liked the feel. A boxy, multi-colored restaurant caught her eye. It sat on pilings above the water. She would have to ask Sarah about it. Farther down the beach, Natalie spotted an open-air café squeezed between two seafood vendors. She slipped in for a cup of coffee.

"Altura pluma," the man said as he gave her a cup. "The beans are grown high in the mountains. It's the best, no?"

"This is the best coffee I've ever had. My God, it is amazing."

"My name is Juan, and I own this cafe. No es grande, but the local people, they like mucho. You here on vacation?"

"I'm staying at a condo just up the beach. I was taking a walk and saw your place. And this coffee is so good."

Juan beamed. "Your name, señorita?"

"Oh, I'm sorry. My name is Natalie."

"Ah, you come back, señorita Natalie. I make you the best tamales in Puerto Peñasco."

"You've got a deal, Juan. And it's nice to meet you."

Natalie thanked him for the coffee and promised she would be back.

It was early afternoon by the time Natalie arrived at Summer Fling. She walked into the store and saw Sarah, who was busy with a customer. After the tourist left, the two hugged.

"I just had to stop in and thank you for last night. I had a blast and it was great to meet all your friends."

"Oh really, anyone in particular?" Sarah teased.

"Well..." She had decided not to talk with Sarah about Peter, but caved at the first mention. "Peter was nice. A little mysterious."

"Natalie, I've worked for Peter for a few years now. He owns half this town, but I honestly can't say I really know him. He's a tough nut to crack. He's charming, friendly, a great boss, hell, he's a genius. But he doesn't let many people into his world."

Natalie hung on every word.

"I'll tell you this, though," Sarah said leaning in. "I've never seen him zero in on anyone like he did last night with you."

"Well, I don't know about that," Natalie answered. "He was very sweet."

"Sweet? The heat coming from you two almost set the room on fire."

"I think Peter Donnelly is a bit out of my league," Natalie answered. "Anyway, I didn't come here to talk about him. I was hoping you could give me some advice on a job. I did some waitressing in college so I thought maybe I could pick up some shifts at that place that juts out over the water."

"The Point? Are you kidding? You should have no trouble getting a job there. Just one of many restaurants here in town owned by Mr. Peter Donnelly."

"Okay, well I didn't know that. I don't think that's a good idea. There's got to be some places that he doesn't own."

"Well, good luck. Most of the tourist attractions are owned and run by Donnelly and Associates," Sarah explained. "What's the big deal?"

"I don't know," Natalie said. "I just don't think it would be a good idea to get involved, that's all."

"Okay, I'm sorry. Didn't mean to overstep, Natalie. I just think you and Peter would make a terrific couple."

"So what do you know about the little café on the beach? The one down by all the seafood vendors?"

"Juan's Café? I've been in there a few times. You want to waitress there? I mean, that's fine if you want to do that, but believe me, the tips at any of Peter's places will probably be triple what you'd pull in at Juan's."

Natalie was intent on keeping a low profile, so Juan's sounded like the perfect place. She decided to stop by the cafe on the way home and see about a job. Besides, Juan had promised her the best tamales in town.

Juan's Café turned out to be busier than Natalie expected, but by her second week on the job, it felt like home. She was getting to know the regulars, and Juan was quickly becoming a good friend. She wasn't making a lot of money, but she liked the atmosphere and the tamales were indeed the best.

"Señor Juan, I have to stop eating your tamales or I will have to retire the bikini," Natalie called out to her boss in the back room as she wiped down the counter.

"Tamales or no tamales, I'm sure the bikini looks great on you."

The voice startled Natalie. She looked up to see Peter Donnelly in the doorway. Her heart began to race.

"Hello, Peter, I didn't expect to see you here. We're in between lunch and dinner right now, but if you're hungry I've got some pull with the owner."

"I could go for tamales and a cold beer, if you can swing it."

"A man after my own heart."

Peter Donnelly chuckled. He was not a patient man by nature, but with Natalie, Peter was careful to go slowly.

So, every afternoon for the next five days, Peter Donnelly, owner of the finest restaurants in Puerto Peñasco, arrived at Juan's Café to eat tamales and spend time with Natalie Summers.

On the fifth afternoon, Peter and Natalie were making small talk when Peter made his move.

"Hey, have you ever been fishing?" Peter asked.

"Nope, I've never really been around the ocean."

Peter took a swig of beer.

"Come out fishing with me," he urged. "You'd love it. Besides, you should really know where fish tacos come from," he added with a smile.

Natalie knew she should decline. She could hear in her mind Jack telling her to be careful, but the words came out anyway. "Okay. You're on."

Saturday morning, Natalie woke early, both excited and a little nervous. She was meeting Peter at the dock in a little over an hour, giving her time for a quick cup of coffee and a shower before heading out. She debated over her outfit, finally settling on a yellow bikini, covered up by shorts and a simple t-shirt. Keep it low key, she told herself. After packing a small beach bag with a towel, sunscreen, and jacket, Natalie took a final sip of her coffee and called Jack.

"Hey, how's Mexico?" he asked, answering on the first ring.

"Fabulous. I'm settling in and loving Puerto Peñasco. Starting to feel like a regular."

"That's great, Natalie. I'm so glad to hear that."

Jack filled her in on the Lombard investigation. Things had slowed down considerably. With Lisa Sullivan on the run, the case was going nowhere.

"Okay, well that's good news."

Jack sensed her mind was somewhere else.

"You okay? You seem a little distracted."

"Oh, no. I'm fine," Natalie responded quickly. "Just a little tired. I think I'll take it easy today. Maybe a nap on the beach. I'll call you later."

Walking to the docks, Natalie thought about what Jack would say about Peter. "It's no big deal," she mumbled, trying to convince herself. Still, she knew Jack would have warned her about getting into a romantic relationship. He would consider it to be too risky for her.

But Natalie reasoned she was just having fun with a friend. What harm could come of that? As she approached the dock she saw Peter standing next to a beautiful, sleek boat.

"There she is," Peter said to a man standing on the bow. "Natalie, I'd like you to meet Captain Dave. He's worked for me for more than a decade and is the best captain on the Sea of Cortez."

Dave Maddox extended his hand to Natalie. He looked the part of a charter boat captain: face weathered by wind and sun, worn shorts, canvas dock shoes, and a well-worn t-shirt and cap.

"Welcome aboard Natalie," he said warmly. "I've heard a lot about you from Peter." Captain Dave had a thick Boston accent and a twinkle in his eye.

She felt in good hands as the two men shoved off from the dock. Captain Dave soon maneuvered the boat out into the open water, settling in at an easy 12 knots, while Peter outlined his personal fishing strategy to Natalie, much to the amusement of the captain.

"Peter, when was the last time you went fishing?" Dave teased. "Better yet, when was the last time you actually caught a fish?"

"Good point," Peter laughed. The two men had an easy rapport and the friendly chiding went on for most of the trip. Natalie sat back and enjoyed the warm sunshine, the steady vibration of the boat, and the comedy show put on by the two men. Before long, Captain Dave slowed the boat, and Peter got busy organizing the gear.

"Today, you are going to catch a grouper. It's a God-awful ugly fish, but delicious," Peter said as he baited the hook and cast her line.

"When you get a bite, you'll feel a tug. When that happens, let me know, and I'll come help."

Before Peter could finish his sentence, Natalie felt a pull on her line.

"Oh my God, what do I do?" Natalie screamed.

The fight was on.

With a lot of help from Peter, Natalie began playing the fish: reel in, release, reel in, release. She was surprised at how tiring the whole process was, but with her adrenaline pumping, she was able to keep at it. Peter reached around her to secure the pole. She felt the warmth of his skin as his muscles tightened and the sweat beaded on his tan arms. The fight was exhausting.

"This fish must be huge," Natalie screamed as she struggled to reel in the line.

"It is a big one," Peter responded, teeth clenched. Working as a team, they finally pulled the grouper toward the boat. Captain Dave was standing by with a net, and he snagged the hard fought catch.

Peter was right—the grouper was the ugliest fish Natalie had ever seen. Still, she was ecstatic at reeling it in. The crew exchanged high fives and Peter gave Natalie a long, warm hug.

The trio spent the rest of the day fishing, drinking beer, and soaking in the sun.

"Have dinner with me tonight," Peter asked. "We'll take the grouper to the Marbella and have the chef make us a fabulous meal, and we'll eat on my private patio."

"I don't know, Peter," Natalie stammered. "I would have to go home to change, and I have no way to get there."

"You can come with me. I'll have Sarah bring something over from Summer Fling. Come on, it'll be fun."

"You might as well give in, Natalie," Captain Dave advised, smiling. "Peter Donnelly is not a man who takes no for an answer."

"Two against one—I'm outnumbered!" Natalie relented. "Okay, I'll go. But promise you won't have Sarah bring anything expensive."

Peter smiled and draped his arm around her shoulder as the waning sunlight danced on the Sea of Cortez. Approaching the harbor at Puerto Peñasco, Natalie felt the excitement of a new life ahead and her past life fading away in the boat's wake.

FORTY

The last of the early autumn snow had melted in Castle Springs and only a few golden leaves remained on most of the trees. Nearly a year after the murder of George Lombard the drama had faded, but the case was not forgotten.

Chuck and Mia pulled into the parking lot of CopyPrint in Castle Springs. Chuck headed inside while Mia grabbed her phone to make a call.

Inside, Chuck found a register without a line.

"Hi, I'm here to pick up an order for Mia Serrano," Chuck said when he got to the counter.

"Okay, let me check in the back," responded the young cashier.

As he waited, Chuck glanced around the shop. He saw a man wearing a roman collar a few feet away. He recognized the priest instantly.

"Hello, Father," Chuck said.

"Good morning. How are you doing today?"

"Doing great, thanks."

"It's another beautiful Colorado day, isn't it?" asked the priest.

"It sure is, Father. I don't believe we've met—my name is Chuck Serrano," he said, extending his hand towards the priest.

"Nice to meet you, Chuck. I'm Father Jon from St. Joseph's Church."

"Oh, St. Joseph's, yes."

Chuck thought back to the parking lot of the church several months earlier when the priest had been talking with Jack Keller. It was more like an argument, he remembered.

"The package for Mia is all done," the clerk said. "All paid, too. You're set to go."

"Great, is the receipt in here? She's a stickler about receipts."

"Yes, sir. It's in the bag," the clerk told Chuck. "And they'll be bringing yours up in just a minute, Father," she said to the priest.

Chuck took the bag and turned to leave. He nodded to the priest and then stopped, reached into the bag, and took out a campaign flyer. He handed it to Father Jon.

"I'm doing some campaigning for Mick McCallister. He's running for Rocklin County Sheriff. He's a good man and will make a wonderful sheriff. I hope we can count on your support."

"Ah, yes," Father Jon said, reviewing the flyer, "I've been following the campaign in the papers."

"There's a rally for him this afternoon at Butterfield Park. It would be great if you could drop by." Chuck winked at him, "There's a free hot dog and a soda in it for you."

Father Jon chuckled, "Well, I may just do that. Thank you, Chuck."

"Great, I'll introduce you to the future sheriff. You'll like him."

"I'm sure I will. You know, I've got a friend that works for the sheriff's department. He's in the Investigations Bureau—his name is Jack Keller. Do you know him?"

"Yes, I do. In fact, my daughter works for the RCSO and was his partner for a time. She's moved back to the patrol division now, so she doesn't see him as much."

"Well, neither do I. Haven't seen Jack in quite a while, actually."

"If I see him, I'll tell him you said to get back to church. In the meantime, I hope to see you at the park this afternoon."

"I'll do my best to come by. Thanks for the invite."

Chuck headed back to the car and found Mia still on the phone.

"How long does it take to put up a bounce house? Okay, as long as it's up in time. We should be there soon," she said, setting down the phone. "How do they look, Dad?"

"Good, I think," he said, handing Mia a flyer.

"Remember when I told you about following Keller? And how I saw him arguing with a priest in the parking lot at St. Joseph's last winter?"

"Yes, wasn't that when you were doing your best Columbo impression and following Keller all over town? I thought you wanted me to forget all that."

"I just saw that priest. He was in the CopyPrint, and we struck up a conversation. He asked me if I knew Jack Keller."

"He just asked you that out of the blue?"

"Well, no, I was telling him about Mick running for sheriff, and he said he had a friend in the department. He says he hasn't seen Keller in a long time. It was kinda odd."

"How so?"

"I don't know. I got the impression that Keller was a regular at St. Joe's. And they had to know each other pretty well to have a conversation like the one I saw. And now Keller doesn't go to church anymore? Anyway, I invited him to the rally. He says he might come."

"That's great, Dad. Mick needs all the support he can get."

All day, Mia's focus had been solely on the "McCallister for Sheriff" rally. Now, as she drove to Butterfield Park, the Lombard case came flooding back to her. Since returning to patrol, Mia hadn't worked an investigation in months. She didn't mind working patrol, but she did miss investigations work. They had been so close to solving the Lombard murder only to have it all slip away along with Lisa Sullivan.

"Mia!" Chuck yelled.

"What?"

"You just missed the turn for Butterfield Park."

Frito made the turn from West Valencia onto the I-19 South in Tucson. Jack was in the passenger seat, the hot wind blowing through his hair. It was almost one o'clock, and the temperature had already crossed the century mark. Frito's truck did not have air conditioning, so all the windows were down. Jack wasn't sure if having the hot air hitting him from all directions was a good idea or not, but Frito seemed to think so, so he went along with the program.

This was Keller's first trip to Puerto Peñasco since Lisa Sullivan's disappearance. He had started to make plans several times since she had gone, but the timing never worked. Jack didn't want to set foot in Mexico until he was confident he wouldn't draw any possible attention to her whereabouts.

Keller had tried to make a case against Scott Lennox without Lisa Sullivan. He had spent months searching the records of auto body shops looking for a link to Scott Lennox. He even trailed him for a few weeks hoping to find something to link him to the death of George Lombard. He had gotten nowhere. The only thing that could make a murder charge stick to Scott Lennox was living on a beach in Mexico, and Jack couldn't wait to see her.

"Thank you for taking such good care of Natalie, my friend," he told Frito. "How has she been doing?"

"She is very good, Jack. You maybe worry too much."

Jack hadn't told him why she had come to Mexico or why she needed a new identity. Frito hadn't asked, and it didn't really matter. As far as Frito was concerned, he was still in Jack Keller's debt.

The two had met eight years earlier when Jack walked into Frito's tile business looking for someone to do work on the bathroom in his condo. At the time, Frito had just landed the tile job for the new Marbella Hotel being built down at the beach. The Marbella job was the largest he'd ever been awarded and with it would come financial stability. However, the project wasn't set to begin for three weeks, so Frito was happy to take on a small job for Jack.

After showing Frito his bathroom, Jack invited him to stay for dinner. Frito accepted the invitation and the two men enjoyed a meal of fresh seafood and talked late into the night. Frito shared his frustration of balancing work with the demands of a young family, a story Jack knew all too well. That night, the two men formed a bond that each would rely on in the years ahead.

That bond soon proved to be a lifesaver for Frito. A few days before his crew was scheduled to start work at the Marbella, Frito was visited by two men from an organized crime syndicate in Sinaloa. They demanded he sign over his business to them or his family would die. Organized crime was rampant in Mexico and payoffs were a part of business, but Frito stood firm and refused the two men.

A few days later Frito returned home from work to find his family had vanished. He was again told that unless he surrendered his business to the crime syndicate his family would all be killed. Frito knew he had no choice but to comply. He signed the papers but was then told he would have to negotiate the return of his family with a man they called "El Coyote."

With his whole world crumbling around him, Frito asked his new friend, the American detective, for help. Three days later, the ordeal was over and Frito's family was back safe and sound. Meanwhile, El Coyote found himself in a Phoenix jail facing murder charges. Frito didn't know what his friend Jack had done, but the problem was solved. The incident changed Frito's life and his priorities forever. He moved his family to a new home and focused his attention on his wife and children. He would be forever indebted to his friend Jack Keller.

As Mia and Chuck pulled into the parking lot at Butterfield Park, they could see Mick and a small group of volunteers working in the BBQ area. It was their third campaign event at the park; Mick had decided early on that his campaign events would be accessible to all and not just well-heeled Rocklin County residents.

His opponent, Jerry Griffith, a retired assistant chief from the Castle Springs PD, had taken a different approach, holding mostly high-priced events at country clubs and high-end hotels. Anyone could attend one of Griffith's events, provided you could pay $250 a plate or more. Griffith's strategy targeted the county's power brokers, while Mick's focus was more of a grassroots campaign. It was a risky move for Mick as he was being outspent nearly three to one. Griffith had spent sixty thousand dollars in just the last two weeks alone on local cable TV and newspaper ads. Mick's campaign had used their limited dollars mostly on campaign literature handed out door to door and at town hall meetings and informal gatherings like the rallies at Butterfield Park.

Despite the lopsided fundraising totals, informal polls showed Mick ahead by a few percentage points. Anything could happen in the last days of the campaign, though, and the race was essentially a toss up.

Mick looked up and saw Mia and Chuck in the parking lot. He waved and headed their way, but was quickly pulled aside to shake hands with a small group of supporters.

"The poor guy gets yanked in a lot of directions, doesn't he?" commented Chuck.

"Yep, but he's got the patience of Job. It's one of the qualities that will make him an excellent sheriff," Mia replied. "Dad, can you get those campaign flyers over to Barbara?"

"You bet."

As Chuck headed off to find Barbara, Mia made her way towards the picnic area to find Mick. She found him looking over notes scribbled on an index card.

"You ready to give your speech?" Mia asked him.

"Yep, let's do it."

Jack and Frito traveled the desolate highway from Tucson to Gringo Pass, crossed the border, and continued on towards Puerto Peñasco. The long drive gave the two a chance to catch up.

"So tell me about Natalie and Peter."

"Ah, my friend. Natalie is señor Donnelly's corazón."

"It's that serious?"

"No sé, mi amigo, but they are together most times. They are the big couple in town."

"Well, I really don't like the sound of that."

Being part of a high-profile couple was the last thing Natalie needed.

By mid-afternoon, the rally was in full swing at Butterfield Park. More than three hundred people came out in support of the candidate and enjoyed a BBQ lunch served by Mick and his crew of volunteers. Afterward, they cheered as Mick hit the main points of his platform in a rousing campaign speech.

Afterward, as Mia and her dad worked the crowd handing out campaign flyers, Chuck spotted a familiar face. Father Jon had taken him up on his offer.

"Hey, Father, glad you could make it!"

"How can I turn down a free hot dog on such a beautiful day?"

Chuck smiled and turned toward Mia. "Father, I'd like you to meet my daughter, Mia Serrano. She's the one I told you about."

"It's so nice to meet you, Father, and thanks so much for coming today."

"My pleasure, Mia. After your dad's kind invitation this morning, I didn't want to miss it."

"Yeah, he can be pretty persuasive."

"Chuck tells me you were partners with Jack Keller. I know Jack from my parish, St. Joseph's here in Castle Springs."

"Jack and I partnered on a case several months back, but now I'm back working patrol. He's a great investigator, though. I learned a lot from him."

"I don't doubt it," Father Jon said. "I first met him when he moved to Colorado from St. Louis. We've become good friends since then. I haven't seen him much lately, though."

"Well, neither have I. We have different schedules and don't really cross paths anymore."

Thanking supporters along the way, Mick approached the group and Chuck made the introductions. "Father Jon, I'd like you to meet the next Sheriff of Rocklin County. This is Mick McCallister. Mick, Father Jon from St. Joseph's Church."

The two shook hands. "Hello, Father, it's nice to meet you. Thanks for coming out today."

"My pleasure. Is it Captain or Commander or…"

"Captain. But please call me Mick."

"Thanks, I will."

"Father Jon was just telling us that he's friends with Jack Keller," Mia added.

"Jack works in my division. As you probably know, he works homicide cases for us."

"Yes, Jack has shared that with me."

"We were very lucky to get him out of retirement several years ago. He's really a top notch investigator—one of the best I've ever seen."

"I can imagine. I haven't seen much of him lately, I'm sure he's very busy."

"Well, he's on vacation right now. Mexico, I think," Mick said. "Jack's got a place down there."

"I'm sure it's a wonderful escape," the priest said.

"He's had it for years but doesn't find the time to get down there very often. It's on the Sea of Cortez, if I'm not mistaken."

"Well, look at me monopolizing your time. You have campaigning to do. Mick, I wish you well in the election and you can count on my support."

"Thanks, Father, that means a lot to me."

"Have a great day, I hope to see you all again soon."

Father Jon headed back to his car. If Jack was in Mexico, was it possible his daughter was there, too?

Jack waved goodbye to Frito outside the condo and let himself in. Natalie was on the back patio and heard the door. Before he could say anything, she rushed to hug her father.

"I'm so glad you're here," she said, holding him tightly. "God, I missed you!"

"Me too, Natalie. My God, I almost didn't recognize you."

Natalie posed for him. "Cute, huh?"

"You look beautiful. And I missed you so much." As they walked hand-in-hand toward the patio, Jack added, "I missed this place, too."

"You must be exhausted. What can I get you?"

"Iced tea, if you have any."

"I can do that. Be right back," replied Natalie as she disappeared inside.

Jack plopped himself down on a lounge chair and looked out at the surf. He had spent some important time here after leaving St. Louis. It seemed so long ago, he thought. It was an important place in his life, where he had begun his life of sobriety. Now, this same place was providing a new life for his daughter.

Jack breathed in the salty sea air as the sun bathed him in warmth. Still, he couldn't fully relax. His daughter was a fugitive. And while the interest in finding her had waned and the media had moved on to other stories, he knew it could change at any moment. It was a fear that haunted him daily.

"Here you go," said Natalie, handing her father his iced tea and breaking his train of thought. "Complete with fresh lemon from Roberto's house."

"Perfect," said Jack as Natalie sat down in the chair next to him. Jack looked at his daughter and said, "Life down here seems to be agreeing with you. So tell me, how are things going?"

"Well, I think you know most of it already. I've been working at the mission school like I told you on the phone. I miss the restaurant, but I love working with the children and they're so sweet. When I first came down here, I was stunned at the poverty just blocks away from all the resorts, shops, and nice homes. Just look at Roberto's family. He and Juanita work so hard and barely make enough to live. I can't believe that his two daughters don't even go to school. I've been trying to convince him to send them to the mission school. If these kids can get a basic education, they can do so much more here."

"How are you able to talk with the kids? I mean, how's your Spanish?"

"Pretty good actually. Luckily, the kids I work with at the school are little and so are their vocabularies, so I've learned along with them. They also know more English than you might expect, and there's another teacher there and she's a big help."

"Wow, Natalie, I'm impressed."

"I guess I have an aptitude for language. Who knew, huh?"

"You sound like you've found your niche."

"I think I have—I care deeply about the people in Puerto Peñasco. I've made some awful mistakes in my life, and I want to make up for it somehow. Helping the local kids here get an education—maybe it's just my small way of making amends. Not enough, I know, but it's the best I can do right now."

"Well, I'm proud of you."

"Thanks, that means a lot to me. You know, sometimes I lay in bed at night and think that less than a year ago I was involved with Scott. I thought I loved him, and I let him talk me into doing something that

I would never have believed I was capable of. I sometimes have nightmares about Mr. Lombard, and I can't get his face out of my mind. But then at the same time, it seems so long ago. I know now that I never loved Scott. I think I just wanted someone, anyone to love, and there he was. He used me, and I can't change that. But I can change the lives of the kids here and maybe that makes up for it in some small way."

"Natalie, I need to tell you something about the Lombard case that I haven't shared with you before."

"What?" she asked, frightened.

"Don't worry," Jack said quickly, calming his daughter. "Just something you probably should know. After Lombard was killed we did an autopsy, standard procedure in any suspicious death. Anyway, the doctor who did the autopsy found George Lombard had cancer. It had spread and… The bottom line is Lombard was dying. He probably had only three or four months to live."

Natalie put her hand to her mouth and the color drained from her face. Dazed, she walked to the corner of the patio and broke down sobbing. Jack gave her a moment and walked over to give comfort.

"You okay?"

Natalie nodded.

"I didn't mean to shock you. But I thought you should know. Maybe to give some perspective."

Natalie took a deep breath. "It doesn't make it right."

"Natalie, listen to me. You've found a new life here, doing great work for people who need your help. You didn't kill Lombard, Scott did. You just helped him cover it up. That's different. You thought you were in love with the guy, and you weren't thinking clearly. Believe me, I've seen people do much crazier things in my career. My point is, you are now in a place where you are doing some real good. You have a new life, and it was Lombard's death that put you here."

"But we killed a man."

"No, Scott Lennox killed a man. And if you two had known he had cancer, Scott wouldn't have concocted this plan to kill Lombard. But we never would have been reunited, and you wouldn't be in Mexico helping kids. You can't go back and change things, Natalie. But a greater good has come from all of this."

FORTY-ONE

Father Jon made the call from his rectory office.

"Hello, I'm trying to reach Father Diego Montanez. Do you speak English?"

"Sí, señor. Who may I say is calling?"

"This is Father Jon Foley, calling from St. Joseph's Parish in Castle Springs, Colorado."

"Very well, Father. Let me ring him for you."

"Thank you."

Father Jon hadn't spoken to his friend in years. The two had been seminary roommates. The familiar voice of Diego Montanez brought back fond memories.

"This is a wonderful day. To what do I owe this great honor, my friend?"

"Hello, Diego, it's been way too long. How are you?"

"I am well. The Bishop blessed me greatly by me assigning me to a mission at this wonderful parish in Mexico. Are you still in Colorado?"

"Yes, I've been here for several years now. It's a busy parish in Castle Springs. Things are good. Where exactly are you in Mexico?"

"I'm in the state of Jalisco. I've been here three years now. In another year, I will see where the Bishop wants me to go."

"We should be better about staying in touch, my friend."

"I agree, Jon. But I'm guessing there's a reason for your call today.

What can I do for you?"

"Yes, I need some help."

"Anything for you, Jon."

"Do you know anyone there in Mexico who might be able to track someone down for me? Specifically, if I gave you a name, is there someone there who could find where this person might own some property in Mexico?"

"Sure, I think I could probably make that happen. What have you got going on there, Jon?"

"I'm not one hundred percent sure, really. It involves one of my parishioners, and I believe he has a place somewhere on the Sea of Cortez. I don't know how many possible places that could mean, but I thought I'd give you a call and see what you thought."

"Well, the Sea of Cortez is large and there are several resort towns. Los Cabos, La Paz, Puerto Peñasco, San Carlos… Those are the largest."

"Do you know someone who might be able to do a little quiet checking if I gave you a name?"

"This sounds serious, Jon. Can you tell me why you are trying to find this man?"

"To be truthful, I'd rather not. At least not right now. It's just a hunch on my part, and I'm not really sure what, if anything, it will lead to… Can you just trust me on this one, Diego?"

"Of course, Jon. You have a name?"

"His name is Jack Keller. He now lives in Castle Pines, Colorado, but he lived in the St. Louis area when he bought the place. He's owned it for several years now."

"How old would he be?"

"I'd guess around sixty or so."

"Give me a few days and I'll see what I can find out."

The last wedge of sun was fading into the Sea of Cortez as Natalie jostled Jack on the patio lounge chair.

"Huh? Oh. I must have nodded off. Wow, look at you."

Natalie, wearing one of her favorite sundresses, took a quick bow.

"It's time for dinner. I took the liberty of digging in your bag and pressed some clothes for you. Our ride is here in ten minutes, so let's get a move on."

"Are we having dinner with Peter?" he asked, stretching.

"Yes, and I need you to look respectable."

"Nag, nag, nag," Jack muttered as he headed toward the bathroom.

The doorbell rang.

"Oops, I'm wrong. Our ride is here now. You have three minutes. I'll be in the car."

"All right, I'll hurry."

When Jack came out the front door, he was surprised to see Natalie and a large, muscular man standing next to a black luxury SUV. The back passenger door was open.

"Meet Miguel, he's our driver."

"Hi, Miguel, I'm Jack," he said, climbing in the back seat. "Wow, this is quite a ride."

"Mr. Donnelly is sorry he could not be here when you arrived, señor."

"Peter's meeting us at the Marbella for dinner," Natalie said, fixing his collar. "You look nice."

Miguel closed the door behind him. When Jack heard the sound the heavy doors made as they slammed shut, he knew. He took a quick look around. The windows and glass partition that separated the front and back seats were laminated polycarbonate—commonly called bulletproof, though technically just bullet-resistant. They were riding in what was essentially an armored car, and Jack quickly wondered why his daughter's boyfriend would need such a vehicle.

"So, just how serious are things with Peter?"

"Why, what did Roberto tell you?"

"Just that you two are an item."

"Like I told you on the phone, we've been spending a lot of time together. He's very special to me, and I know what you must be thinking, but it's not like that. He's not like Scott."

"I'm not thinking anything. I just want what's best for you."

"I know you do, and there's nothing to worry about."

They rode in silence the rest of the way to the Marbella, both thinking about Peter Donnelly.

When Natalie first told him of her involvement with Peter, Jack called a friend in D.C. His buddy was able to gather some intelligence on Peter Donnelly. He was 42 years old and born in Newport, Rhode Island. He attended Brown University in nearby Providence where he earned a masters in international business. His police record was clear, short of a couple traffic violations. Financial records showed Peter Donnelly was worth more than forty million dollars.

So why the fancy armored SUV? Jack knew Mexico could be a difficult place to do business, especially for Americans, but did that warrant such a vehicle? Corruption in Mexico was commonplace in government, construction, and labor, and there was always the presence of organized crime. If his daughter was going to be a constant companion of Mr. Donnelly's, maybe it was a good thing the guy had a nice armored car. Still, the whole idea made him nervous.

A few minutes later they pulled into the entrance of the Marbella Resort. The building and grounds were beautiful and looked like a Mexican oasis.

"Gorgeous, isn't it?" Natalie said as they pulled into a giant portico. "Oh look, there's Peter!"

A doorman walked quickly to the SUV, opening the doors for both Jack and Natalie.

"Welcome to the Marbella," said Peter, extending his hand. "It's wonderful to finally meet you, Jack. I've heard so much about you from Natalie."

"Yeah, nice to meet you, Peter. And thanks for inviting us to dinner."

"My pleasure. I'm sorry I wasn't there when you arrived, Jack. Business, I hope you understand."

"No worries."

"Right this way."

The three walked through the opulent lobby to the elevators. Jack eyed the beautiful marble and tile. This should have been Frito's job, he thought.

"So, Jack, how was your trip?"

"Hot and dusty, as usual. But worth it. I'm just happy to see Natalie and the beach again."

"Well, the chef has something special planned for us. I hope you're both hungry."

"Starving," said Natalie.

"I'm feeling like a burger, how about you guys?"

The campaign rally at Butterfield Park had run long and it was getting dark. Mick talked with the few remaining supporters while Chuck, Mia, and the others cleaned up and packed everything away. By nightfall, the candidate, Mia, and Chuck were alone in the parking lot under a beautiful full moon. They had all been so busy they hadn't had time to eat. All three were famished.

"Burgers? I thought you were trying to eat healthy, Dad."

"Ah, come on, Mia. YOLO. Let's go to Crave." Crave was a popular new burger bistro not far from the park.

"YOLO? What the hell is that, Dad?"

"Come on, Mia, get with it. YOLO. You only live once."

"And where, may I ask, did you pick that up?"

"I know a lot more than you think I do, young lady."

Mick laughed. "He did work his tail off today, Mia. And so did you.

I'm with Chuck on this one, let's splurge."

Mia looked at the two men in her life and realized she had little choice but to go along.

"All right, but I'm hitting the gym tomorrow. And I'm counting on you, Dad, to make sure I go."

The dinner rush at Crave was long past and they were able to get a table and order right away.

"I think the rally went well today, what do you guys think?" asked Mick.

"We had a good turnout," Chuck said. "And we handed out every last flyer. People seemed to have a good time, and your speech, short and sweet, seemed to click with people. I would call the day a success."

"Do we have the team of people set up to make calls on election day reminding folks to get out and vote?" asked Mick.

"Yep, we've got nearly a hundred people signed up," responded Chuck. "I think I got at least twenty signed up just today."

"We need to hit our social media efforts really hard. We've only got ten days until the election," Mia added.

"I've been really pleased with the Facebook and Twitter efforts. I knew this social media stuff would be big, but I had no idea how effective it could be," said Mick.

"I will touch base with Andy—he's been coordinating all that stuff," Mia said.

The waitress soon arrived with the food. The booth was filled with the scent of burgers, fries, and onion rings.

"Chuck, there's one more thing I need you to do for me."

"What's that, Sheriff?" Chuck asked.

"Pass the ketchup."

"These scallops are simply amazing. Best I've ever had," Jack said.

"Glad you like them, Jack. We buy them from a guy who catches them off the shore just south of here."

The tapas style feast consisted of one exceptional dish after another, and Peter, Natalie, and Jack enjoyed it all from the private patio at the top of the Marbella. The views of the Sea of Cortez were spectacular, with stars lighting up the sky and a full moon glistening off the water.

"So Peter, what initially brought you to Puerto Peñasco?" Jack asked.

"Probably the same things that brought you here," Peter said. "The sea, the beach, a relaxed lifestyle you don't find in many places. It's a perfect place to escape, don't you think?"

Jack and Natalie shared an unsure glance.

"After all, isn't everyone really running from something? Could be a dead-end job, some stressful situation, a bad relationship… I look at Puerto Peñasco as a refuge."

"If you boys will excuse me for a moment, I have some freshening up to do."

Both gentlemen stood as Natalie rose from the table.

"Natalie tells me you have many business interests here."

"Yes, that's true. I've been very fortunate and have enjoyed some success here. It all started with a restaurant down in the port. We really catered to the tourists, providing authentic local cuisine with an emphasis on fresh seafood, and the concept worked. I opened a second restaurant, then a third, and so on. From there, my company moved into the charter fishing business. It became clear to me that people were willing to spend large amounts of money for a high-end experience. Clean boats with friendly crews, great food, comfortable accommodations, you get the picture. From there we got into real estate, then hotels—first the Bonita, the small place just down the row."

"And then this place, the Marbella?"

"This was my dream. Several years back I went down to Cabo, and while I was there I took notice of the many beautiful high-end hotels along the beach. Puerto Peñasco was missing that kind of luxury, so I made it my mission to build one here."

"Marbella—is that Spanish for something?'

"No, actually it was my wife's name. She died of cancer several years ago and I wanted to honor her memory."

"Oh, Peter, I am so sorry. I didn't know about your wife."

"Thank you, Jack. It was a very difficult time. She was only 35 when she passed."

"The place is certainly beautiful. You should be proud of what you've created here to honor her memory."

"Thank you, Jack."

The two men looked out onto the dark sea until Natalie returned. Peter stood, pulling out the chair for her.

"Your father was just asking me about my time here in Puerto Peñasco."

Jack offered, "I have to say, what you've built here is pretty impressive, Peter. Not many people could pull this off."

"Well, thanks, Jack. You are too kind."

"Do you mind if I ask you a personal question, Peter?"

"Not at all Jack, what is it?"

"I couldn't help but notice that the car you sent today for Natalie and me—am I correct in saying that it was an armored car?"

"Armored car?" Natalie asked. "What are you talking about?"

"Your father is very observant, Natalie. And yes, the car that brought you here tonight, the one you're in most of the time, Natalie, is designed for security. We have three such vehicles. Remember, this is Mexico. We are a hotel that is frequented by government officials, movie stars, musical artists, professional athletes..."

"Any organized crime figures?" Jack asked.

"Well, I really have no way of knowing about that. We don't ask for a resume when we take reservations. But keep in mind, security is a constant concern in everything we do."

"Peter is a bit overprotective of me," Natalie added with a trace of embarrassment.

"I was just curious, and I apologize if I came off a bit nosy," Jack said.

"Not a problem, Jack. And if Natalie were my daughter, I would want to know as well. But now, Natalie, I think it's time to show Jack his surprise."

"Oh, yes! You're going to love it."

"What surprise?"

"You're staying here, tonight," Natalie told him. "Peter wants to give you the Marbella experience."

"But—"

"We brought your bag. I sneaked it out while you were getting ready, so you have no excuses."

"Yes, Jack," Peter told him. "Please, I'd like you to be our guest. You'll love the Marbella."

"I'm sure I will. Thank you for dinner, by the way. It was fantastic."

"It was my pleasure. Natalie, shall we show your father his room?"

Jack had been in a few penthouse apartments and high-priced homes before but nothing prepared him for the extravagance of the Viejo Suite at the Marbella.

"What do you think?" asked Natalie.

"Oh my God, it's amazing," stammered Jack.

"Jack, welcome to our finest suite here at the Marbella. I hope you enjoy your time here."

"Wow. That's about all I can say. It's unbelievable."

The suite was enormous. There were floor to ceiling windows throughout, all providing panoramic views of the Sea of Cortez. The furnishings were modern Mediterranean, and the entire suite had a comfortable yet elegant feel. A huge balcony featured a large dining area and an outdoor master suite complete with a king size bed and television for relaxing under the stars. Inside, there was another master suite, with an en suite bath nearly as large as Jack's apartment. It had a Jacuzzi tub, steam room, and sauna. Off the main parlor was a large kitchen and a wine cellar the size of a large bedroom.

"I don't know much about wine," Jack said, taking a bottle from one of the racks, "but if I decide to fall off the wagon tonight, what would this one cost me?"

"You have good taste, Jack. I'm not exactly sure, but I believe a bottle of a 1990 Chateau Margaux runs $4,000 here in the suite."

Jack shook his head as they walked back into the main parlor where Natalie was waiting.

"Beautiful, huh?"

"It's certainly impressive. I don't know what to say. What does a room like this run, if you don't mind me asking?"

Peter responded, "Fifteen thousand a night, twenty on weekends. But the room comes with lots of extras, anything from golf at our private club to sports fishing, as well as complete spa privileges and private in-room treatments. Anything our guests desire, we provide. The rate is actually quite competitive, Jack. A comparable suite in Cabo would run twenty-five to thirty thousand per night."

"Well, on my cop's salary, I could afford about fifteen minutes in here," Jack added.

Peter and Natalie smiled, pleased they could provide Jack with something special.

"Well, the suite isn't being used right now, so we want you to enjoy it. Relax. Play some golf, get a massage, or just enjoy the view."

"My God, are you sure you don't have anyone wanting to stay here? I mean, if Brad and what's-her-name show up—I mean, I can go back to the condo. I wouldn't want you to lose any business, Peter."

"That's a deal, Jack. If they drop by we'll boot you out of here."

Natalie jumped in, "You deserve this. You've done so much for me. So please accept Peter's hospitality and stay in the suite, okay?"

Jack looked at Natalie and then Peter.

"All right, but if some hot shot celebrity shows up, seriously, I'll just sneak out. There has to be a back door in this place, right? I mean, it might take me half an hour to find it..."

"Very good, enjoy it," Peter said. "We'll let you get some rest after your long trip."

Natalie hugged Jack. "I'm so glad you're here. I'll call you in the morning."

Before Peter left, he turned to Jack and asked, "Tomorrow, if you have time, I'd like it if you and Natalie could join me again for dinner."

"Sure, Peter, that sounds great."

Out of earshot from Natalie, Peter asked quietly, "And I'd like to talk with you privately beforehand, if you don't mind."

"If Brad and his wife don't show up, I'm sure I can fit you in."

FORTY-TWO

Exasperated, Mark Archer sat across the large wooden desk from Sheriff Cole Connelly. He had asked for a meeting to plan the sheriff's retirement ceremony. Connelly was a very popular figure with the rank and file of the RCSO, and Archer knew it would be an emotional time for many. But the sheriff was having none of it and instead was focused on organizing the piles of paperwork that covered his desk.

"Look, how about I just quietly clean out my office, shake some hands, and get the hell out of here?"

Archer tried to convince him there were certain things expected from their leader on such an occasion.

"If you really want help with my retirement, you can persuade my wife to go to Scottsdale so I can play a little golf in the sun. But she wants to go to Florida and see the grandkids. Can you find me some numbers that show it rains too much down in Florida this time of year? I gotta convince her…"

"I'll see what I can do, Sheriff. So do you want input in planning this ceremony or should I just plan it myself?"

"Lieutenant Archer, we've worked together for what? Ten, twelve years?"

"Yes, sir."

"So you know when I don't give a rat's ass?"

"Yes sir, I do. I'll put things together and just tell you what time to be there."

"Perfect."

"And because you're such a good boss, I'll see if I can't find a great fare to Arizona. Mrs. Connelly loves a good deal."

"Good thinking, Mark. I like that."

"I'll get on it, sir," Archer said, smiling as he got up to leave. He was going to miss the old man.

"One other thing," Connelly said, pushing a piece of paper toward Archer. "See if you can get this in tomorrow's paper."

Intrigued, Archer scanned the handwritten statement.

"You're endorsing Mick McCallister?"

"He's a good man. Now let me know if you find a deal on those Scottsdale tickets. No luggage fees, either—I don't want to pay $200 to get my clubs there."

Father Jon was surprised to hear back from his friend so quickly.

"Hello, Jon. I've got some information for you."

"Wow, Diego, that was fast."

"My friend made some inquiries and learned that someone named Jack Keller purchased a condo in Puerto Peñasco eight years ago. The U.S. address he gave was in St. Louis, so that seems to match up."

Father Jon grabbed a pen and began scratching down the details. "Puerto Peñasco? Where is that and how do you get there?"

"It's on the Sea of Cortez, an hour or so south of the Arizona border. Closest big U.S. city would be Tucson. There aren't many direct flights into Puerto Peñasco, so you can get there by car or by shuttle bus. Catching one of those shuttles in Tucson is probably your best bet."

"So, that means a border stop for people coming from the U.S. down to this town, correct?"

"Yes, you will need your passport."

"Have you got an address for the condo?"

"Sure, it's 1030 Portofino Way in Puerto Peñasco."

"Diego, I can't thank you enough for doing this for me."

"You're welcome, but I have to tell you, I'm a bit intrigued."

"Look, I'll tell you all about it once things come together. Is that fair?"

"Sure, that's fine."

"I'll be in contact. Thank you, my friend."

Father Jon hung up and immediately dialed his friend Monsignor Thomas Sutton. Sutton was retired but lived in a neighboring parish, and was still happy to provide backup when needed. As he waited, he typed in the URL of a discount travel site on his computer.

"Hi, Monsignor. It's Father Jon. How are you doing? Good... Hey, I was wondering if you would be kind enough to fill in for me here at St. Joe's for a few days. I need to leave town..."

It was mid-morning by the time Jack Keller woke from his deep sleep. He slowly sat up and took in the pristine view from the Marbella.

He shuffled to the master bath and splashed his face with cool water. In the parlor, a breakfast tray had been set out on the table with fresh fruit, an assortment of Mexican breads, and a pot of fresh coffee. Jack poured himself a cup and sat down at the table, taking in the enormity of the room in the sunlight. The coffee was piping hot. It must have been delivered just minutes ago, he thought.

Jack then remembered that Natalie had promised to call in the morning, and he realized that he may not have heard the call. He went to his suitcase and dug out the burner phone. Sure enough, he had one missed call and one message.

"Hey, I hope you're still sleeping. I'm at the mission school and just wanted to invite you here so I can introduce you to the kids. If you don't sleep too late, maybe we can grab a quick lunch. Maybe tamales? I can get away during lunch period from 12:15 to 1:00. If not, I'll see you tonight for dinner."

Jack smiled at the thought of seeing Natalie in action with her kids. He looked at his watch and saw that it was just after 9:30. He had plenty of time to get to the school, he thought. Jack called down to the front desk.

"Buenos dias, señor Keller, how can I help you?"

"I was wondering if I could get a cab to the mission school, maybe around 10:15 this morning."

"We have a driver for you, and he's standing by to take you anywhere you'd like to go."

"Well, thank you very much," he said, glancing out at the sea. A fishing boat caught his eye.

"You're quite welcome. Is there anything else I can do for you?"

"Come to think of it, Mr. Donnelly mentioned there might be an opportunity to do some fishing."

"Certainly, I can have the captain ready for you at your convenience."

Jack thought about it. Donnelly had offered and it might be rude if he didn't accept.

"Would it be okay if I brought a friend?"

The Pueblo, Colorado *Young at Heart* seniors group had been planning their bus trip to Puerto Peñasco for more than a year. The week long trip, billed as the "Run to the Sun," would allow the seniors an opportunity to stock up on low-cost Mexican drugs that ordinarily required a written doctor's prescription in the states. As an added bonus, organizers had planned a couple of stopovers at Indian casinos along the way known for loose slots and generous buffets.

After the bus pulled up to the modest beachside motel in Puerto Peñasco, Nick Fetzer, Sergeant-at-Arms for the group, began coordinating the offloading of luggage, as his wife Carol went in to fetch the room keys. As the men sorted through the luggage piled alongside the coach, they eyed the slick, black SUV cruising by.

"Next time, we go in one of those, Fetzer," Nate chided him. "That's traveling in style."

Jack chuckled at the sight of the pasty senior citizens unloading luggage from a tour bus. He realized he was nearing the age where he'd qualify to go on a trip like that but vowed to himself to never wear socks with sandals.

A few minutes later, the SUV arrived at the mission School where Jack asked Miguel the driver to wait with the car. As Jack walked into the modest two-story brick building he could hear the sounds of the children's voices echoing from inside.

"Buenos días, señor. I am Father Fidel, and you must be Jack. Natalie has told us much about you. Please come in, welcome to our school."

"Thank you, Father," Jack replied. "It's nice to meet you. Natalie has mentioned you many times."

"Gracias señor, we are very blessed to have Natalie as part of our staff. She is wonderful with the children and is doing a fine job helping them learn to speak English. Come, let me take you to Natalie's classroom."

Father Fidel walked Jack down a long hallway, passing several rooms. As they passed by an open door with a sign that read "Office," a female voice called out to them.

"Padre Fidel, teléfono."

"Oh, can you excuse me, Jack? Natalie is in classroom number two, down near the end of the hall. Please, go right in. I know she's expecting you."

Jack thanked the priest and walked the rest of the way down the hall, stopping just outside the door of her classroom. He quietly peeked in and watched his daughter for a minute or so and was impressed with her patience and the genuine rapport she had with the kids. Natalie finally noticed him, smiled, and ushered him inside.

Father Fidel took the phone call in his office. "Of course, Father Jon, you are welcome to stay in our rectory."

Such requests were very common, and when asked, a parish priest almost always offered a room to a fellow traveling priest. Many American clergy had discovered the beauty of Puerto Peñasco and visited each year. Father Fidel enjoyed the company.

"You're from Colorado, you said? Well, that's fine. We will see you tomorrow then."

"Niños, vengan acá. Tenemos un invitado especial," Natalie said as she gathered the kids around in a circle. Jack awkwardly sat in a tiny chair. Natalie chuckled at her father as he tried to get comfortable, with his knees nearly touching his chest. A little boy plopped himself down on her lap and looked shyly at Jack. Natalie instinctively put her arm around the child, offering comfort while at the same time working to settle the other kids. It didn't take long. The kids clearly loved Natalie.

"Ninos, quiero presentantarles a un famoso policía de los Estados Unidos, el señor Jack Keller," Natalie said, introducing him to the class.

"Señor Keller, would you like to read a book to the kids?" Natalie asked her father with a sly grin.

"Natalie, it's been a long time since my high school Spanish class. I'm not sure I could pull off story time en español."

The kids giggled and Natalie smiled, too.

"But I'll give it a go."

After their time in the classroom, Natalie took her father to lunch at Juan's Cafe, where she introduced him to Juan and all the regulars.

After lunch, Natalie returned to her classroom, and Jack met up with Frito for an afternoon of fishing. With Captain Dave at the helm, the trio had a great time on the water, landing a couple of nice sized Dorados, commonly known as Mahi-Mahi. Captain Dave let Jack know the chef at the Marbella could make a fabulous meal from the catch. Frito told the two that he'd be taking his catch home to his wife, adding that he'd put her mariscos up against the Marbella's chef's anytime.

On the way back to port, the three shared stories, jokes, and ice cold horchata. Once docked at the pier, the pair thanked Captain Dave for the afternoon of fishing and walked back to the parking lot where Miguel was waiting with the SUV.

"Nice ride, amigo," Frito said, nodding at Jack.

Jack looked at him, offered a shrug and a smile, and climbed in the back seat. "Thanks for coming, Frito," Jack said. "I'll call you mañana."

FORTY-THREE

Mick and Mia marched into the house with boxes filled with campaign materials—buttons, signs, and bumper stickers—all the things they carted from one campaign stop to the next. The two had spent the afternoon shaking hands at the mall and then visiting a large manufacturing plant. By the end of the day, they were exhausted and ready for a glass of wine and a nice dinner.

They dumped the boxes in the front hallway and headed for the kitchen. "Hey, Dad, we're home. Something smells good!"

"Hi guys. I picked up some pizza," Chuck said with a grin. "Keeping it warm in the oven. Why don't you open a bottle of wine?"

Mick's cell phone buzzed. "McCallister," he said. "That's great news! Thanks for letting me know, Mark. Okay, talk to you soon."

"What gives?" Mia asked as Mick ended the call.

"That was Mark Archer. Tomorrow morning Sheriff Connelly is going to announce that he's endorsing me for sheriff. Mark says Connelly wanted to wait until it was close to the election for maximum impact."

"Wow, that's fabulous, Mick, congratulations!" Mia responded excitedly.

"And there's more. Archer says he talked to Anita Sanchez from the paper. They conducted a telephone poll and the numbers have us up by six points, plus or minus three," Mick grinned.

Mia handed a glass to each of the men in her life, and raised hers. "Here's to a new sheriff in town!"

"Your chef is amazing," Jack said to Peter as they relaxed after dinner on the balcony of Jack's suite.

"I think a little credit should go to our fisherman, don't you, Natalie?" Peter said.

"Here, here," she added, holding up a glass of wine in a toast to her father. "The mahi-mahi was delicious. But if you gentlemen don't mind, I'm going to slip inside and do some work I need for school tomorrow. Can you manage without me for a little while?'

"Of course. Jack and I will be just fine."

Natalie gave each a quick kiss and went inside. Peter watched as she disappeared into the suite.

"Jack," he said quietly. "I'm glad we have a few minutes alone. I have something I'd like to talk to you about."

"What's on your mind, Peter?"

"As you know, Natalie is a very special woman, and I love her very much. I never thought I would find anyone after my wife passed, but I have. I intend to ask her to marry me, and I'd like your blessing."

Jack didn't know what to say, his emotions mixed; he certainly wanted the best for his daughter, and while he had some concerns about Peter and his business dealings, he did seem to treat her well. At the same time, he was concerned about her past life and what would happen if Peter ever learned of the events that transpired in Colorado. He knew it wasn't his place to tell Peter about her past, but if marriage was in their future, perhaps it would be best if Natalie did. It was a conversation he would need to have with his daughter.

"Peter, I know you two have grown close over the past several months, but I didn't see this coming."

"Your daughter means the world to me and you have my assurances that I will be a wonderful husband to her. So do I have your blessing?"

Jack didn't respond. In addition to his concerns about Peter, he was also worried about the attention a high-profile marriage would bring to his daughter. Being married to a man like Peter would likely put her in the spotlight.

"Jack, am I to interpret your silence as a 'no' to my question?"

Jack took a deep breath and realized there was little he could do.

"Of course you have my blessing, Peter. I can see Natalie loves you very much, and I wish the two of you nothing but the best. I know you will be a great husband to her."

"Wonderful," Peter said, relieved, and reached over to shake Jack's hand. Both looked inside to be sure Natalie wasn't in view.

"I take it she doesn't know?"

"No," Peter answered, "I'd like to ask her tomorrow night. I'm planning a little get together at the beach house."

"Works for me," answered Jack.

"I want to pop the question at the place we first met."

"Nice touch, Peter," Jack said.

"Thank you, Jack. I'm so glad you can be a part of it. And thank you for your blessing. It means a great deal to me."

"My pleasure, Peter. But I do have one request."

"Anything, Jack."

"Please don't take offense. I'm very grateful for your hospitality here. The Marbella is amazing, but I'm just a simple guy and if you don't mind, tomorrow I'd kinda like to go back to my place. I miss it a little."

Peter chuckled. "No offense taken, Jack. But I should warn you, Natalie's planned a little something for you for tomorrow afternoon here at the Marbella."

"Like what?"

"Don't let on I told you. You'll have to act surprised." Peter laughed.

"Okay, Peter, what am I doing tomorrow?"

"You, sir, are booked for a spa day."

Jack lay on the king size bed in the giant master suite struggling to sleep. His arms ached from battling the Dorado and his mind raced contemplating Peter's marriage proposal. While Jack was happy his daughter had found a new life, he knew the old one could come back to haunt her at any time.

Peter had the means to give Natalie the world. Jack could only offer fatherly advice from an imperfect father.

FORTY-FOUR

Colorado seniors Nick Fetzer, Nate Goldstein, and Buck Wells had broken off from the rest of the *Young at Heart* group and were enjoying lunch and a few beers at Juan's Café. They were scheduled for an afternoon fishing trip and were busy discussing a wager. As they were setting the ground rules, Natalie walked in.

"Geez, look at that, will ya… She's gorgeous," Buck whispered to the other two, as they quietly watched Natalie order her lunch at the front counter.

"It's simple," Nick told them. "Everybody throws in twenty bucks and the biggest fish takes it all."

"What does second place get?" Nate asked.

"Nothing, ya putz," Nick responded. "There's only three of us."

The seniors struggled to focus as Natalie passed their table carrying her lunch on a tray.

"How are you today, young lady?" Nate asked.

"Good, thanks," Natalie said, pulling out a lesson plan to study in hopes of sending a message that she was too busy to talk. The message wasn't received.

"Excuse me, miss," Buck said, "but you sure look familiar."

Nick elbowed him. "What kinda line is that?" he whispered under his breath.

Nate added, "No, he's right. You do look familiar, miss. You're not from Colorado, by chance? We just got in from Pueblo."

Natalie's heart stopped. "No, sorry," she said, shaking her head to emphasize the point.

"I could swear I've seen you before," said Buck. "I wouldn't forget someone as pretty as you."

"You're embarrassing this poor woman, leave her alone," Nick chided, finishing off the last of his third beer.

"Well, if you don't mind me asking, where are you from?" Buck asked her, turning his chair toward Natalie.

Natalie suddenly struggled to get a breath. She panicked and just wanted to get out of there.

"Um, I'm from Missouri. Sorry, I just realized I'm late for an appointment."

"I've been to Branson, are you from there?" asked Nate.

"No, sorry," Natalie said as she stood from the table. Her bag caught the tip of her chair, spilling the contents on the floor.

"Let me help you," Nick offered.

"No, thank you, I've got it. Sorry. I'm really late."

Natalie shoved everything back into her bag and rushed from the café, leaving her lunch behind.

"Jesus," Nick said. "Neither of you morons know how to talk to a pretty woman. That was an embarrassment."

"Yeah, whatever, Casanova. I'm getting another round," answered Nate.

"All right guys, biggest fish wins, twenty bucks a man, pony up."

Just around the corner, inside one of the many shops along the busy malecón, Muriel Hardaway and Carol Freel bartered with the shopkeeper over the purchase of some Mexican pottery.

"Por favor, dos dollars, American," Muriel said loudly.

The shopkeeper, who spoke perfect English, played along.

"Por todo?" he asked, swirling his finger around the stack of bowls.

"Sí, for all of them."

As the bartering continued, Natalie rushed into the small shop, quickly grabbing an oversized straw hat and a large pair of sunglasses. She moved to the counter, hoping to pay for the items and get out quickly.

"Veintiocho," the shopkeeper told the tourists.

"Disculpe, señor," Natalie interrupted, holding up the hat and glasses with one hand and offering a twenty-dollar bill with the other.

"Sí, gracias," the shopkeeper responded, taking the cash happily.

"Do I know you?" Carol asked Natalie. With her heart racing, Natalie quickly put on the glasses, responded with a "No, sorry," and rushed out of the shop.

"Did you see that woman, Muriel? She looks like someone I know. I just can't place her."

"You're right. She looks like someone from back home," Muriel answered.

Carol stuck her head out of the shop, looking down the malecón, then glanced back at Muriel.

"Where have I seen that woman before?"

Natalie rushed back to the mission school and locked herself in the staff bathroom, closing the stall door behind her. Just as she sat on the toilet seat a buzz came from the cell phone in her bag. With trembling hands she pulled out the burner phone, but saw there was nothing displayed on the screen. She dug through the bag again, searching for the smartphone she used locally. On the screen was a text from Peter.

"All set 4 tonight. Can't wait...luv u," it read.

Peter, my God, she thought... What if he found out, what would he do? Natalie suddenly felt more trapped than when she was in

Colorado. In the span of an hour, she felt as though she had completely lost control. She always knew there was the possibility someone could recognize her, but fear and reality were starkly different. Where could she go, she thought? She had to do something, maybe her father…

Natalie grabbed the burner phone and dialed. "Please pick up," she whispered to herself.

The call went to Jack's voicemail. She hit redial again and again but got his voicemail each time. One more time, she thought, and dialed the number.

"Please pick up."

At Spa Marbella, Jack leaned back into the shampoo basin. He was scheduled for a haircut, manicure, and massage and while he knew this was supposed to be relaxing, he really just felt silly.

"Relax, señor, we'll take good care of you, just lean back," the beautician told him.

His reticence about the procedure faded rapidly as the woman began to massage his scalp.

"Is okay, señor?"

"Ah, yes. Gracias."

Down the hall in the men's locker room, Jack's burner phone buzzed again and again inside locker 16.

Father Jon's trip to Puerto Peñasco took nearly twelve hours, and it was late afternoon by the time he arrived at the mission church. Father Fidel welcomed him warmly.

"I'm so glad you could pay us a visit. I always enjoy it when American priests come down for a little getaway. Let me show you to your room where you will be staying."

"That sounds great, Father Fidel. Thanks again for putting me up for a couple of days."

"My pleasure, and please, just call me Fidel."

"Thank you, I will do that. Actually, once I get settled in my room I was hoping you could give me a little assistance. I'm hoping to meet up with an old friend here in town. I have an address, and I was hoping you could give me directions."

"Got a minute, Captain?" Mark Archer asked, poking his head in Mick's office.

"Sure, what's up?"

"I just wanted to stop by and wish you luck on the debate tonight."

"I was just going over my notes preparing for it. I spoke with Tracy Ladd this morning and she outlined the format they plan to use. She said they will have three reporters asking questions and a phone operator taking questions from people watching from home."

"Yep, that's the plan," Archer said. "Keep your answers short and to the point. You've got a lot of experience on TV, so this should be a cakewalk. Got any questions for me?"

"I think I got it, Mark, thanks. Oh, I'm curious, what's your take on the News-Press poll?"

"Anita Sanchez tells me they did a pretty big sampling. You never know, but with a six point lead and an error rate of three points either way, I'd say you're in pretty good shape. Unless, of course, you screw up this debate, then it could go either way."

"Thanks for the vote of confidence. I'll keep that in mind if I actually win this damn thing. I've always thought your office should be down in the dungeon. You know that space next to the shooting range?" the Captain teased.

"Duly noted. You're gonna be fine."

"Thanks again, Mark."

Unable to reach her father, Natalie sat in the bathroom stall, trembling. She'd been in Puerto Peñasco for nearly a year without any issues or problems. Why was she suddenly being recognized? Had something happened with Scott Lennox? Was her face back on the news? She had to get back to the condo and find out.

Natalie snuck out the side door of the mission school and began walking a circuitous route through the local neighborhoods to avoid the tourists. As she reached the condo, Natalie stopped dead in her tracks, quickly ducking behind an old truck parked on the street. There was a man in black pants and a short sleeve black shirt knocking on her door. She peered around the truck to gain a better look. Who could it be? The Mexican authorities? Maybe a detective from Colorado? Her heart pounded beneath the thin sundress, now drenched in sweat. Should she run? Where to? She would only draw attention to herself. She felt trapped, like a caged animal.

Father Jon knocked again, but there was no answer. He wasn't sure if Jack was inside and didn't want to come to the door or if there was simply no one there. But he had traveled more than a thousand miles and he wasn't ready to leave just yet. The priest looked around at the cars in the parking lot and along the street, but they offered no clues. All the vehicles but one had Mexican plates; the other was from California.

He stood on the porch and continued to knock, thinking about what he would say to fugitive Lisa Sullivan, assuming that his hunch was right and she was there. He would tell her that he knew she was wanted by the authorities in Colorado, and that she needed to turn herself in. It just seemed better that way; if she would voluntarily turn herself in, she stood a better chance at a lesser charge, and ultimately face less time in prison for her role in Lombard's death. If he simply alerted Colorado authorities, and they went to Mexico to make the arrest, things for Lisa Sullivan would likely turn out far worse.

Father Jon felt he owed that much to Jack, given he only learned about Sullivan's involvement in the murder through their conversation on Castle Trail. Further, if she did turn herself in, Jack's involvement in the entire fiasco wouldn't have to be revealed. She could simply walk into the sheriff's department and say she was tired of running and wanted the ordeal to end. Father Jon considered it a good trade off, though he knew Jack would likely never see it that way.

He rapped on the door again but got no answer. Perhaps Jack or Lisa were out on the patio. He took the path around the building to the beach side. He knocked on the glass patio door but still got no response. Holding his hands up to block the sun, he peered in through the glass. He sighed in frustration. No one was home.

"Can I help you, sir?" a man called out from the beach. "Are you looking for somebody?"

The man looked to be American and was older, probably in his seventies. He wore shorts and a golf shirt and was well tanned. He approached the patio.

"Oh, yes, thank you," Father Jon told him. "I'm trying to find my friend Jack Keller, but he doesn't appear to be home. I guess I should have called first."

"Ah, I thought you might be up to no good. Sorry, Mister."

"Father, actually. Father Jon Foley. I'm visiting from Colorado," he said, offering his hand.

"Oh, nice to meet you, Father. I'm Herb Whitten. I live two doors down. So you're here to see Jack, Natalie, or both?"

"Well, actually I'm looking for either one," he responded, wondering who Natalie might be.

"I haven't seen Jack for a couple days, but Natalie's been around. She usually gets home from work around five. So she should be here in a bit."

Father Jon glanced down at his watch and saw that it was just after four.

"Okay, I think I'll wait for them. I appreciate the help."

Father Jon looked around the patio and then at the beach, wondering how he'd kill the time.

"You're more than welcome to join me for happy hour, Father. I was about to pour myself a cool one. You interested?"

"That's very kind of you, Herb."

After all, he had nothing to do and looked a little silly on the beach in long black pants. Maybe he could learn something. The pair walked to Herb's unit and climbed a set of stairs to his deck.

"What would you like? I've got anything and everything in my bar inside—pick your poison."

"Actually, a Diet Coke would be great, if you have one."

Herb was disappointed. He had hoped to enjoy a cold beer or highball with the Padre, but whatever, he had some Diet Coke.

"I can do that. Be right back."

Herb disappeared through his sliding glass door and returned a minute later with the soda in one hand and what appeared to be scotch or bourbon in the other.

"Cheers," said Father Jon, raising his glass.

"And Roebuck," responded Herb.

"Excuse me?" said the priest.

"Sorry, old habit. I'm retired from Sears. That was something we all said back in the day when I was a hard-working executive stiff."

"That's very funny. I'll have to remember that one."

"So where did you say you're from again, Father? You don't look like you're from around these parts."

"Castle Springs, Colorado. It's a town south of Denver. I have a parish there."

"Well, good for you. I'm sure that's challenging work... being a priest and all."

"Yeah, it has its moments."

"So, how do you know Jack and Natalie?"

"Actually, Jack is from my parish. He's always after me to come down for a little visit. Great little place here, it's my first time to Puerto Peñasco."

"You should have seen it fifteen years ago when I moved here. It was a little slice of heaven. It wasn't crowded and prices for everything were dirt cheap, but now the tourists have discovered it, and they flock here like lemmings."

"I guess you can't really keep a place like this a secret for very long."

"Yeah, I guess. Things really changed down here when the Hollywood types started coming and hanging out. That brought the media, and then the whole world hears the name of a town they never knew existed before."

"Yeah, I can see how that could happen. So, you mentioned that Natalie usually gets back around five?" asked Father Jon.

"Give or take. Usually she's with her boyfriend. He's the rich guy in town, owns most of everything around here. It's easy to see the two of them together, as beautiful as she is."

"Yeah, that she is," responded Father Jon, now more confident than ever he'd found Lisa Sullivan.

Herb offered more small talk, giving Father Jon a rundown on the history of Puerto Peñasco, and throwing in a little bit of the town gossip.

Father Jon feigned interest, marking time with Herb on his deck while waiting for the woman named Natalie to show up.

"I'm going to pour myself another one, can I freshen your drink, Father?"

"No, I'm fine, but thanks."

Herb shuffled back inside the condo and returned quickly with another drink—this one larger than his first.

"So, when did Natalie move in down here? I remember Jack telling me about it, but I can't seem to recall," Father Jon asked, feeling a bit guilty about the fib.

"Oh, she's been here for a while now. Let me think… It could be close to a year. But hell, you get to be my age and everything blurs together. You know what I mean, Father?"

"Oh, indeed I do."

The timeframe fits, he thought. This woman Herb calls Natalie shows up in Puerto Peñasco around the time of Lisa Sullivan's disappearance. It had to be Sullivan; she's changed her name to protect her true identity. It made perfect sense. He wondered if she had changed her appearance—maybe a new hair color or hairstyle, or some cosmetic surgery. He had seen her picture many times; so even with a new hairstyle, he was confident he'd recognize her. She was not a woman one easily forgot.

"Yeah, she met up with Peter Donnelly not long after she arrived in town. He's a big player here and fell hard for her from what I hear. I think they met at one of his parties at his house about a quarter mile up the beach. The place is enormous, and he likes to throw parties there from time to time. In fact, I think he's having another one tonight. I saw them setting up while I was out on my afternoon walk."

Father Jon peered at his watch. Perhaps the best plan would be to return to the rectory and try to find her at the boyfriend's house later that night.

"You say those parties Mr. Donnelly holds—they're right on the beach?"

"Yup. They put lights up on the patio and make a big bonfire. It's always a pretty swanky affair. One night, I was walking by and they invited me in for a drink. You can't miss the place. Take a walk the right time of night and you might get invited, too."

"I may just do that, Herb. In fact, I'd better get on my way. Thank you for your hospitality. It was a real pleasure meeting you, I hope to see you again."

"Any time, Padre, you have yourself a good one."

Father Jon began the walk back to the rectory. He hadn't recalled ever crashing a party, even as a teenager. Tonight would be a first.

Afraid to go inside the condo, Natalie eyed a cab and quickly flagged it down. She slumped into the back seat.

"Hotel Marbella," she said as she reached into her purse for her cell phone. Again, the call to her father went to voicemail. "Rapido, por favor," she pleaded to the driver.

Jack couldn't remember the last time he was this relaxed, and the thought of checking his cell phone for messages simply hadn't crossed his mind. The ninety minute massage had done the trick—and given all the stresses and concerns that were weighing on him, he was surprised at how easily they had melted away.

As he checked out of the spa, Jack tried to offer a tip but got nowhere.

"That is not necessary, Mr. Keller. I hope you enjoyed your day with us."

"I really did, it was great."

"I'm glad to hear that. The front desk has notified us that your bags have been transferred, and your driver is waiting in the lobby."

"Oh, great, thank you. And I gotta tell you, I think I'm as relaxed right now as I've ever been. Thank you for everything."

"It's our pleasure, sir. I hope you come back and visit us again at Spa Marbella."

"I may just do that."

Jack left the spa and walked across the lobby to the entrance of the Marbella where Miguel was waiting with the SUV.

Just as the SUV pulled away, Natalie's taxi pulled up to the front gate.

FORTY-FIVE

"Señor Donnelly, everything is set for the party this evening."

"Thank you, Juana," Donnelly said.

"And señor Pacheco is here to see you."

"Please send him in," Peter told her from behind the large, Spanish desk in his home office. The room was fully equipped with high-tech accessories including a high-definition television mounted on the wall tuned to an American business channel. Stock ticker symbols crawled across the bottom of the screen.

The visitor knocked on the open door. "Señor Donnelly?"

"Manuel, my friend, please come in."

"Thank you. I hope you like what I have selected for you and Miss Natalie. But I brought several other rings for you to look at as well," he said, tapping the attaché case in his lap.

Manuel Pacheco was a local jeweler that catered to tourists visiting Puerto Peñasco. He opened his first store in the port area fifteen years earlier, selling mostly inexpensive baubles and trinkets. His business changed dramatically after Peter Donnelly invited him to open a shop within the Marbella Hotel to cater to the high-end vacationer. Peter saw something in the young man that made him believe he would be a good fit at the Marbella. Manuel owed his success to Peter Donnelly and was hoping he would be pleased with the engagement ring he had designed specially for him.

"I'm sure I will love it, but most importantly I want Natalie to love it."

"Of course," he replied, nodding and pulling a small, elegant box from his case.

"Wow, it's beautiful."

"The diamond is a near flawless, four carat princess cut. An exquisite gem, really. The aquamarine gemstones on either side are as you requested, to match Miss Natalie's eyes and the Sea of Cortez."

"You've outdone yourself, Manuel. It's perfect."

Jack arrived home, opened the doors to let the breeze in, dropped onto the sofa and nodded off. The buzz from his burner phone brought him back.

"Hey."

"Where have you been?" Natalie asked, clearly panicked.

"You sent me to the spa, remember? I'm back at the condo now. Why, what's wrong? Where are you?"

"Was the man there?"

"What man? There's no man here."

"There was a man at the door of the condo earlier. I'm afraid he's with the police."

"Whoa, why do you think the police were here?"

"There were these tourists in town and they were from Colorado. Everywhere I went they looked at me and said I looked familiar."

"Did anyone say anything specifically about the Lombard case?"

"No, but they knew. They knew!"

"Knew what? Did anyone ask if you were Lisa Sullivan?"

"No, but they knew. And then there was this man at the door. I'm so afraid."

"Natalie, I need you to calm down and tell me what happened. Tell me about the people in town. You said they were tourists?"

After she calmed down, Natalie was able to tell Jack about her run-ins with the Colorado seniors, as well as the man at the door of the condo.

"Look, we went over this before," he told her gently. "Things like this can happen. That's why it's important to keep a low profile and be aware of your surroundings at all times. The tourists have probably already forgotten you—maybe they noticed you were American and were just making conversation. And as far as the man at the door—it could very well have been a neighbor looking to borrow some sugar, who knows? But I really don't think you have anything to worry about."

"Are you sure?" Natalie asked, calming down.

"Yeah, I'm sure, but I'll see if I can check it out. Where are you right now?"

"I'm at the Marbella. I tried to come home, but then I saw the man…"

"Okay. Just stay put until I check on things. As soon as I know what's going on, I'll give you a call."

"Okay, so you don't think I've got anything to worry about?"

"I'm sure things are fine, but just to be safe stay at the Marbella until you hear back from me. Okay?"

"Okay, sorry if I freaked out a bit."

Once off the phone with Natalie, Jack called Frito. He had family and friends everywhere, including some who were tight with the local federales. If there was something brewing, Frito could find out what it was.

"Ten minutes to air," barked the floor director at Castle Springs Cable.

The studio was small and cold. The set for the debate was a small riser with two director's chairs. Captain Mick McCallister sat stage left and the other chair was empty as candidate Jerry Griffith had yet to arrive. Few were surprised as Griffith had a habit of showing up at the last minute to campaign events.

Moderator Tracy Ladd sat at a small desk stage left of the riser. A table for the reporters was positioned right of that and faced the candidates: from left to right sat Anita Sanchez from the News-Press, Marisa Coleman from KUCU-TV in Castle Springs, and Rich Gordon from KNPG News radio.

"What if he doesn't show?" Gordon asked Ladd, glancing at his watch.

"Then I guess you guys will be asking questions of Captain McCallister and an empty chair."

The reporters chuckled, almost wishing for the chance. Just then, the doors swung open and candidate Jerry Griffith ambled in.

"Nice of you to join us, Jerry," Ladd said. "If you just sit right there next to the captain, we'll get you mic'd up."

"Mick, good to see you," Griffith said, extending his hand. He had a seedy, used car salesman look—both in appearance and personality. His light blue sports jacket and plaid tie didn't help.

"Anita, Marisa, Rich, good to see you, thanks for coming," he said, offering a quick wave to the three seated at the table.

"Five minutes!" called out the floor director as Ladd went over the ground rules one more time for Griffith's benefit. The live, televised debate would run one hour and then be aired several more times on local cable in the days leading up to the election.

Mick eyed himself in the monitor and sat up straight. He wore a dark navy suit with a white shirt and a green tie Mia had picked out for him. She'd said it made him look presidential.

"Fifteen seconds!" the floor director called out. "Stand by!"

"Dad, it's starting!" Mia called out from the living room. "Hurry up!"

"I'm coming," Chuck said as he rushed in with a big blue bowl of popcorn.

"I can't believe you made popcorn."

"What? You don't want any?" Chuck replied, "More for me, then."

"Butter?"

"Of course."

"Lemme try that," Mia said, grabbing the bowl. "There's Mick. Doesn't he look handsome in that suit?"

"Very nice. I'll get another bowl," Chuck said.

"It's Frito," said the voice through the front door of Jack's condo. Jack peered through the peephole and saw his friend standing on the porch. He opened the door and let Frito inside.

"I called my cousin. He knows everything that happens here."

"And what did you find out?"

"Nada. Only thing that happened today was a tourist bus headed north broke down a few hours ago. The federales charged the driver a couple hundred dollars to call a mechanic. He said the bus got fixed and left town. Otherwise, nothing going on in Puerto Peñasco, and he would know."

"That's what I thought," Jack said.

"You okay, señor Jack?"

"I'm fine, Frito. Natalie just got a little spooked this afternoon."

"No hay problema. I keep my ears open."

Jack called Natalie with the news.

"Oh, thank God," she said. "I was so scared."

"Looks like it was nothing," he said, trying to offer some comfort. "But it's a good reminder for you. Maybe you shouldn't be so high profile around here."

"Are you saying I shouldn't be with Peter?"

"Not at all. Look, we can talk about it tonight at the party," Jack told her.

"Oh no, the party! Look at the time! I don't even have a dress here!"

After finishing her call with Jack, Natalie immediately dialed Sarah at Summer Fling to see if she could run a dress by the Marbella on her way to the party. Sarah was happy to oblige. After all, she brought outfits to the Marbella for high society women all the time. Natalie had certainly become "high society" in Puerto Peñasco.

FORTY-SIX

J ack finished getting dressed and took a Diet Coke out onto the beach to enjoy the sea breeze until it was time to go. He was still struggling with Peter's engagement plans, but it certainly was a beautiful night for a proposal.

"Hey, neighbor, how's it going?"

Jack turned and saw his neighbor Herb waving from his deck.

"Good, Herb, how about you?"

"Doing great, thanks. Hey, did you meet up with your friend the priest?"

"I'm sorry?" Jack said.

"Your priest friend from Colorado came by earlier. Said his name was Jon Foley—a helluva nice guy."

Forty-five minutes into the debate and no clear winner had emerged. Mick had come off as more professional, but Griffith had focused on his lengthy law enforcement career and it seemed to resonate.

"We have a question from a caller in Lynnbrook," Tracy Ladd told the candidates. "She would like to know, if elected, what changes you would make to the sheriff's department. Chief Griffith, let's start with you."

"The RCSO under Jerry Griffith would be a department that gets things done," he said firmly. "Take this Lombard murder case, for example. The way the captain here has handled it, well it's just not very good police work. It's been almost a year, and they're really nowhere on the case. At one point, they had a suspect in custody, and yet they let him walk out of jail. Meanwhile, you have a woman on the run and the RCSO has done nothing to get her into custody. As sheriff, I won't rest until those responsible for the Lombard killing are brought to justice."

Ladd jumped in. "Captain McCallister, would you like to respond?"

"The Lombard case is complicated, and—"

Griffith cut him off, "C'mon Captain, every murder case is," making quotes with his hands, "complicated. That's a cop-out, and you know it."

"Not at all, Jerry. The Lombard case is complicated, but we will bring the people responsible for the death of Mr. Lombard to justice. Now, if you want to talk about open cases, we should talk about the Garcia gang killings. Those took place nearly twenty years ago in Castle Springs. There's never been an arrest in those cases. And what about the retaliation murders of Chen Liu and Bobby Nguyen? Again, there have been no arrests made by the CSPD in those homicide cases."

"That's not the same thing, and you know it..." interrupted Griffith, but the captain would have none of it. He was on a roll.

"You say you're running on your record, but you want to pick and choose what parts of that record the voters should consider. And I'm guessing you don't want to talk about three of your officers suing your department over promotional policies that discriminate against minorities."

Mick was firm and measured in his attacks. Griffith was clearly rattled. Sweat began to bead on his upper lip, his face slowly turning a crimson color.

"Those lawsuits were settled out of court, and the department admitted no wrongdoing!" Griffith barked at Mick. "And as for my record, in the thirty-one years I served at Castle Springs PD, we had a total of eleven homicides, but we only lost one good citizen. And in that case, the suspect was convicted and is in prison today."

There was dead silence. It took a second or two for the full weight of Griffith's words to sink in to those sitting in the studio.

Tracy Ladd couldn't believe what she'd just heard and wasn't going to let it go. "Chief, could you clarify for us what you mean when you say there were eleven people murdered, but only one was a good citizen? Are you suggesting that as sheriff, murder cases involving victims with criminal records will be treated differently? I think we're all aware that in the James Ponder murder, where you got a conviction, the victim was white. In the other ten cases, the victims were either Latino or Asian. Are you saying their families don't deserve justice?"

"Woohoo!" Chuck shouted as he leapt to his feet, spilling the popcorn onto the floor. They didn't care and exchanged high fives.

"Thanks for being such a dumbass!" Mia yelled at the TV.

Sasha was jolted from a deep sleep on the couch but seized the opportunity to quickly gobble up the popcorn. Griffith stuttered a denial and tried to backtrack from his comments, but the damage was done.

It was Jack's first visit to Peter's beach house, and not surprisingly, the place exceeded his expectations. Peter saw him from the patio, immediately excused himself from his guests, walked into the house, and greeted Jack with a quick hug.

"Do you think she has any idea?" Peter asked.

"I talked with her on the phone an hour ago. She has no clue," Jack assured him. "She was running a little late, though."

"I'm used to that, Jack. Please, let me show you around."

Peter gave him a quick tour of the house. The place had the same feeling as the Marbella—elegant but relaxed. After the tour, they walked out to the patio where a crowd was gathered around the fire pit.

"Everyone, I'd like to introduce you to Natalie's father, Jack. He is visiting us from Colorado."

The guests all raised their glasses towards Jack. After meeting everyone, Peter pulled Jack aside.

"My plan is to walk Natalie down to the beach during dinner and pop the question there. I'll announce it to the group when we return, assuming she says yes."

Father Jon had no trouble finding Peter's beach house. Herb had said that it was just a short distance up the beach from Jack's condo, and while it was not yet completely dark, the patio lights and glowing fire pit made it easy to find. He approached the house from the beach, careful not to be noticed, stopping some fifty yards away. After watching the guests for a few minutes, he spotted Jack with a gentleman who seemed to be familiar with everyone present.

He figured the man had to be Peter Donnelly, the one Herb said Lisa Sullivan, or Natalie as he called her, had been dating. As Jack and the man talked, a member of the wait staff approached and said something to the two. The man quickly left and went back inside the house, leaving Jack to mingle with the guests. A few minutes later he came back, this time with a woman. The pair held hands as they greeted the guests.

Father Jon wandered along the shore to avoid suspicion and angled for a better view. The woman was striking, that was certain, but her hair looked different from what he remembered from Lisa Sullivan's photographs. The couple crossed the patio together beneath a string of lights. The light cast upon her face for just a few seconds, but it was enough for Father Jon to be certain that it was indeed Lisa Sullivan. He wondered if Peter Donnelly knew the truth about Lisa and her troubles in Colorado. But to Father Jon, it didn't really matter.

Jack watched Peter and Natalie work the crowd. He struggled whether or not to tell his daughter who had been at their door earlier in the day. After his talk with Herb, Jack was certain it had been Father Jon, and the priest wasn't likely to go away. Still, Jack didn't want to ruin Peter's proposal. He would deal with Father Jon tomorrow.

Lost in thought, Jack felt a tug on his arm.

"Jack, you look like you're a million miles away. Is everything all right?" asked Peter.

Jack gazed at Peter and then at his daughter. They were a beautiful couple.

"Oh, I'm fine. I just cannot get over how great your place is, that's all. Here we are, practically neighbors, and this is the first time I've ever been here," replied Jack.

"Well, it will be the first of many visits, Jack. Oh, where are my manners? You have nothing to drink. What can I get you, Jack?"

"Oh, a Diet Coke would be great. Thanks, Peter."

"I'll be right back," Peter replied and turned towards the house.

Once Peter was out of earshot, Jack asked Natalie, "Are you recovered from today?"

"I think so, but those tourists scared me to death," she replied quietly. "You were right. No matter what I do or where I go, I'll never be able to escape what happened in Colorado. Living here I somehow convinced myself I was free, that I had managed to escape my past. Now I'm not so sure that running away is the answer, but I don't see any alternative. I'm just trapped in this lie. Maybe—"

As Natalie was whispered her concerns, the two heard the sound of a man loudly clearing his throat as a shadowy figure approached.

"Hello, Lisa, my name is Father Jon Foley. I'm from St. Joseph's parish in Castle Springs, and I don't believe we've ever met," he said, extending his hand.

A look of utter disbelief crossed Natalie's face. She didn't respond or shake the priest's hand. The sound of her old name brought a wave a nausea.

"You're the man outside the condo today," she said blankly.

Before Father Jon could respond, Jack grabbed the priest by the arm and pulled him toward the beach, away from the rest of the guests. Natalie stood there on the patio, staring, too stunned to move.

"What the hell are you doing here?"

"I think you know, Jack. I've been very patient with you. But you don't return any of my calls, so I've decided to force the issue. It's been almost a year, and the time has come for you to do the right thing."

"Oh, for God's sake. Are you still hung up on that?"

"Your daughter is a fugitive, and she needs to turn herself in."

"And what if she doesn't?"

At least Jack wasn't denying the woman was Lisa Sullivan, Father Jon thought.

"Then I will return to Colorado and notify the authorities. I met your boss the other day at a campaign rally. I'm sure Captain McCallister and your former partner Mia Serrano would be interested to hear what I have to say."

"Father, I could have her out of Mexico and hidden somewhere else before the authorities in Colorado could get here. It's not like they can call down here to the local police and have her detained. The police here don't work that way. Things here take time; there are channels you have to go through, and they are certainly open to the occasional bribe."

"Jack, do you really want her to be on the run for the rest of her life?"

"Better than the alternative."

"But you're forgetting something. If she doesn't turn herself in, and you force me to take action, then your involvement in all this comes out. Your career will be over. I would guess you could even be facing some prison time for aiding and abetting. And if she decides to run again, you know it's just a matter of time before she's caught. She won't have your help anymore; she'll be on her own. And we both know she won't last long. And when she does get caught, she will be facing a much stiffer prison sentence than if she turns herself in voluntarily. Come on, Jack, you have to know that."

Jack stood, shaking his head.

"I don't care what happens to me. It doesn't matter, Father; you don't understand what's going on here. She met someone, a man she loves and who loves her back. That man has a ring in his pocket, and tonight he's planning to propose marriage. This is supposed to be the happiest night of her life. Now you want me to walk over there and tell her it's all over? Bullshit, it ain't gonna happen, Padre."

"Perhaps we should ask her. It's really her decision, Jack, not yours."

"She has a whole new life here. My God, she works at a school helping local kids get an education so they can hopefully make something of their lives. Father, don't take all that away. Remember the 'greater good?'"

There was that phrase again, Father Jon thought. The same one Jack had used in Colorado.

Both men stared at one another defiantly.

"I'm going over there, Jack. I need to talk to her."

"No, you're not. It ain't gonna happen. You are going to get off this beach and go back to Colorado. Do you understand me?"

Father Jon ignored him and started toward Natalie. Jack moved to cut him off.

"Don't do this, Jack."

The pair were quickly headed to a physical confrontation but were interrupted.

"Hello, I don't think we've met," Peter Donnelly said. "I'm Peter Donnelly. Is there a problem here?"

As if in slow motion, Natalie felt her new life slipping away. She didn't know how or why this priest was involved, but it was clear he knew who she was. The realization crashed down upon her. The charade would soon be over. But she wanted to end it on her terms.

She walked directly toward them. Her eyes locked with the man who had tracked her to Mexico.

"Lisa, it's time to do the right thing," Father Jon said gently.

"Lisa? There has obviously been some kind of mix-up, Father. This is Natalie Summers," offered Peter.

There were somber faces all around him. Peter realized something was very wrong. "Can someone please tell me what the hell is going on?"

"Peter, I need to tell you something," Natalie said.

"What? What is it?"

"My God, I don't even know where to begin."

"Natalie, what is it?"

Tears began flowing down her cheeks.

"Please, forgive me, please, please, forgive me, Peter."

"For what? What did you do? I don't know what's going on..."

"My name isn't Natalie Summers. It's Lisa Sullivan."

"What?"

"My name is Lisa Sullivan, and I'm here in Mexico because I'm hiding."

"Hiding from what?"

"Peter, I am so sorry... I'm hiding from the police. I can explain."

"The police? Your father is a cop... How can you be hiding from the police?"

"Peter, let me explain," said Jack. "Lisa got caught up in a bad situation in Colorado, and the police are looking for her. I helped her come here to Puerto Peñasco."

Peter looked incredulously at Jack and then at Lisa.

"What bad situation? Did you rob a bank or something?"

Lisa shook her head, "No, nothing like that."

"Then, what?"

Jack began to offer an explanation, but Lisa cut him off.

"Let me tell him. I owe him that much." Natalie took a deep breath and began. "About a year ago, I was involved with a man in Colorado. I lived there, near Denver. I thought I loved him, but really, I didn't. I realized that later but only after it was too late."

"Too late for what? Did he hurt you?" Peter asked, his body tensing.

"No… It wasn't that. He was married—he lied to me about that. I only found out about his wife long after the relationship had started."

Lisa realized just how stupid she sounded, falling for a married man. She was embarrassed retelling the story to Peter, but she knew the worst part of it had yet to be told.

"So… Why are the police after you?"

"The man I was involved with had a business that was having financial difficulties. He was looking for a way to solve his money problems, divorce his wife, and marry me—at least that's what he told me."

"Did he commit fraud? Embezzle money? What?"

"A few years ago, to help the company financially, he brought on a business partner. But that didn't really help, and so he came up with an idea that would solve all his problems."

"And what was that?"

Lisa paused, finding it difficult to tell the next part of the story. Jack stepped in.

"The guy then, on his own…"

Lisa interrupted, "That's okay. Let me tell it. I need to start owning up to things… The guy, his name is Scott Lennox, plotted to kill his partner and collect the life insurance money. He said with the money he could walk away from the business, get the divorce, and be with me."

Peter's eyes widened. He looked like he was going to be sick.

"Scott killed him, and I helped him cover it up."

Lisa was spilling everything. It had been stewing inside her for so long, she just wanted to purge herself of the secrets and lies.

"Scott made the death look like an accident, like his partner had been hit by a car. Scott ran him down, and then we staged it to make it look like I had accidentally hit him. He was already dead, though. The police came and interviewed me, and at first they believed it was an accident. Eventually, they tried to arrest us, but they only caught him because I ran away and came here. That's when I met you. God, I am so sorry, Peter. I love you so much, and now everything is coming apart."

Peter didn't move, his eyes fixed on the waves as his dream crashed on the beach.

"I meant to tell you, but it was never the right time. I was scared that you'd leave me. I couldn't bear the thought of you not being in my life. I fell in love with you the night we met... You had me by the time we sat down for dinner."

Peter turned to Jack. "And you've been hiding her down here? Doesn't that break some moral code? Some sort of police oath?"

"I've made some mistakes in my life, Peter, but this isn't one of them."

"Seems like a pretty big one to me, Jack."

Father Jon interrupted.

"Look, I'm certainly no expert on the criminal justice system, but listening to all that has been said here, I may have some ideas how to best proceed."

"I'd like to hear it," answered Lisa.

"First off, you must turn yourself in. That's imperative and non-negotiable. If you don't, I will go public with all this. It's the right thing to do, and it has to be done. Period."

Jack started to object, but Lisa stepped in.

"I want to hear the rest."

Peter's mind was reeling. Twenty minutes ago, he was planning his proposal. Now his life had been turned upside down.

Father Jon continued, "You turn yourself in, saying that you are tired of running and you feel the need to set things right. You don't tell anyone where you've been, and you do not acknowledge that Jack is your father. There is nothing really that connects all those dots. You get yourself a top-notch attorney who can negotiate the best possible plea bargain. He stresses the fact that you were only an accomplice in this crime and that Scott was the sole mastermind behind the murder. He tells the court that you have a clean record and that you are truly sorry for your involvement in this horrible crime. He stresses to the court that you returned to Colorado voluntarily because you knew it was the right thing to do."

Lisa turned to Jack. "Do you think this is possible?"

"Yeah, it could play out that way. But you never know how plea bargain deals might go. Sometimes the DA wants to play hardball, and that's what concerns me. You're a pretty good catch for him—one that he and the RCSO might want to play up to the media and the public. But they need to be careful, though, because having you back in custody wasn't really due to anything they did. That could be an angle the media plays up. One wildcard in all this is Election Day is just a few days away. The RCSO will have a new sheriff—probably my boss Mick McCallister, and the DA is in a dogfight to keep his job. He may not even win re-election from what I hear, it's too close to call."

"I don't know about the politics," Father Jon said. "But I can't allow you to wait. I'm sorry, Lisa, but you need to go back to Castle Springs right away."

Peter held out his hand, bringing the discussion to a halt. "I'd like a few minutes alone with Natalie. Do you mind?"

"No, of course not," answered Jack.

"Okay with you, Father?"

"Certainly."

Peter silently guided her to the beach. They stopped short of the waves lapping on the shore and stood eye to eye.

Lisa had grown to love Peter deeply, but had no idea how he'd react. She ached at the pain she had caused him.

"Natalie… Can I call you that?"

"Of course."

"You will always be Natalie to me, no matter what happens."

"Okay, Peter."

"I'm trying my best to process all this, but my God—I'm numb."

"I know. So am I."

"Not exactly the way I pictured this day ending," Peter added, quietly touching the small box in his jacket pocket.

"I'm so sorry, Peter. I should have told you. I came so close so many times. I just couldn't do it. I was so scared that you'd leave me."

"You should have told me. If I had known all this it wouldn't have changed anything between us. It just would have allowed me to prepare for if and when this day ever came."

"So, what do you think I should do?"

"If our relationship isn't built on trust and honesty, we have nothing. You need to do what's right and live the truth. I can't make you any promises, but I can say that I love you very much. But we can't build a life on a lie. You should go. I can only hope that someday you'll come back to me, and I hope I can be here for you."

Natalie saw the pain in his face.

"Just know, I love you," she said. "I always have. I'm so sorry."

"I'm sorry, too. Now go."

She turned and gazed at the moonlight reflecting off the water. Natalie stole a final glance at the man she loved and walked back up the beach to her father. Jack put his arm around his daughter and pulled her close.

Together they left Puerto Peñasco toward a new reckoning.

FORTY-SEVEN

Lisa did her best to hold her emotions in check, mostly staring straight ahead, sitting between the two men that helped her escape to Mexico. Now, the three were crammed into the cab of Frito's truck, making their way north. She was leaving the place she thought of as her home and leaving behind the man she loved. She had no idea when or if she would ever return or if she would ever see Peter again. The pain of leaving him was raw, but Lisa's resolve was strong. It was time to do the right thing for her father and for herself.

Frito dropped the pair at the airport in Tuscon where Jack picked up a rental car for the rest of the trip to Colorado. Jack drove the rest of the way, very careful not to draw the attention of the highway patrol. He had rehearsed a story about how he had tracked Lisa down in the event they were pulled over and she was recognized. He wouldn't need the story, as they made long trip without a hitch.

The hotel was one of a dozen located just off Pena Boulevard near the Denver airport. Jack knew that hundreds of travelers went through the place each day, and the staff would be too busy to remember faces. Besides, they wouldn't be needing much time.

After checking into the hotel and getting Lisa settled in the room,

Jack returned the rental car to the airport and retrieved his pickup from the long term lot. He stopped off at a nearby strip mall for new burner phones and something to eat.

"Hope you're hungry. I grabbed a pizza on the way back," he said to Lisa upon his return.

She didn't respond.

"I also got you another phone—one you should use for the attorney. If you pop open the soda, I'll serve up the pizza. Then, when you're ready you can make the call."

"I'm scared," Lisa said.

Jack hugged his daughter. He held her close, feeling her warm tears through his sleeve. "I know, sweetie, everything's going to be okay."

Danny Velasco was a far cry from the slick, well dressed, defense attorneys that smiled from billboards off the freeway. He was fifty pounds overweight, balding, and wore ill-fitting, off-the-rack suits. He was, however, a hell of a lawyer with a reputation for playing hardball with prosecutors and securing favorable deals for his clients. Jack Keller had seen Velasco work his magic on more than one occasion.

Divorced and the father of two grown children, work consumed his life. On this particular Friday night, he was sitting in his apartment watching a movie on cable and looking over a case file when his cell phone rang.

"Danny Velasco."

"Mr. Velasco, my name is Lisa Sullivan, and I need an attorney. You were recommended to me."

"Lisa Sullivan? I'm sorry, your name sounds familiar, but I can't place it. Have we met?"

"No, we've never met, Mr. Velasco. The Rocklin County Sheriff is looking for me in connection with the George Lombard murder."

Velasco certainly recalled the case that captivated Coloradans months earlier. He could still picture the woman RCSO had sought in connection with the investigation. He also remembered Branch Kramer's bloody mouth.

"Right, of course. The Scott Lennox case. So, what can I do for you?"

"I want to turn myself in, and I need your help to do this. I want to stay out of prison, and I want Scott Lennox to pay for what he did."

"I don't do pro bono work. Can you pay?"

"Yes."

"Can I ask who referred you?"

"I'd rather not say."

"Where are you now?"

"I'm in a hotel near DIA."

"Good. Do you have time right now to tell me about the case?'

"Yes, I can do that."

"Okay, let's start from the beginning. Tell me everything…"

Lisa carefully and methodically told Velasco the story, from the time she first met Scott to the trip back from Mexico. He told Lisa he needed to make a call and that he'd get back to her shortly. Lisa gave him the number to the new burner phone.

Velasco flipped through his contacts for Dave Baxter's personal cell number. Generally, he dealt with assistant DAs, but this time, he'd go straight to the top.

"Baxter."

"Dave, Danny Velasco."

"Hey, Danny. Listen, I'm walking into a fundraiser right now," he replied, irritated. "The election, you know?"

"I think you'll want to hear me out on this one, Dave. I have a new client you may be interested in talking to—her name is Lisa Sullivan."

"Hang on."

Velasco suspected Baxter was finding a quiet place to talk. It was nearly a minute before he came back on the line.

"You're in contact with Lisa Sullivan?"

"I am, and she may be willing to give up her boyfriend in the Lombard killing."

"I have a campaign speech in twenty minutes, let me call you once I finish with it. If we can get something done quickly, I may be open to a deal."

Of course he's interested in a quick deal, Velasco thought. The election was four days away. He had the DA just where he wanted him.

Jack and Lisa were both startled by the buzz of the phone.

"Go ahead, let's see what Danny has to say."

Lisa put the call on speaker. "Hello?"

"It's Danny Velasco. I talked with the DA. We're going to negotiate a proffer hearing. Do you know what that is?"

"A proffer? No, I don't know what that is," she replied, turning to Jack.

He gave her a thumbs up.

Velasco continued, "That's when the DA gives you immunity for a short period of time in order to hear your testimony in the case. Based on that testimony, the DA will either agree to a deal or not. Your testimony has to be completely truthful. Either way, you get to walk out the door when you finish the hearing. If we agree to a deal, then you'll have to testify at trial. If we don't, then you're back to where you are now. There's no real risk and you get to decide. That's why they call it 'Queen for a Day.' Listen Lisa, this is what I do. I get clients good deals. Do you understand?"

"I think so."

"So do you want to move forward?"

Lisa again looked to Jack for guidance. He nodded.

"Yes, I do."

"I will do everything in my power to keep you out of prison. You stay put until you hear from me. It'll probably be mid to late morning tomorrow before I call you again. Once things are in place, I will have one of my assistants come and pick you up and bring you to the DA's office in Castle Springs. Sound okay?"

"Yes, that sounds good. Thank you for your help." Lisa hung up and turned to Jack.

"Okay, the wheels are in motion. You gonna be okay?" he asked.

Lisa nodded, trying to contain her emotions.

"You want me to stay with you?"

"No, I've got to do this on my own. Besides, you've taken enough chances. I've got to stand on my own two feet now."

"Okay, but call if you need me," Jack told her.

"So, when will I see you again?" Lisa asked as Jack prepared to go.

"In all likelihood, tomorrow sometime. It sounds like this thing will happen fast, and typically they will have the lead investigator present for the proffer hearing. If I am there, you can't let on."

"I know. But having you there will help."

They hugged tightly.

"It's gonna be okay."

"I know... I love you, Dad."

The words caught him off guard. "I love you too, Lisa," he whispered. "See you soon."

Jack waited until he was down the hall before allowing the tears to fall. By the time he reached his truck, he was nearly sobbing. He couldn't recall Lisa ever calling him "Dad" as a child, and he certainly never heard the words "I love you" from her before.

Inside the truck, Jack Keller struggled for the strength to turn the ignition. The emotions churned deep inside him, welling up until he could no longer hold them back.

FORTY-EIGHT

The district attorney's office filled the fourth, fifth, and sixth floors of the county courts building in the RC Justice Center complex. On weekdays, the office was buzzing with activity, but on a Saturday morning, the place was deserted except for a small group huddled in a large corner office on the sixth floor.

"C'mon, Danny, get real. I can't let her walk," said Baxter after hearing Velasco's pitch.

"Dave, I told you what she's prepared to offer as far as testimony against Lennox. She's handing him to you on a fucking silver platter. Five years probation is more than fair."

"She pleads accessory to murder, ten years suspended," Baxter said flatly.

"You're wasting my time. Do you want her disappearing again? She's proven she knows how to do it. You guys didn't have a clue where to find her. My client has a mind of her own, and I'm telling you she'll be in the wind in a heartbeat if the deal isn't to her liking."

"Jesus, RCSO is going to flip out."

Velasco wasn't sympathetic to Baxter's concern. "With all due respect, Dave, your election is no sure thing, so your current relationship with RCSO is the least of your worries right now. But if you can pop Lennox before the election, it could be just what you need to put you over the top."

Baxter was irritated at Velasco's arrogance, but the DA was nothing if not pragmatic. He knew Danny was right; he and his client were holding all the cards at the moment.

"Obstruction, five years suspended, two probation. And the deal goes away after today."

"Okay, then, I'll have her here in an hour."

Keller stood outside the Justice Center building waiting for McCallister. The captain had called some forty-five minutes earlier saying the DA had requested a one o'clock meeting regarding the Lombard case, saying it was important.

McCallister was none too happy about it. He was called away from the campaign and time was short. Baxter had simply told him there was a development in the case but offered no other details. As he and Serrano came around the corner toward the entrance, Keller shot them a quizzical look.

"What is she doing here?" he asked, unlocking the door with his RCSO ID card.

"What do you think, Jack?" Mia snapped as they entered the elevator.

"I really don't know."

"Jack, knock it off. It's her case, too."

"Whatever you say, boss," responded Jack, shrugging his shoulders.

The trio left the elevator and walked through the glass doors of the district attorney's office. As they approached Baxter's office, a clerk appeared.

"Conference room. They're waiting."

Dave Baxter, Deputy DA Phil Killebrew, and a stenographer were standing over the conference table. Danny Velasco and his client were sitting at the table, facing the doorway.

The door swung open and McCallister, Keller, and Serrano all marched in.

"Okay, Dave, what's so important?"

"Everyone, I think you all know Lisa Sullivan."

"Holy shit," the captain muttered.

Sullivan had changed her hair color and was deeply tanned, but there she was. They were in the same room with the woman they'd spent nearly a year searching for.

"What are the rules here?" Keller asked the DA.

"Miss Sullivan is 'Queen for a Day,'" Baxter said.

McCallister couldn't contain himself, "Dave, can we have a word?"

Baxter looked around. He didn't like McCallister's tone but thought it best to react calmly. "Sure, Mick, we can talk in the hallway."

The two left the others in the conference room and faced off down the hall, out of earshot.

"I feel a bit railroaded here, Dave, and I don't appreciate it. What kind of deal are you offering her?"

"Come on, Mick, we do proffers all the time. This is a good deal for both of us. It will enable us to bury Lennox for doing the murder. Yeah, Sullivan makes out on the deal but so what? She wasn't the mastermind behind it. And I don't need to remind you the election is in three days. We can go re-arrest Lennox and make a big splash with this story—and it may just help us both. If we don't like the story and don't think she can get us a conviction, we can back out."

"I don't give a fuck about the election. What are we offering her?"

"Obstruction on the statements at the accident scene. Five years suspended, two probation. Now don't go all high and mighty on me, Mick."

Mick took a deep breath, "We need to do what's right, and offering her immunity for her testimony is bullshit. You know it, and I know it."

Baxter shook his head. "You have a lot to learn, Mick. The deal is done. Right now, you and your team need to get her testimony and make sure that statement is iron clad. Let's get to it."

Testimony given under a proffer agreement is protected from prosecution. Danny Velasco had secured immunity for Lisa in exchange for her testimony, but there was a caveat. If the investigators found inconsistencies or felt the story wouldn't hold up in court, Lisa Sullivan would walk away and the deal would be rescinded. The process of piecing together her testimony took nearly ten hours.

"Okay, Dave," Velasco said, exhausted leaning back in his chair. "My client delivered. We have a deal, right?"

"Give us a minute, Danny," responded Baxter.

Baxter, Killebrew, McCallister, Keller, and Serrano gathered in the DA's office.

"I'm confident that we can get at least manslaughter, possibly murder two," Baxter said.

"Manslaughter?" McCallister said angrily. "Are you kidding me? It's premeditated all the way and Lennox did it for financial gain. This is a murder case!"

"I'd rather go with what we are sure of and that's manslaughter."

"Dave, we need more from her. I can't accept this deal."

Baxter's anger was building as he eyed McCallister.

"That almost sounds like a threat. Tell me I'm mistaken, Captain."

"You're hearing me loud and clear. She's an accessory to murder and we can't let her walk in exchange for just manslaughter on Lennox. He'll be out in four years, if we're lucky."

"May I remind you all that you had almost a year to find Lisa Sullivan and came up with nothing. If we back out now and she walks out that door, she's gone for good and so is our case on Lennox."

"We'll find her," Serrano chimed in.

"Oh, you'll make an effort this time, Investigator? Forget it, you had your chance. Now this is my ballgame."

Tension and silence filled the office until McCallister spoke up. "There is another option. It could give us what we need for murder one."

FORTY-NINE

"**A**re you fucking kidding me, Dave?"

Baxter had taken Velasco down the hallway, leaving everyone else behind in the conference room. He wasn't happy with what he was hearing from the DA.

"Look, Danny, I know it's not exactly what we've been discussing today, but we haven't signed off on anything, and I think we need more from your client before we agree to immunity. We're not getting as much from her as you promised."

"I don't believe you. I negotiate in good faith and then you renege on the deal?"

"It wasn't a done deal, Danny. We've gone over the testimony and it really only amounts to manslaughter on Lennox. We need a murder conviction here and Lisa Sullivan can still give it to us."

"And you want my client to wear a wire and go meet with the guy who murdered a man?"

"Yes, and don't forget she played a significant role in that homicide. Look, when she wears the wire we will have law enforcement standing by everywhere to ensure her safety. We do this kind of thing a lot, Danny. And if she does this she won't see a day in custody. It's what she wants, you said that yourself."

"I don't like this, Dave, not one bit."

"Look, Danny, I need this," Baxter said, and in a lowered voice offered, "I'm just asking for a little consideration here."

Velasco couldn't believe the audacity of the district attorney. Was he really asking him to compromise his client's interests? Danny shook his head as the options and angles played out in his mind. If he threw Baxter the bone he was asking for, it could prove helpful down the road. The DA would owe him big time and the leverage wouldn't hurt the next time he needed to cut a plea deal, assuming he was still the DA. If everything went down as proposed, this might even help Baxter win reelection. That was a good chit to have and who knew when he might need to cash it in. It wasn't like they were reneging on jail time, they just needed her to wear a wire to snag the boyfriend.

"So help me, Dave, if anything happens to my client it will be a career ender for you. I will hang you by the balls from the fucking foul pole at Coors Field. And one more thing. You can forget probation. Misdemeanor obstruction, five years suspended for the false statements, and she walks when this is over. Period."

"Okay, Danny, fine. And nothing's going to happen to her. She'll go in, get him to say something incriminating, and then get the hell out. Easy peasy."

Baxter and Velasco walked back to the conference room where the others were waiting.

"I need a moment with my client," Velasco said, nodding to Lisa. "Let's step out into the hall."

Lisa's eyes got big, and she fought the urge to look to her father. The attorney and his client left and walked down the hallway.

"Look, the DA wants to play hardball, and he says he won't give you immunity unless you wear a wire. He wants you to meet with Lennox and get him to admit that he killed Lombard."

"What are you talking about?"

"I'm sorry, Lisa, but he's adamant. Without the wire, there's no deal. Now, if you are dead set against it, you are free to walk out of here. I don't know that returning to a life on the run is what you want, but you still have that option."

"I can't do that—I can't face that man. Forget it, no deal."

"Then you will need to disappear again. But if you agree, they'll also drop the probation. Lisa, a suspended sentence on a misdemeanor is a glorified parking ticket. You walk when this is over. You'll be free."

Boxed in, Lisa considered her attorney's advice. She had felt a sense of relief when she had returned from Mexico, like a giant weight had been lifted from her. Things with Peter had ended horribly, and she desperately hoped to make things right. But now, Lisa felt the rug had been pulled out from under her. She wished she could somehow talk it over with her father.

"If I agree to wear this wire, how do I know I'll be safe? Scott is obviously a violent person capable of murder. How do I know he won't hurt me?"

"The RCSO will have people everywhere. If he tries anything, which I think is pretty unlikely, then they will be there in a heartbeat. Remember, they need you and your testimony in court. The last thing they want is for something to happen to you."

"If I agree to do this, then what's to keep them from going back on their word again?"

"We'll go in there right now, have them write it up, and all parties will sign off on it. Done deal."

Lisa closed her eyes. "All right, I'll do it."

By Sunday afternoon, things were in place. The RCSO command vehicle was stationed in an industrial park a few blocks away from Lennox Ice. Inside, Jack and Mia went over the plan with Lisa.

"So, you've had no contact with Lennox since you fled Colorado?" Mia asked.

"No, nothing at all."

A tall man dressed in police fatigues walked in, carrying a bag. Mia looked up and nodded at the man, then looked back at Lisa and said, "This is Sergeant Low from the Electronic Surveillance Unit. He's got a special phone for you that will allow us to record everything that is said. Right now we need you to text Scott and then get him on the phone to set up the meeting."

"What should I say in the text?" Lisa asked nervously.

"Let's keep it simple. Just text, 'this is Lisa, we need to talk.'"

The sergeant handed Lisa the phone. She took a deep breath, punched in Scott's number followed by the letters, and pushed send. It didn't take long to get a response.

"OMG can u talk now? Are u alone?"

"Call me, we need 2 meet," Lisa texted back.

The phone rang immediately, startling Lisa.

"It's okay. Just keep it short and this will all be over soon," Mia said as she put on a pair of headphones. Low and Jack did the same before the Sergeant gave her the cue to pick up."

"I need to see you, Scott."

"Where are you?"

"Scott, I need help. We need to talk."

"Anything you need, baby, you know I'm here for you."

Lisa rolled her eyes in disgust. "Not on the phone. Can you see me tonight?"

"Of course, where?"

"I don't want anyone to see us. Your office at 8."

"I miss you so much, babe."

Lisa looked sick, she was filled with anger and revulsion.

"Just meet me, okay, Scott?"

"Okay, I'll be there at 8."

Lisa ended the call. The sergeant checked to make sure the call had been recorded and gave a thumbs up.

Mia called Mick to let him know the Lennox "take down" was on.

By 7:00, everyone was in place. A pair of investigators had trailed Lennox throughout the day, and were now down the block from his house ready to alert the team once he was en route to meet Sullivan.

Back in the command vehicle, Bob Brandon, a tech from the RCSO information technology unit, attached a tiny wireless microphone to a button on Sullivan's coat. Mia, Jack, and Mick looked on.

"So there's no wire, just that tiny microphone?" Lisa asked.

"Yep, we've come a long way," Brandon explained. "There's a tiny transmitter in there and we have receivers set up at the ice company and here in the truck. The mic is virtually impossible to spot."

Brandon moved over to a console to test audio levels. "Count to ten for me, Lisa. Just a normal speaking voice."

Lisa complied as Brandon listened in his headphones. "All good here, Captain," he said.

"Just give Lennox the same act you gave me on the highway that morning, and we should be good to go," Mia said.

Lisa didn't respond, but Jack wasn't going to let the comment go.

"For God's sake, Serrano, giving attitude to the state's material witness just before an undercover operation is a pretty stupid ass thing to do," he said sharply.

Mia glared back at him. Sensing the mounting the tension, Mick turned to Brandon and said, "Take Sullivan outside for some fresh air."

"Sure, Captain. C'mon, miss," he said, helping Lisa out of the truck and leaving Keller, Mia, and Mick alone.

The tension in the truck was approaching a boil. Mia played the first card. "You always come to her rescue, don't you, Jack? Makes me wonder why."

"Jesus, Mia, we've been down this road before—you and your bullshit accusations. I was just making the point that upsetting a key witness before we send her out to confront a killer isn't the best way to play it. Just saying."

The two cops both moved a step closer to each other, forcing Mick to put himself between them. Facing his senior investigator, Mick put his hand firmly on Jack's chest.

"Jack, that's enough," he said quietly.

Jack glared at McCallister, stepped back and grinned. "We all got secrets, don't we, Mick? We all have stuff we'd just as soon not share, right? Something that makes you bend the rules... not break them, just bend them. You and Mia know all about that, don't you? And really, who does it hurt if in the end we get our guy—put a cold-blooded killer behind bars. Voters like that. They like it when cops catch the bad guys. So, we do our job and all the bending the rules stuff stays tucked away. No reason to talk about it, right?"

"Are you threatening me?" Mick demanded.

"Of course he is," Mia interjected. "Go to hell, Jack."

"Mia, this is between Jack and me."

She backed off.

"No threat, Captain. Just pointing out that we all have our secrets. Like say, a junior investigator gets promoted because she's banging the boss. Or that same—"

In an instant, Mick swung at Keller, landing a punch to his left jaw. Keller staggered but didn't go down. He started to move towards Mick, but thought better of it and stopped himself.

No one spoke for several seconds. Blood trickled from the corner of Jack's mouth. He wiped it away with back of his hand.

"Don't you ever speak to me like that again, Keller, or you'll be writing fucking parking tickets for the rest of your career. Understood? And whatever issues the two of you have I am telling you to get over them, right fucking now! Got it?"

Keller nodded and looked towards Serrano.

"Got it," Mia answered.

"Good," Mick said. "Jack, get cleaned up. Then get Brandon and Sullivan back in here. Let's go over everything again. No fuck ups."

On schedule at 7:15, two snipers set up on the roof across from Lennox Ice. Undercover teams were stationed near the entrance, positioned behind garbage and recycling containers. Two additional undercover cars were parked nearby, each with two deputies slouched down out of view, ready to respond in the unlikely event a pursuit should occur. Serrano and Keller would take their positions just outside the entrance once Sullivan was inside.

At 7:48, McCallister's phone buzzed. It was a text message from the team covering Lennox's house. "The iceman cometh," it read.

McCallister chuckled, then reached for his cell to call Chuck Borman, the lieutenant in charge of the SWAT team to tell him Lennox was en route.

"Here we go, Ms. Sullivan. Just play it exactly as we've instructed," Mick told her. "Any questions?"

"No," she replied, nervously. She wanted to look at her father for some reassurance, but looked straight ahead. Lisa knew she couldn't risk it.

Scott Lennox peered frequently into the rear view mirror of his Lexus sedan. It hadn't occurred to him to watch for police. He was more afraid his wife would tail him.

He thought of Lisa waiting to meet him at the office, and became aroused. He imagined the plans they had made together coming to fruition. He smiled and cranked up the stereo as he pulled the Lexus onto the interstate toward Lennox Ice. He turned up the radio and sang along with Tripp Barnes's new country hit.

"Welcome back baby, we both know that you missed me...
You couldn't stay away, so come on then let's play...
We both know, you wanna go, don't take it slow...
Just let your pretty hair down and come and kiss me."

As their suspect pulled into the lot at Lennox Ice, the undercover officers alerted McCallister who in turn called Borman. He cued Mia and Keller.

"Lennox just pulled in."

At 8:04, Lisa arrived at Lennox Ice in an undercover RCSO car procured from drug seizure operations. The sight of Scott's Lexus sent her heart racing in fear. Still, she kept her cool and parked close to the entrance as instructed. The position of her car would offer additional cover to the SWAT team if needed. She climbed the steps of the loading platform and found the office door unlocked.

Her stomach turned at the sight of him. He stood confidently, arms extended. "Welcome back, baby," he said.

Just like the song.

Lisa felt nothing but hatred and anger. The man who had used her and taken so much of her life stood there smugly, acting as if nothing had happened.

But she did what she had to do. "It's so cold out there," she said, setting down her purse and pulling off her hat. It seemed odd to be making small talk but it was all she could muster.

"Wow, I like your new hair. God, you look sexy. I have missed you so much," he said. "Don't worry, I'll warm you up, babe. Just like before."

He came forward and kissed her. This would be far more difficult than she had imagined, but she knew she had to play along and get him to admit to the murder.

"Scott, I just had to see you. I miss you too."

"I've missed you more than you'll ever know. Where the hell have you been hiding? Ah, forget it—it doesn't matter. Now that you're back, we can make it all happen. The cops have nothing on us. We can do all those things we talked about. Just you and me… It's just about us now," Scott said, extending his hand to stroke her cheek.

Lisa was repulsed, but had to carry on. "Scott, how are we going to get out from under this? I want to be with you, but I'm so tired of running. You have no idea what it's like to be worried every second of every day. It's a living hell."

"We can make this work, don't worry," he said. Lennox put his arms around her and began to kiss her neck.

Lisa retreated slightly from his advances, looked him in the eye, and continued, "God, I wish we could take back what we did. I still have nightmares about it. I see Lombard's face in my dreams. I hear the sound of when you hit him with the car. Why did he have to die, Scott? Why?"

"It was the only way… You know that. The insurance money paves the way for our new life, it can still happen. They will have to pay out on the policy eventually. It will just take a little more time."

"I don't know how much more I can take of this. I miss you so much."

"I'll get an attorney and have him force the insurance company to pay. They can't keep stringing this along. Once I have the money, our new life together will start. You just gotta be patient."

Tears flowed down her cheeks. "I'm out of money, and I'm so tired of running."

Lennox pulled her close. Lisa let several seconds go by before cutting to the chase.

"Why did we have to kill him, Scott? I'd give anything to go back and change things. I can't live with myself knowing what we did to that poor man."

Scott held her closely, responding, "It's all been for you since the night we met. From the moment I set eyes on you, everything was about us being together, don't you see? That's why Lombard had to go. But I needed your help."

"You needed my help to kill him? Why did you get me involved, Scott? Why?"

"I needed your help to secure our future. And it's going to work, Lisa. The police have nothing. We can be together. You have to know I did this all for you. George was between us and our future, so I had no choice."

"You had to run him over?"

"Yes, and you had to help me set up the story. Don't you understand? It was all for us."

Lisa wanted to be sure the cops would have enough to make their case so she pushed a little harder.

"So you killed George Lombard for me?"

"Yes, Lisa, just like we talked about."

Lisa grabbed her hat and purse and turned to the man who caused her so much misery. "Goodbye, Scott. Rot in hell."

Lennox didn't move. His mind struggled to catch up as Lisa moved quickly. She was through the door and down the stairs to the parking lot in seconds. Lennox sprinted after her, gaining with every step. "Lisa, wait!"

Lisa slipped and dropped her keys. Scott was closing in. She left the keys and ran as fast as she could toward the street. Lennox bounded down the stairs from the loading dock and headed toward her.

In the command vehicle, McCallister grabbed his radio and shouted, "Go, go, go!"

SWAT officers stationed on the nearby roof began to zero in on Lennox with their high-powered rifles, while officers on the ground rushed in from the street. Jack and Mia quickly maneuvered their vehicle to block the exit from Lennox Ice and rushed in on foot, guns in hand.

"Freeze, Lennox!" A voice echoed from a megaphone, somewhere above. "On the ground!"

Scott stopped cold next to his car. Stunned, he realized it had all been a setup. Anger exploded from inside of him as the deputies moved quickly towards him and Lisa ran. The scene seemed to unfold in slow motion.

Lennox grasped at his only chance for escape. In a heartbeat, he jumped into his car, shoved it into gear, and gunned the engine. The deputies on the ground jumped out of the way of the speeding car. Snipers opened fire from above. The rounds pierced the Lexus as it accelerated toward Lisa.

The deputies screamed out to her, but it was too late. The car struck her from behind, tossing Lisa's body like a rag doll onto the hood of the car and over the roof. She dropped in a thud on the pavement not far from where George Lombard had come to rest nearly a year ago.

The Lexus turned sharply and slammed into a metal garbage bin, setting off the airbag. Officers swarmed the car with guns drawn as Mia and Keller rushed to Lisa Sullivan.

"Lisa!" Keller screamed. "Lisa!!!"

FIFTY

The headline on the front page of the News-Press read, "RCSO BUSTS LENNOX; Gunfire, Confession and Witness Deal in Lombard Murder Arrest." The byline belonged to Anita Sanchez, and the story covered the night's events, complete with quotes and photos from the scene. A quiet, last-minute deal struck between Mick McCallister and Sanchez gave her photographer the perfect vantage point to capture Lennox being loaded into an ambulance.

The story made the front page of every Colorado paper and was the lead on every Colorado TV newscast. But the News-Press had the most extensive coverage, thanks to the tip from McCallister. In each article, Dave Baxter offered a glowing account of the work done by his office and RCSO Captain Mick McCallister in getting Ms. Sullivan to admit to her 'small role' in covering up the killing and convincing her to "testify against the actual killer, Scott Lennox."

The media outlets were satisfied—they had another sensational murder trial to cover, and the beautiful Lisa Sullivan would be part of the prosecution's effort to put away a cold blooded killer.

Captain Mick McCallister was on his way to a last-minute campaign event when his cell phone rang.

"Hey," he said, "I saw the front page, nice work."

"I just called to say thanks." It was Anita Sanchez.

"Don't mention it," McCallister said.

"Hey listen, I'd like to be able to call you on things after you're elected sheriff tomorrow, if you don't mind. Future stories, stuff like that. I think we can have a really great working relationship."

"Absolutely, I look forward to it."

"Great, and thanks again for the heads up on the Lennox deal. It was a great story for us."

"No problem, we'll talk again soon."

While Mick McCallister was new to politics, he did understand the world of give and take. It was a savvy move on his part to give Sanchez the heads up about the Lennox takedown, knowing his photo would land on the front page of the paper the day before Rocklin County voters were set to elect a new sheriff. He had played his hand well.

At Rocklin County Community Hospital, Scott Lennox lay in a room on the second floor, recovering from two gunshot wounds to the shoulder. He was lucky to be alive. The CSI team determined that two rounds fired by SWAT officers had penetrated and passed through the driver's headrest of his Lexus, just missing Lennox. Either shot would likely have been fatal. McCallister ordered a 24/7 security detail to ensure that Lennox wouldn't attempt to somehow leave the hospital or try to harm himself. One deputy was stationed inside his room, while another stood guard outside in the hallway.

Lisa Sullivan was in a room on the fourth floor with a deputy stationed outside her door, as well. She had suffered a broken hip, wrist, and tibia and had undergone six hours of surgery overnight.

Danny Velasco was standing outside Lisa's room when Keller and Mia arrived.

"How's your client, counselor?" Jack asked.

"Pretty good, all things considered," Velasco told them. "The doc says she should be ready to testify before the grand jury in a couple weeks. She may have to do it in a wheelchair, but she should be good to go. I spoke with Dave Baxter this morning, and he said they will be adding attempted murder to the charges against Scott Lennox. You can stick a fork in him, he's done."

Just then Jack's cell went off and he excused himself. "Peter, thanks for calling me back," he said, disappearing down the hallway.

"Can I talk to her?" Mia asked.

"She's pretty doped up and not making a lot of sense right now."

Just then, a nurse walked past and into Sullivan's room.

"That's Doris. She sorta runs the place. If you want to talk to my client, she has to give the okay."

Mia walked to the doorway and poked her head in. "Excuse me, I'm Mia Serrano, and I'm an investigator with the RCSO. Any chance I can get a minute with your patient?"

"Right now I need to change some of her bandages. Can you come back later?"

"Oh, sure, that'll be fine. Sorry to be a bother, my mom was a nurse and I know how overworked you are."

It was a fib, but there was no harm in getting friendly with Sullivan's nurse, Mia thought.

"How long ago was your mom in nursing?"

"Oh, quite a while ago. She's passed now. But I know what a difference she made for her patients and how much they loved her for it."

She was laying it on a little thick, but Doris was listening and seemed appreciative.

"Your mom was right. Although it's even harder now with all the budget cutbacks. I don't even have the help I need to care for this patient. I don't know how they expect me to do this by myself. It's a two person job."

"Can I help?"

"Well, I need to change her bandages. Do you mind?"

"Not at all. What should I do?"

"When I roll her onto her side, if you could just hold her there while I put on a fresh dressing, that would be a huge help."

"I can do that."

"Wait," she responded, surveying the bandages on the tray. "There's no tape. I'll be back in a minute."

Lisa groaned and twisted in an effort to get comfortable.

With the nurse out of the room, Mia bent over the bed rail to get close to Sullivan.

"Lisa, can you hear me?" she whispered.

Sullivan mumbled, nodding her head slightly in agreement.

"Lisa, Jack's here. Do you want to talk to him?"

A slight smile appeared on the corners of her dry, cracked lips.

"You know Jack real well, don't you?"

Again, a smile.

Mia tried quickly to come up with the right questions. She looked back at the door.

"You love him, don't you?"

Again, Lisa nodded slightly and shifted in the bed. "Yuh, heesh my…"

"The things you have to do to find tape around here," announced Doris, as she returned.

Mia jumped. Lisa groaned, shifting again in her bed.

"Lisa, we're going to change your dressing now," the nurse said, before turning to Mia. "Just hold her right there and keep that gown up."

"Got it," Mia said, following the instructions.

Doris bent down and focused her attention on Lisa's back and hip.

"So they say our patient here helped you get that Lennox fella. Who was that man he killed? Weren't they business partners or something?"

"Yes," Mia responded. "His name was George Lombard."

296

"Laahmbahrd," Lisa moaned. "Hhhyaad cancer. Ah didint nahw. Caancer."

"Cancer? No, honey," Doris said, looking at Lisa, "you've got some broken bones and some ugly bruises, but there's no cancer. You're gonna be just fine."

The nurse finished with the dressing. "You can let her down now, hon."

Cancer? How did Lisa Sullivan know Lombard had cancer? There was only one person who could have told her.

Keller. That bastard.

Mia let Lisa's body roll back on the bed. As she did, Lisa cried out in pain.

"Ahhhhhh!"

"Her pain meds are wearing off," Doris told her. "I'll be back with a shot."

Mia looked down on Lisa Sullivan with disdain. Her intuition had been right all along. Sullivan had killed a man with her married boyfriend and gotten away with it. Then as police closed in, she lured Keller into her web. She and Keller deserved one another and Mia was committed to bringing them both down.

Lisa's eyes fluttered as she fought to remain conscious. Mia made sure the door was closed and then leaned in close.

"I was right about you all along. You're nothing but a whore—first Lennox and then my partner. This is not over..."

"Hurrrrthh. Owww," Lisa moaned.

"Now you know what George Lombard felt the moment you and your boyfriend killed him in cold blood."

"Laaambaahrd. Canswer! Owwwww!," Lisa bellowed. "Daaaahhhdy!," she yelled incoherently. "Daaaaaahhhhhhhd!"

Lisa began to flail on the bed, her face contorted in pain and confusion. "Helpppp," she whimpered. Then cried out again loudly. "Daaaaaahhhhhhhd!"

Mia stepped back from the bed, shaken by the scene and unsure what to do. The beeps of the pulse monitor chimed in fast rhythm.

"Daaaaaahhhhhhd!" Lisa screamed. "Daaaahhhddddeee!"

The air rushed from the room as the door pushed open and Keller burst in.

"Lisa!" he called out, pushing past Mia and leaning over his daughter.

"It's okay, babe. It's okay," he said holding her down. "Everything's okay now."

Jack stroked her hair and Lisa's fit subsided. Comforted by his touch, she gazed up at him and said "Daahd."

Lisa's demeanor continued to calm as she looked at her father and the beep of the pulse monitor dropped to a more regular pace. The room became silent as Jack turned to Mia. His eyes were defiant.

His stare shook her to her core. Mia's intuition, theories, and conclusions in the murder case of George Lombard were instantly shattered.

"Oh my God," she said.

FIFTY-ONE

The silence in St. Joseph's church was broken only by hushed voices reciting a litany of Hail Mary's. There were just a handful of people present, each with their head bowed in reverence. An elderly woman appeared from the small door, walked to a nearby pew, knelt, and joined the others in prayer.

A tall figure with thick, dark hair sprinkled with gray rose slowly and went inside.

"Forgive me, Father, for I have sinned. It's been nearly a year since my last confession…"

The curtain pulled away, exposing the priest behind the screen.

Father Jon smiled.

"It's good to see you, Jack."

ACKNOWLEDGEMENTS

While driving on Interstate 5 in the fall of 2009, I noticed a large ice truck in the lane next to me. I looked over at the big eighteen wheeler and it struck me: I wonder if you could put a body in there in an effort to fool investigators as to the time of death. I know what you're thinking… Why would anyone have a thought like that driving down the interstate?

After nearly thirty years working within the California criminal justice system, I probably look at things a little differently than most people. The idea of keeping a body frozen in that truck stayed with me as I continued down the interstate, and when I returned home later that evening I sat down at my laptop and just started typing. I had no outline or real idea where I was headed, but I just knew there was a story there. A few hours later, I had the first dozen pages of Icy Betrayal in hand.

The rest followed in fits and starts, with sometimes months going by without a word being written. Finally, over the course of 2013, I pounded out the rest of the story. I hope you enjoyed it.

There are so many people to thank for giving me the encouragement I needed to finish this book. I'd write a handful of pages and quickly send them off to select friends and family to get their feedback. Mostly they told me that I had to "hurry up and finish the damn story" as they were hooked and wanted to see how it would end. Those kind words kept me going.

Specifically, I'd like to thank the following people for their support and encouragement:

Tom and Barbara Laubacher, Marvin Petal, Rich Gualano, Steve Low, Laura Rainey, Mark Keith, John Higgins, Laura Greaves,

Anita Gergen, Ron Calkins, Mike Palmieri, Tom and Mona Neuhaus, Monica Schoenfeld, Robert Garcia, Martin Remmen and Doug Saint.

A special thank you to my editors Dan Green and Erin Clark and their marketing team at OMG Media in Monterey—their assistance was invaluable.

I want to thank my wife Giselle, my two older kids Jessica and Michael, and my youngest Alyssa; who along with her college roommate Nikki Voest would meet me regularly for breakfast on the campus of California Lutheran University to share their thoughts on my writing. Their insights were a tremendous help.

ABOUT THE AUTHOR

David Keith has nearly thirty years of experience in criminal justice and policing. As the longtime spokesman and community affairs manager with the Oxnard Police Department he publicly handled high profile cases including more than 200 homicides. Considered a leading expert in media relations, David trained officers and staff from over five hundred police agencies across the nation in media communications, community outreach and crisis management.

David lives in Southern California with his wife Giselle.

Made in the USA
Charleston, SC
20 June 2015